THE DRAGON'S MEMORY

Lochguard Highland Dragons #10

JESSIE DONOVAN

Mythical Lake Press, LLC

The Dragon's Memory

Copyright © 2022 Laura Hoak-Kagey

Mythical Lake Press, LLC

First Print Edition

Cover Art by Laura Hoak-Kagey of Mythical Lake Design

ISBN: 978-1944776367

Books in this series:

Lochguard Highland Dragons

The Dragon's Memory Synopsis

Logan has loved Emma for years. But after he stole a kiss when they were teens and she brushed it off with a laugh, he tried to settle for being her friend, especially once he realized she wasn't his true mate. However, no matter how much time passes, he can't seem to get over her. Deciding to leave Lochguard and finish his doctor studies, Logan hopes that with space he can forge a new path. As a sort of farewell, he agrees one last time to help her with her geocaching—a modern form of treasure hunting—adventure. Except during the excursion, he pushes

Emma out of the way to save her life and gets hit on the head, knocked unconscious, and nearly dies.

When Logan wakes up and doesn't recognize or remember Emma, her world tilts. If her best friend being gone isn't enough to worry about, this different Logan keeps looking at her with heat in his eyes. Years ago, she'd pushed him away to avoid her greatest fear—falling in love. However, as he helps her on her treasure hunt, each touch, whisper, and kiss tempts her to take the plunge. It takes everything she has to resist him, especially since his memories don't seem to be returning.

As the stakes and danger amp up in her quest to find the final clue, Emma soon finds herself falling for Logan. Will she finally give in and risk her heart? Or will Emma find a way to resist Logan and watch him walk away to prevent any sort of pain in the future?

The Stonefire and Lochguard series intertwine with one another. (As well as with one Tahoe Dragon Mates book.) Since so many readers ask for the overall reading order, I've included it with this book. (This list is as of May 2022 and you can view the most up-to-date version on my website at www.JessieDonovan.com)

Winning Skyhunter (Stonefire Dragons Universe #1)
The Dragon's Discovery (Lochguard Highland Dragons #6)
Transforming Snowridge (Stonefire Dragons Universe #2)
The Dragon's Pursuit (Lochguard Highland Dragons #7)
Persuading the Dragon (Stonefire Dragons #12)
Treasured by the Dragon (Stonefire Dragons #13)
The Dragon Collective (Lochguard Highland Dragons #8)
The Dragon's Bidder (Tahoe Dragon Mates #3)
The Dragon's Chance (Lochguard Highland Dragons #9)
Summer at Lochguard (Dragon Clan Gatherings #1)
Trusting the Dragon (Stonefire Dragons #14)
The Dragon's Memory (Lochguard Highland Dragons #10)
Taught by the Dragon (Stonefire Dragons #15, 2023)
The Dragon Recruit (Lochguard Highland Dragons #11, TBD)

Short stories that lead up to *Persuading the Dragon / Treasured by the Dragon*:

Meeting the Humans (Stonefire Dragons Shorts #1)
The Dragon Camp (Stonefire Dragons Shorts #2)
The Dragon Play (Stonefire Dragons Shorts #3)

Semi-related dragon stories set in the USA, beginning sometime around *The Dragon's Discovery / Transforming Snowridge*:

The Dragon's Choice (Tahoe Dragon Mates #1)
The Dragon's Need (Tahoe Dragon Mates #2)
The Dragon's Bidder (Tahoe Dragon Mates #3)
The Dragon's Charge (Tahoe Dragon Mates #4)
The Dragon's Weakness (Tahoe Dragon Mates #5)
The Dragon's Luck (Tahoe Dragon Mates #6, TBD)

Chapter One

Logan Lamont trailed behind Emma MacAllister and the two Seahaven dragonmen she'd roped into helping her yet again, barely noticing the steep climb and crunch of gravel beneath his feet. It was hard enough to not stare at her swaying, round arse ahead of him, but as he curled his fingers into fists, he fought the urge to toss Emma over his shoulder and carry her home, away from the two bloody annoying dragonmen who looked at her like she was a treat to be licked from top to bottom.

Clenching his fists harder, he tamped down his desire to lock her inside his bedroom for days and never let her out, knowing he could never act on it.

After all, Emma had never been his, had refused him before, and at this point, he was fairly sure she'd never change her view of him.

But he still had a huge weakness where she was concerned—Logan would always help when she asked him. Even if he wanted more than friendship, she was still one of his best friends, someone he'd known his whole life. She was one of the youngest of the older MacAllister siblings, one who always seemed to get away with bloody reckless shite that only Logan seemed able to tame. At least, to a small degree.

Which was why he was here now, following her on yet another damn geocaching chase, hiking up a steep incline to the top of a mountain when he should be home, studying for his next doctor's exam.

His inner dragon, the second personality inside his head, spoke up. *When are we leaving for Edinburgh again? Maybe then you'll finally find another female and fuck her.*

That's not the reason we're going.

His inner beast sniffed. *Aye, I know. Doctor studies. But it's been years since our last female, and I barely remember what it's like to have a hot, tight pussy around our cock.*

Shut it, dragon. We're not doing this now.

His beast reluctantly fell quiet, at least for the moment.

Not that he had much time for solitude as Emma turned toward the taller of the two Seahaven lads and gave him a flirtatious smile.

It took everything Logan had not to punch something.

Emma grinned up at Andrew and gestured toward the mostly sheer rock face next to her. "It's time for another climbing competition, don't you think, Andy? This time, a fair one, where you don't give me a head start and let me win."

The dark-haired Andrew MacKay grinned back, the bastard sneaking in a slow perusal of Emma's body, as if judging her ability to best him but truly was probably undressing her with his eyes.

Logan clenched his jaw and tried not to crack a tooth.

Andrew replied, "I don't think a wee lassie such as you could win in a fair contest."

Emma tilted her head. "So that means you accept my challenge, aye?"

Andrew put out a hand to shake. "Provided I get to select where it happens, then aye, I'll take your challenge."

As soon as Emma placed her hand in Andrew's, the Seahaven bastard tugged her closer and Logan narrowed his eyes. If the bastard tried to kiss her, he might need to toss him off the mountain.

He missed whatever they said when his dragon chimed in. *I still say toss her over our shoulder, carry her off, pin her to a wall, and show her how we're more than a friend.*

Don't start. You know I kissed her before, and all she did was laugh at me, to the point she could barely breathe.

His inner beast sniffed. *Aye, and that was years ago,*

during our teens. I still say you should try kissing her now, as a grown male.

Not wanting to hash this out yet again with his dragon, he mentally growled, *It doesn't matter. She's not our true mate, and I've accepted it. After next week, we won't see her for a while and I'll forget her.*

I doubt you'll ever forget her.

That may be true. After all, Logan had been in love with Emma for a good chunk of his life. Ever since she found him reading a book by himself while everyone else played football or tag or other games when he'd been ten and she seven, he'd been charmed by her energy and optimism. As they grew older and Emma always smiled and came to him for advice, or to merely share a laugh, he'd become more enamored. Which had resulted in him daring to share his feelings at nineteen and Emma laughing at him, saying he was basically her brother and it was like kissing a dead fish.

That should've been the end of his obsession for her, it really should have.

And yet he had never been able to truly sever their friendship, craving her lightness and recklessness more than air. Through the death of his parents, his brother's disappearance, and all the shite the clan had been through over the years, Emma had been the constant light, the one who had always been able to improve his mood.

The only female who invaded his dreams and made him wake up with a hard cock and frustrated desire.

Going to Edinburgh for the next year or two was the only way he was going to fucking recover his sanity. If he was to ever find someone else, a female who wanted him and looked at him as if she could never get enough, then his friendship with Emma needed to become *only* friendship, and nothing else.

Especially since for months, while accompanying Emma on her modern-day treasure hunting adventures called geocaching—where people left clues that sometimes incorporated technology to locate and figure out the next one—he'd had to watch her rope one male and then another into helping her. The two Seahaven MacKay brothers— dragonmen from the Scottish splinter clan that lived near the northern coast of Scotland—had been the worst, though. Emma had flirted endlessly, and Andrew MacKay, in particular, had flirted back, the male's glint determined for more than exchanging mere words.

Thank fuck Logan was leaving Lochguard to take up his doctor studies in Edinburgh next week. She couldn't ask for his help any longer and he wouldn't have to seethe at watching her flirt with other males, oblivious to his torture.

His dragon sniffed. *Stop your whinging. It's giving me*

a headache, especially since we haven't shifted today yet and I want to fly.

As soon as this is done, dragon. I promise.

Until then, keep your jealousy in check. I want to nap.

His inner beast curled up and dozed, and Logan merely kept up his pace with the others. He was only there in case of a medical emergency. Even if he wasn't a doctor yet and was only a trained nurse, it was more than enough for minor injuries.

Deciding to focus on what his future brought instead of what it didn't, Logan ran through his latest studies, the ones he'd been reading ahead of his first scheduled training shifts in Edinburgh. There was only one university and hospital in the UK that accepted dragon-shifters medical students, and he was determined to impress and succeed.

The distraction worked, to the point Logan nearly ran into the older MacKay brother, Dean, when everyone else had stopped in the middle of the trail. Andrew motioned toward a rock face of about twenty feet high and looked at Emma. "This will do, aye?"

Logan eyed the stone, noting how there was a ledge above, one they couldn't see the top of. Used to being the voice of reason with Emma, he stated without preamble, "I don't know if you two should. We can't see what's above, and two dragon-shifters racing toward the top, shaking things loose, could cause rocks to fall."

Emma waved a hand. "Och, Logan, you're such a worrier. I've been on this mountain before, and it's fine."

He moved to stand on Emma's other side and raised an eyebrow. "How long ago was that?"

She glanced away, revealing how she didn't want to answer. She muttered, "Three years or so."

He grunted. "Then you know as well as I that one winter, with snow and ice, can easily move things around once it melts."

Andrew snorted. "Don't worry so much, aye, Lamont? It's just a short jaunt. Besides, Emma's clue should be just up there, if the GPS is correct."

Emma smiled at the Seahaven lad, no doubt already thinking of how to wind him even more around her finger.

The dragonwoman was good at that.

She nodded. "I agree with Andrew. It's just a short climb and we'll be done before you know it."

She flashed the bastard a smile and Logan resisted rolling his eyes. Emma always did this— charm or hedge others into agreeing with her. It didn't work on him, though. "I'm supposed to be here to make sure everyone goes home in one piece. I don't want to risk someone getting bashed over the head and possibly falling down into that loch down there to drown."

Emma raised an eyebrow. "I'm not a novice, Logan. I've scaled numerous walls before."

The steel in her eyes said she wasn't going to budge. But he also knew Emma's stubbornness got her into all kinds of trouble on a regular basis.

His cautious, protective nature was about to warn some more—even contemplated hauling her away by force—but Andrew moved into position and motioned for Emma to come over. "Come on, lass. He gave his warning, and my brother can note it if needed. Now, let's go."

He glanced at Dean, hoping for someone else to see how bloody stupid this was since the male was a Protector, but Dean merely shrugged. "It's only twenty feet. And both of them have reflexes to move out of the way if a rock falls or breaks off."

Logan was outnumbered. Before he could try to find a way to convince them to see reason, Emma and Andrew were in position. Right before Dean could say, "Go!" he noticed a decent-sized rock falling toward Emma. For a beat, he thought it odd given how they hadn't started climbing to knock anything loose.

But then his instincts took over. Grabbing Emma about the waist, he swung her out of the way. He'd barely noted how she'd fallen to the side, on her knees, when a blinding pain struck his head. Suddenly he was weightless, falling through the air, and blackness creeped over his vision. He was barely aware of crashing into the water before the world went dark.

ONE SECOND EMMA MACALLISTER had been about to best the cocky Andrew MacKay and the next she was on her knees watching as Logan fell over the side of the mountain and crashed into the water of the loch below.

For a beat, she expected him to pop his head out of the water and give her one of those disapproving frowns of his, the ones that he always had when he was right and she was wrong.

Ones he had given far too often.

But he didn't surface, and panic clawed at her heart. Logan was her best friend and he couldn't die. He just couldn't.

Without thinking, she told her dragon, *Like we practiced, aye?*

Aye.

Then she jumped into the air and imagined her nose elongating into a snout, wings growing from her back, and her limbs lengthening to complete her change into her dragon form.

She had barely a few feet above the water's surface before she could use her wings to move a little to the side of where Logan had fallen and dove into the loch.

The water was cold even in late summer, but she barely noticed. No, she did her best to scan the water, looking for Logan.

Just as she was starting to worry she wouldn't find him, there he was, at the bottom of a shallow area, his body slack and his mouth open.

With a cry, she moved toward him, scooped him up carefully, and swam toward the surface. She jumped and hopped to get to the shore as quickly as possible. Laying him down, she could see the MacKay brothers still too far away to help.

And Logan lay still, not breathing.

Completing the fastest shift in history, she moved next to Logan. "You won't die on me, Logan. I won't let you."

She pinched his nose and breathed into his mouth before doing the chest compressions she'd been taught during one of Logan's first aid classes.

Moving back, she waited a beat to see if he'd cough up water, but he didn't.

Fighting her panic, she repeated the steps again. And again.

She was about to start crying when on the fifth repetition Logan choked up water. She tilted him to the side until he stopped and gulped in greedy draws of air.

However, despite his breathing, he was still unconscious.

Searching his head, she found the gash caused by the rock and tried not to panic at the blood on her fingers. Thanks to her brothers all but trying to kill each other as lads, she knew head wounds bled a lot.

And yet, seeing Logan pale, breathing shallowly, and unmoving, it hit her that her recklessness had finally hurt someone close to her, as her mum had always warned it might do.

Her inner dragon spoke up. *We need to get him help. Focus on that.*

Forcing her heated eyes not to spill with tears, she looked for the Seahaven brothers. Dean was still up where they'd been at the sheer rock face, but Andrew was racing down the trail. She shouted, "Call someone on Lochguard. He needs a doctor."

Andrew ran closer to her. "I already did. But we have bigger problems and need to think about moving to someplace safer."

Still gripping Logan's lax hand in hers, she couldn't look away from one of the dearest people in her life, but she managed to ask, "Why? That could hurt him or make his condition worse."

Andrew frowned. "I know, but my brother noticed someone moving at the top of the ledge. He thinks the falling rock was no accident."

She'd known going after this particular find would be dangerous—it was worth more than anything she'd tried for before—but never had she thought it'd end up with someone trying to hurt her.

It seemed the unspoken geocaching code didn't matter a damn thing for this competition.

She finally tore her gaze from Logan's slack face and looked at Andrew. "But surely if there was someone on that ledge, they can't hurt us now we're down here, aye?"

Andrew shook his head. "Maybe, maybe not. All it would take was a dart of some sort with the right sort of drugs, or a real gun, and we'd be fucked. Dean suggested taking cover."

Emma looked back at Logan. Had his breathing grown shallower?

Swallowing back the fear choking her throat, she croaked, "Aye, then let's move. But carefully."

The Seahaven male nodded. "There's an old boathouse further down the loch. It should give us some protection for now since it's stone and I doubt anyone has grenades or missiles, or anything like that."

She wanted to dismiss it, but those invited to this particular geocaching contest were some of the most skilled. It'd taken her years to get to a level to be invited to the top-tier competitions, ones where the treasure at the end wasn't some joke toy or cheap piece of jewelry.

No, this time the find was worth £500,000. And rumors she'd heard on the internet meant some of the players would do anything for the money, even if it was frowned upon.

Anything.

And to think she'd dismissed them as paranoid; she'd been so bloody naïve.

Her dragon huffed. *Think of that later, and tell Faye and Grant about it. For now, let's just get our arses to safety.*

Somehow she and Andrew managed to carry Logan between them and move slowly down the edge of the loch, constantly looking over their shoulders for danger.

It wasn't until they were in the old, musty boathouse that would barely fit the three of them, with Logan laid down on a pile of some sort of sheet coverings, that she shivered. Andrew took off his shirt and gave it to her. She smiled wobbly and tossed it on to cover her nudity before she resumed stroking Logan's wet hair off his face. She murmured, "I'm so sorry, Logan. Truly. If—no, when—you wake up, you can lecture me as long as you like and I'll listen this time, I promise."

He lay still, unmoving except for the rise and fall of his chest.

Only because she needed to remain alert, in case of a threat, did she not start crying or breaking down. Seeing strong, solid Logan so pale and helpless was killing her.

She didn't know how long she sat there, doing her best to fight the tears that wanted to fall, when she heard the familiar voice of Brodie MacNeil, one of Lochguard's Protectors.

He popped his ginger head inside, and Emma blurted, "Tell me you brought a doctor."

"Aye, Dr. McFarland is just behind me."

A beat later, Brodie motioned Andrew away and Dr. Layla McFarland rushed into the room.

And at the worried frown on Layla's face, tears finally streamed down Emma's face. "It's my fault."

The doctor merely raised her dark brows and went back to examining Logan. "Just tell me the facts of what happened, Emma. And don't leave anything out."

She stumbled through it, somehow getting out the events until she reached the present and blurted, "Will he be okay?"

Layla stood. "Let's get him back to Lochguard."

Emma didn't like the non-answer. "Will he?"

Layla gave her a sympathetic look. "He's alive, and his heart beat is fairly strong given the shock to his body by nearly drowning. But until I can scan him for brain trauma, I won't know for certain." She reached out and squeezed Emma's shoulder. "I'll do everything I can, aye? Logan's dear to me too."

Emma only had the strength to nod. Brodie and another Protector named Cooper managed to get Emma to stand and make her legs work before they maneuvered Logan onto a stretcher. Needing something to keep her mind from thinking the worst would happen—that Logan would never wake up again—she asked Brodie, "Dean MacKay says he saw something after Logan fell into the loch. Have you talked with him and learned anything?"

Brodie shook his head. "Not yet. Iris went to chat with him and scout the area." Brodie smiled at her. "Don't worry, Emma. If there's someone who did this deliberately, Iris will find them."

Even though she wanted to go with Logan, she knew that her energy would be better focused on giving Iris the information she needed. "If that's the case, then I need to talk with her."

Brodie and Cooper reached the area where a dragon sat waiting next to a long, flat basket of sorts, one used to transport injured people via dragon wing. Brodie asked, "Do you know who might've done this?"

"Maybe. I'm not sure, but I need to talk with Iris."

Brodie grunted. "Not here. Back on Lochguard. Let her scan the area and look for clues, or even people, before rain comes and washes everything away." He studied her a beat and added softly, "Besides, you look about ready to fall over, lass. Come home, get warm, and then you can tell us everything."

She wanted to argue, but Brodie was one of the males immune to her charm, even if she had enough energy to use it. Besides, she was exhausted and still trying not to fall completely apart at seeing her best friend pale and lying on a stretcher. She nodded. "I'll come with you and talk with Iris later."

And before she knew it, Logan was in the

carrying basket with Layla next to him, everyone else had shifted except for Iris and Dean, and they were flying back toward Lochguard.

Chapter Two

P ain throbbed throughout his entire body, but most especially in his head. Add in the darkness, and it felt as if he were in hell.

He didn't know how long he stayed there, in the blackness, struggling to open his eyes, when a low humming filled the room. It was female, but that's all he knew.

The longer she hummed, the more relaxed he felt until he knew he needed to see who made the sound.

Bit by bit, he forced his eyelids open until he could see a beautiful female sitting next to him, typing away on a laptop. She had dark hair, blue eyes, and full, pink lips. Lips he couldn't help watching as she hummed along.

He also wouldn't mind strumming his fingers over her smooth, pale skin to see if it were as soft as it looked.

He must've made a noise because the female looked at him, squealed, and jumped up. After quickly putting her computer down, she was at his side, stroking his forehead.

Each stroke sent a rush of heat through his body, banishing the pain.

Then the female started crying, a huge contrast to her smile. "You're awake, Logan. You have no idea how happy I am to see your brown gaze again." She sniffled and stroked his skin some more. "Or just how sorry I am that you got hurt."

He frowned at both her tears and her words. "Who's Logan and why are you crying?"

Her fingers stilled and he nearly growled, wanting her to stroke him some more.

After wiping her cheeks with her free hand, she whispered, "You're Logan, Logan Lamont."

He rolled the name around in his head, but it didn't ring any bells. "If you say so."

Her brows drew even closer together, and he resisted the urge to reach up and caress it away. Even if he had no bloody idea who she was, he wanted to ease her hurt, protect her, and keep her by his side. Something inside him screamed that she was his.

She blurted, "Do you know who I am?"

He raked her face, lingering on her full lips, down to her breasts and back up again. "A bonnie angel sent to watch over me?"

She huffed. "Don't tease me right now, Logan. It's

Emma, the female who irritates you more than anyone else alive. Although I promise to be better. No more putting people in danger, or thinking I know everything. You were right, and I should've listened to you." She stroked his forehead again. "You have no bloody idea how sorry I am."

For a beat, he merely reveled in her light touches on his skin, his cock slowly coming to life.

Needing to tame the beast and not scare her away, he said slowly, "Emma." Aye, he liked how her name sounded on his lips. "I wish I could say I remember you since I have no idea how someone could forget such a bloody beautiful female, but I don't know you."

She opened her mouth, closed it, and then tried again. "Are you teasing me to get back at me? Aye, I know I deserve it, but could you please cut it out? You're scaring me."

Her pupils flashed to slits and back to round. Something about the action was familiar, but he couldn't place it. "Why would I want to scare you? I'm telling the truth—we've never met. Although I hope we'll be spending plenty more time together in the future."

Worry and confusion danced in her eyes. "You truly don't know me?"

He hated to say something that would probably upset her—the thought of making her cry made his heart pound—but he wasn't about to lie to her. She'd figure it out soon enough. "No, lass. I don't know you."

She removed her hand from his forehead and he wished he had the strength to reach for it and bring it back. But merely talking with her was making him more tired by the second.

She took a step away, and then another, until she reached the door, opened it, and spoke with someone in the hall. "Fetch Dr. McFarland."

Even after she closed the door again, she kept her distance, looking at him with pain and guilt.

He didn't like any of it—the emotions or her distance.

Before he could think of what to say to bring her back to his side, a female probably in her midthirties walked into the room, her black hair pulled back from her face. Given the lab coat and clipboard, she was probably a doctor.

Strange how he could remember things like that but he had no idea what his name was.

Because ever since the lass had called him Logan, he'd tried to remember it and hadn't been able to.

The doctor stopped near his bed, and Emma finally took a few steps nearer and yet still too far away for him to touch her. She said, "He doesn't remember me."

The doctor's brown eyes met his gaze. "Do you know who I am?"

He tried to place her dark hair and brown eyes,

but it was as if he'd never seen her before. All he could think about was how she wasn't as beautiful as the lass called Emma.

The doctor gently gripped his wrist and took his pulse. And unlike when Emma had touched him, he didn't feel as if he needed to haul her close and kiss her.

Finally, the doctor spoke. "I'm Dr. Layla McFarland." She waited a beat before continuing, "I can see you're tired and need rest, but I'm going to ask a few questions, aye?"

"Fine," he gritted.

She frowned at his terseness, but he didn't bloody care. His entire body ached, it seemed he couldn't remember anyone's name, and Emma was standing much too far away from him.

Dr. McFarland pointed to the item draped over her neck. "What is this?"

"A stethoscope."

She pointed toward the rectangular object mounted to the wall. "And that?"

"A telly."

"What are the early signs of dragon hormone deficiency?"

Without thinking, he answered, "Fatigue, thinning hair, mood swings, difficulty with shifting into a dragon, and low blood pressure."

"And your name?"

Unlike everything else, he didn't have an answer, just a bloody big vat of nothingness. "I don't know."

"Who is Phillip Lamont?"

Again, a big void of nothing. "I don't know."

"Hmm."

Anger flared. "Just bloody tell me what's going on and why the fuck I can't remember my name, or anyone's name for that matter."

He noticed Emma frowning at him, but he ignored it to focus on the doctor. She finally answered, "You have partial amnesia."

He growled, "I surmised as much, oh great one. But will it go away?"

The doctor sighed. "The temper is new." He growled again, but she straightened taller and continued, "Sorry. Now back to your condition—you have a type of amnesia where you retained practical knowledge but not your name or those of others. And you probably can't recall any memories, either, aye?"

She waited for him to answer and he tried to remember anything from before he woke up. A mother, or father, or even a friend. Hell, even his first fuck or how he knew Emma. However, there was only a big, fat void of nothing.

It was both frustrating and terrifying. Not that he'd let it show it scared him a little. "No."

The doctor nodded. "I'll have to run more tests, of course, to figure out the extent. But for now, it's going to be a confusing time until your memories return."

Emma spoke up. "Will they return?"

The doctor looked over at her. "Most likely, although when it comes to the mind, I can't guarantee anything." She turned her gaze back at him. "For now, you'll stay here at the surgery until you're strong enough to leave. And even if you don't remember, your name is Logan Lamont."

He grunted. "I don't really like it."

The doctor's lips twitched. "Aye, well, that was your mother's doing, not mine. It'll be easier for everyone, including you, if you answer to it, though."

He wasn't sure how he felt about the doctor trying to be funny.

However, she apparently wasn't done because her tone became firmer as she said, "It's time to rest. We can chat more when you wake up, but not before. Sleep is the best medicine for now, since I didn't find anything else amiss apart from some bruises and minor cuts. The bump on your head will take the longest to heal, but dragons heal swiftly. Speaking of which, I do have one more question—do you have an inner dragon?"

His knowledge of a species who could turn from human forms into dragons and back again rushed into his head. "I know of them, but am I one?"

The doctor tilted her head. "I think that answers my question. No matter, time for you to rest, aye?

Don't fight it, either. I'm not above medically inducing a coma if I have to."

He narrowed his eyes, not liking the steely orders. "Fine, whatever you say. For now."

The doctor chuckled and moved toward the door. Emma picked up her computer and was about to sit again, but the doctor spoke. "No, Emma. I need to chat with you in private and he needs his sleep."

The beautiful blue-eyed lass stared at him a beat before whispering, "I'll be back to check on you again later, Logan. I promise."

As much as he didn't care for the name Logan, he didn't mind it as much when she said it.

And then she was gone and the room became a hell of a lot colder and emptier.

Not wanting to lay in wait like some infatuated puppy for her return, he tried to force his mind to work properly, to maybe remember something about himself. Even just what foods he fancied, or if he had any sort of hobby.

However, his mind turned even foggier the harder he tried to recall anything. And before he knew it, the male everyone insisted was named Logan Lamont let his exhaustion embrace him and fell asleep, dreaming of the dark-haired female who'd looked so concerned and pained, and he wondered why, exactly, and how he might be able to chase the emotions away.

EMMA SILENTLY FOLLOWED Dr. McFarland out of Logan's room and down to her office at the end of the hall. She motioned for Emma to sit, and once they were both settled, Emma blurted, "It's not permanent, is it?"

"I don't know, Emma. I wasn't lying when I said the mind can be unpredictable. In most cases, aye, memories come back. But we can't constantly push him to try and remember, as that will only frustrate him. Promise me you won't do that."

Maybe some would take offense, but Emma knew herself well enough to know she could be a wee bit demanding when she wanted. So she sighed. "I'm going to try. Although there must be things we can do to help him. It sounds as if he doesn't even have his dragon."

Dr. McFarland bobbed her head. "Aye, it seems that way, at least for now. Although I'll have to run more tests, like I said, to have a better understanding of what's going on."

She plucked at the material of her trousers. "What can I do to help?" The doctor studied her, and Emma added, "I need to do something. It's my fault he was hurt, and now he doesn't have his memory? I-I need to do something to help make this right."

The female's gaze softened. "Aye, I understand your feeling. But all you can do in the present is visit him, try to entertain him, and not be too forceful. You have to remember that he doesn't know who he is, and his personality could be different as a result. He seems to have a temper now, and I'd rather not see how far it goes."

Emma sat taller and said with conviction, "Logan would never hurt me, or anyone, and you know it."

Dr. McFarland leaned forward and propped her arms on the desk. "I want to believe it, but until we can observe him further, you need to be careful around him, aye? If you can't do that, then I'll have to put a moratorium on you visiting him."

The thought of Logan suffering alone did something to her heart. "No, I'll do whatever you say. He's my best friend and I won't abandon him."

"I know, lass. I know." Dr. McFarland leaned back in her chair. "I'll send a message when you can come and sit with him again. For now, go home. And no, don't argue with me. You've barely slept the last two days and I won't have you falling ill as well."

The thought of going home to the small place she'd recently moved to and shared with Kaylee MacDonald, her refuge from the insanity of her family, triggered every bit of tiredness and strain she'd held back to rush forth. "Aye, I'll go. But I need to know if anything changes. Anything."

The other dragonwoman's eyes softened. "I know, Emma."

Not wanting to endure the doctor's kind look—

she most definitely didn't deserve it after her brashness and selfishness had nearly killed Logan—she quickly left and headed home.

Her dragon finally spoke up. *Now's not the time to be sad or depressed.*

If not now, then when? Logan's alive but doesn't remember anyone. And if he doesn't regain his memory, then it's as if we lost our best friend too.

Perhaps. But we can't change the past. Accept it and form a new plan, like we always have before.

She wanted to, oh how she wanted to.

But Emma was tired, and angry at herself, and she suddenly longed to see the one person who seemed to love her no matter what sort of shite she pulled—her mum.

Too exhausted and emotionally drained to fight the need to see her mother, she changed her path and was soon standing at the door of the cottage she'd grown up in, and until recently, had been her home.

Even if her mum and new stepdad always told her to just come in, she wasn't going to risk walking in on them half naked and going at each other. She'd done that once and was scarred for life.

So she knocked and a beat later her mother's dark hair and blue eyes met hers and she instantly pulled Emma into a hug. "Come, my lassie. Let's get you some tea and biscuits and you can tell me what has you on the verge of tears."

She might be twenty-three and far past the point

when she should cry on her mum's shoulders, but right then and there, she didn't care. She let her mother guide her into the living room and help her sit down.

Despite wanting to keep it together for at least a little while, as soon as her mum asked, "What happened? Is Logan okay?" Emma burst into tears.

Her sweet, gentle mother didn't bat an eyelash and wrapped her arms around Emma's shoulders, soothing her with strokes and soft words until Emma was calm enough to answer, "Logan doesn't remember me or anyone else. Dr. McFarland doesn't know if his memory will come back or not. And if it doesn't?" She sniffed and tried to calm down, but she couldn't stop her tears. "Oh, Mum. You kept warning me and I kept ignoring you, dismissing you as being overprotective. And now look what I've done. I nearly killed my best friend and he might never regain his full memories. All because I was too busy trying to impress the Seahaven lads with a stupid race. I'll never be able to forgive myself."

Her mum brushed the hair off her face and replied, "Logan is alive, and it's still too early to tell if anything's permanent, aye?"

"But what if it is? He's…different. And rightly angry at not knowing things." She searched her mum's eyes. "If he never regains his memories, then how can I ever make that right?"

Her mum took her face in her hands. "Oh,

Emma. The fact you admit you harmed him and feel guilt is a good start and shows how much you care." Her mother released her face and took one of her hands in hers. "Just try to be the friend he needs right now, aye? And see how that goes. Consistency will probably be comforting to him, and you can try to provide that. And the best way might be to treat him as a new friend, one you're just getting to know. He'll probably like that more than you demanding he remember something or other, as if he's deliberately not trying hard enough." She smiled. "A young male's pride can be a delicate thing."

She searched her mother's steady gaze. "Do you think approaching him as a new friend will work?"

Her mother shrugged. "It's worth a try, aye? Besides, you may fool others with your outrageous comments and constant flirting, but I know you have a huge heart, Emma. One that can tell what someone needs to smile or feel better for a few minutes. Use that with Logan, and I'm sure it'll help him."

Her mother was one of the few people in her family that knew of Emma's penchant for visiting pensioners on Lochguard and assisting them with whatever tasks they needed help with. She didn't do it for the praise, but rather because she liked making others smile, or light up at some company, or sigh with relief at getting some help they were too proud to ask for.

It was ultimately to help those she visited that

she'd taken on the risky geocaching contest in the first place. But even if she still wanted to one day build a human-dragon senior center and help further build relations between Lochguard and the humans that way, she'd find a different pathway to her goal. One that wouldn't hurt anyone else.

And until she helped Logan as much as she could, she would put her dream on hold.

She nodded. "I won't stop until I can find out what makes this new version of Logan laugh or smile. It's the least I can do."

Her mother searched her eyes. "Just don't push him too hard, Emma, if he starts to remember anything."

"I'll try, unless he needs a little fire lit under his arse." Her mother opened her mouth, but Emma beat her to it. "Logan never was one to hold back from telling me hard truths. He might need the same, but I'll only do that if I think he can handle it. That's the best promise I can give right now."

"Aye, well, I trust you know him better than I do." Her mother squeezed Emma's hand in reassurance. "With that sorted, are you staying for supper with me, Jake, and Sophie?"

Sophie was her much younger sister, not even two years old, that her mother had had with Jake Swift, Emma's new stepfather. As much as Emma loved her little sister, being patient and silly for her would take too much effort in her current state of exhaustion.

Emma shook her head. "I'm knackered and need some sleep, especially if I'm going to solve the puzzle of new Logan when I see him next."

"Then I'll ensure Connor delivers you some food, and I won't take no for an answer."

Connor was her eldest brother and mostly ran their mum's restaurant these days. He was overprotective like all her brothers, which meant he drove her crazy, but he was also a bloody good cook. "I won't turn him away. I can burn toast, so I'll take any help I can get."

Her mother chuckled as they both stood. "Aye, I remember a certain birthday breakfast you made me when you were ten. Burnt toast, warm marmalade, and ice-cold tea strong enough to grow hair on my chest."

Emma frowned. "I spent an hour putting it together."

"I know, my dear. And that's what mattered." She winked. "I don't love my children based upon their culinary skills."

Despite everything, she laughed. "Good, because then Connor would never stop bragging."

Her mum chuckled. "Aye, that's true. Although Jake would probably beat him in a cooking contest." They finally arrived at the front door and her mother added, "We're always here if you need us, Emma. Don't let your stubborn pride keep you from asking for help."

She nodded, kissed her mum's cheek, and headed toward the wee cottage she shared with Kaylee.

While her family would always be there to help if she asked, Emma had fucked up and hurt Logan. So unless absolutely necessary, she was determined to set it right on her own.

Well, at least as right as she could make it.

But to form any kind of plan or strategy, she needed sleep. So she did exactly that, her head barely hitting the pillow before exhaustion took over and she embraced oblivion.

Chapter Three

Logan had spent the last day enduring several visits from people who tried to tell him he was indeed Logan Lamont, and offered memories as if they'd help him.

First from a male who looked a lot like him, but older, and had claimed to be his brother, Phillip.

Then various nurses had stopped by, claiming to have worked with him for years.

At least their visits had revealed why he could answer basic medical questions without thought—he'd been a nurse studying to become a doctor.

But the least annoying visitor had been the blond male who'd called himself Finn Stewart, the leader of Clan Lochguard.

He'd been the only one to talk with him as if he didn't expect him to instantly remember the last twenty-odd years if he merely tried hard enough to recall it.

But even the easygoing male's visit didn't ease the irritation he felt at not seeing Emma again.

He'd learned her name was Emma MacAllister, an IT expert for the clan, and one a few years younger than him. She also had a big family but, most importantly, she didn't have a male of her own.

Which had made him relax more than anything. Because he'd dreamed of her constantly and was determined to see if she'd kiss him. Maybe as a plea to see if a fairy tale would happen, with a kiss restoring everyone.

It was ridiculous, aye, but for some reason he couldn't stop wanting to take her mouth with his, revel in her taste, and make her moan.

So when Emma finally walked into his room, wearing tight-fitting jeans showing off her long legs and a top that hugged her slight curves, he had to push aside every erotic dream he'd had of her to keep his cock at bay.

She stopped at his bedside and smiled down at him. "You're awake. Good." She held up a deck of some color-coded cards. "I thought we could play a game, if you're not too tired."

"I've been in this bloody bed nearly every moment since you were here last. I may be sore, but if anyone tells me to sleep more, I may have to punch them."

She snorted. "I'd always heard males made the worst patients, and I see you're no exception."

He grunted. "If you lost your memory and didn't even recognize your own bloody name, you'd be irritated too."

Pain flashed through her eyes, but it was gone before he could blink. He didn't think he'd imagined it, but even if he had, Logan knew he never wanted to see that emotion in her gaze ever again, if he could help it.

He didn't fully understand his protective instinct surrounding the female. But they just felt…right.

Emma cleared her throat and waved the deck of cards around in the air. "Well, you've never played this game before, so I'll need to teach you."

She moved the little table thing that rolled to hang over his bed and shuffled the cards. "What is it?"

"It's called Uno, which means one in Spanish. My stepdad introduced the game to my family and it's become a favorite. It's not quite the same intensity and full-out battle with two people, but I thought we'd give it a go anyway."

He watched her long, graceful fingers as she shuffled the deck. He wondered what it'd be like to have those fingers caressing him instead of a pack of cards that couldn't enjoy it.

Grateful for the table covering his groin, he finally replied, "How do you play?"

As she explained about how it was based on colors or a card with the same value, unless he had a wild card to change the color played, he somehow concentrated on the rules instead of her lips. Barely.

When she finished, he asked, "So what does the winner get?"

She raised her brows. "Bragging rights. That's enough, aye?"

He adjusted his seat on the bed. "No, the stakes are too low. I say we make it more interesting."

She tilted her head and studied him a beat. "Do you, now? And what, pray tell, would you ask for?"

He didn't hesitate, "For a kiss."

She blinked. "What?"

"You heard me—a kiss. With you, specifically."

Her eyes darted to his mouth a second and back to his eyes. She bit her lip—he restrained a groan at her teeth clenching her plump flesh—and replied, "I don't know if that's a good idea."

He hated her hesitation, but he couldn't just order her to give it to him. "What, are you afraid of losing?"

She stood a wee bit taller. "Of course not. Whilst there is an element of luck, I'm fairly good at the strategy part."

"Right, then it shouldn't be a problem."

After studying him a second, she asked, "And what do I get if I win?"

He searched her eyes. "What do you want, angel?"

She blinked at his endearment, but it's how he saw her—the dark-haired beauty who'd been there when he first woke up.

After clearing her throat, she said, "For you to watch an entire movie with me in one sitting."

It seemed an easy request. But for some reason the thought of staring at a television for an hour or two wasn't…desirable. Almost as if he'd rather do anything else.

Not that he could figure out why. Maybe she'd picked that boon on purpose, to see if it'd irritate him.

Still, Logan was in it to win it, so he put out a hand. "Aye, let's shake on the terms."

She put her hand in his and shook. However, before she could let go, he tightened his grip and gently yanked her closer until her face was a few inches from his. He noticed her pupils flashed a little and her breathing quicken, which only made blood rush to his cock.

He ignored it to murmur, "I look forward to claiming my prize." Logan deliberately looked at her lips and Emma's tongue darted out to lick them.

Resisting a groan, he met her eyes again. She tugged on her hand and after a beat, he released her.

She tried to shuffle the cards again, but they went flying everywhere and she had to pick them up.

Logan smiled. Even if he'd never played before, he sensed unsettling an opponent helped with winning.

Even if they hadn't started, he'd made his first play and he'd do whatever else it took to win. Because he was determined to claim her sweet lips no matter what.

As EMMA shakily gathered up the fallen cards, she tried to calm her racing heart.

But no matter how many deep breaths she took, she couldn't forget the heated look Logan had given her a moment before.

Logan, of all people, staring at her as if he'd devour her, given the chance.

For years, Emma had never really thought of him as more than her friend, her best friend, the one person whom she could always lean on, no matter what. Not since the one incident in their teens that had sent her fleeing in panic from him.

But when he'd pulled her face close to his and stared at her lips, a rush of heat had shot through her body, surprising her.

Logan was an attractive male with his blond hair and deep-brown eyes, she knew that rationally; it was a fact. However, since reaching adulthood, she'd never really noticed his broad shoulders or his chiseled jaw, or how his hair looked soft and she wanted to run her fingers through it.

Until now.

Because now, as he stared at her lips, she stared at his. And a sudden longing to kiss him coursed through her body, scaring her for so many reasons.

The same reasons that had sent her fleeing from him the first time he'd kissed her when she'd been sixteen years old.

Her dragon spoke up. *Forget those childish fears and give him a chance. Maybe he has the right idea—kissing would be nice.*

You're just saying that because you want me to finally have sex with someone.

Her beast sniffed. *It's long past due. And I've been bloody patient.*

For most dragon-shifters, her inner beast was right. Dragons craved sex, a lot, and usually started experimenting early on.

However, despite what everyone thought of her, about how she flirted and slept with every male she came across, she never had.

Not that she held her virginity as some precious thing, or any such rubbish. No, it was because she was afraid of something much, much worse. Something that sharing her body could help make a reality.

Emma was terrified of falling in love and losing it, like what had happened to her mother.

She'd seen firsthand how losing a beloved mate could destroy a person, make them barely function and struggle to come back from their grief. While Emma knew her mother had always loved her, for the first few years after her dad's death, she'd had a hard time understanding why her previously laughing mum often stayed in bed, or went through the motions with barely paying attention to her children, or why she'd find her remaining parent secretly crying at night when Emma had trouble sleeping and went looking for comfort.

Her dad's death had devastated her mother, nearly destroying her. And even if eventually her mum had become more herself, Emma had vowed never to risk it.

So she flirted and teased, making people think she slept around, all so no one would guess at her greatest fear.

And while tempted once or twice, she'd never felt the all-encompassing urge to strip her clothes off and throw herself at a male as she just had with Logan's heated look.

It fucking terrified her.

She finished gathering the cards and finally replied to her dragon, *Not now. I need to win so Logan won't kiss me and we'll have to watch the movie. That might remind him of how much he hates watching TV when he'd rather be reading a book.*

Her dragon growled. *Maybe you should let him win. Kissing him might be nice. More than nice, actually.*

He's not our true mate, you know that. So why are you acting this way?

Maybe I'm tired of waiting for you to realize sex, and love, and all those sorts of emotions are worth the risk to experience them.

Not wanting to argue with her dragon yet again about it, she constructed a mental maze and threw her roaring beast into it. There. Now she'd have a wee bit of peace so she could concentrate.

Standing up, she shuffled the cards one last time, took a deep breath, and met Logan's brown-eyed gaze. The blatant desire and heat there made her blink, but she somehow found the strength to ignore it and deal the cards. Once she flipped the top card from the pile, she motioned to Logan. "You go first."

"Is this a practice round?"

She raised an eyebrow. "Not so cocky now, aye? I thought you were going to win, whatever it took. That says you don't need one."

The corner of his mouth ticked up, making his face even more handsome.

Wait. No. Logan wasn't handsome, not like that.

He replied, "Fine, then we'll play without a practice round. Although if you forgot a rule and try to introduce it later, it means we start over."

She finished rearranging her cards into color

groups and then numerical order. "Aye, fine. I told you everything, though. I don't need to cheat."

As they played, Logan did well enough. But soon she had him holding a massive amount of cards in his hand whereas she only had three.

But her confidence vanished when he piled on the cards until she had about twenty bloody cards in her hand, so much so they had to reshuffle the discard pile just to have more cards to play.

He smirked as she finished shuffling. "You were too confident, and I pounced. I don't think you're going to recover."

Scanning her cards, she formed a strategy. "We'll see, Logan Lamont, we'll see."

Not much teasing went on as they both tried to best the other. The result was that an hour later, they still hadn't finished the game.

Emma sighed. "This could go on quite a while. That's the downside to only having two players, is that the game can keep swinging back and forth forever."

"Giving up, are you?" His eyes went to her lips. "I'll gladly take your forfeit."

When his gaze didn't move from her mouth, her nipples tightened at the same time wetness rushed between her thighs.

She tried not to squirm as she wondered what was wrong with her. How could a pair of brown eyes she'd seen thousands of times in her life suddenly be intriguing, and sexy, and make her want him to look at more than just her mouth. Such as maybe her naked body.

No. This was Logan, for crying out loud. The boy she'd had to drag away from a book merely to come outside, or who had constantly scolded her for running wild when she shouldn't have.

He was most definitely not a sexy male she wanted to explore with her hands, or her tongue, or her lips.

He just *wasn't.*

Emma cleared her throat. "Of course not. Let's keep playing."

But it wasn't long before Emma was losing rather badly. Mostly because she kept sneaking glances at Logan's solid jaw, or his broad shoulders, or even his defined forearms.

Bloody forearms? Aye, she was slowly going mad.

The distraction worked to his advantage until before she knew it, Emma had lost.

Logan smirked. "I won, angel."

Taking a deep breath, she tried to calm her racing heart. The best way to handle this was to merely accept his kiss without reacting to it. If she played the bumbling, cold fish, he'd give up. After all, the tactic had worked before, when a male had thought she wanted more than flirtations.

Laying her cards down, she nodded. "Aye, you did. Ready to claim your prize?"

He smiled slowly, making her lower belly flutter. How had she never noticed how handsome he was when he smiled?

Logan shook his head. "Not now. I'll claim it at a later date."

"Pardon?"

He shrugged. "I'm tired right now and I want to make it worth my while when I finally get to kiss you."

"But—"

"You didn't say it had to be claimed right away, aye? I'll let you know when I'm ready for it."

Pushing past her surprise, she studied his face and finally noticed the darkening circles under his eyes as well the slight shaking of his hands.

She'd been so absorbed in winning the bloody game that she'd forgotten how Logan had nearly died a few days before.

And considering she'd been the cause, she should've remembered that.

Gathering up the cards, she replied, "Of course. You need to rest, and no, don't start growling at me for mentioning it. I can see your exhaustion in every movement of your body. And if you truly want to be in fine shape to claim your prize, you need to heal."

When Logan merely bobbed his head, she knew he was more exhausted than he let on. She clicked her tongue. "Do you need anything before I leave? Don't hold back and try to be all macho about it either. You always tell me how I need to learn to ask for help, so you should follow your own advice."

As soon as she said it, Emma mentally cursed. She'd been doing so well at not hinting about his past and merely being the friend he needed.

Logan's gaze shuttered and she couldn't tell what he was thinking. He grunted. "I need to piss, but I can manage that on my own."

He pushed the table aside, gingerly rose from his bed, and walked slowly toward the attached toilet, slamming the door in his wake.

Well, now that was quite the dismissal. However, she gathered her cards and left, doing her best to brush it off. She'd try again tomorrow and be more careful when it came to mentioning the version of him before losing his memories. Unless he asked about it, of course, but she didn't think he would.

Although she had another task to add to her list as well—distract him enough so he'd forget to claim his kiss. Emma didn't mind paying her debts, but she was afraid that if she let Logan kiss her, it might change everything forever. And she most definitely didn't want to risk that.

Chapter Four

Logan woke up the next day to find the male claiming to be his brother, Phillip, sitting in a chair next to his bed reading a book.

The male's hair was light brown to Logan's blond, but he had the same deep-brown eyes and defined jawline. Although only a couple years older than him, Phillip had lines around his eyes and mouth as well as some gray streaks in his hair.

He thought something must've prematurely aged him, but he was afraid to ask what. Every time someone revealed a part of his life from "before," Logan grew frustrated at himself.

Sometimes even a wee bit terrified. Because what if he didn't like who he'd been? He had no bloody idea if he could change it, if it turned out that way either.

Logan must've made a sound because Phillip looked up and smiled at him. "You're finally awake. I was hoping that would happen before I had to go watch my son for a bit."

He did his best to keep his voice polite. Just because his life was in shambles didn't mean he had to take it out on everyone else. Instinctively, Logan knew he wasn't a full-blown arsehole. "What do you want?"

Phillip laid aside his book and leaned forward a fraction. "First, let me say I'm not here to push at you to remember me. I was a wee bit frantic the first time I saw you after nearly drowning. It's not every day a male nearly loses his little brother."

Sensing it was an apology, he nodded and Phillip continued, "I will say this, though—when I needed your help the most, you gave it without worrying about the risk to yourself. So I'm going to do the same, if it comes to it, regardless if you remember me or not."

Not for the first time, Logan wished he knew why all these strangers were so dedicated to him.

However, a headache started behind his eyes as he tried to remember the older male who looked so much like him, so he stopped trying. "Thank you."

Phillip nodded. "Aye, well, here's the other reason I wanted a wee chat with you before I had to leave. You see, Layla is going to release you in the next couple days or so, but only if you agree to stay with someone for a while. You may never get your memory back, and I get that. However, in the meantime, you need to get settled into the clan. And both Finn and Layla agree that for now, it'd be helpful to have someone ease you into life on Lochguard, aye? I've come to see if you want to stay with me and Yasmin. We do have Jacob, and he still cries at night sometimes, but it's not too bad. What do you think?"

Logan knew from his brother's first visit that Yasmin was Phillip's mate and Dr. McFarland's younger sister. Jacob was Yasmin and Phillip's young son, meaning he was supposed to be Logan's nephew.

None of which triggered any sort of memory or sense of family. His head throbbed behind his eyes a few beats. After a deep breath, he replied, "I appreciate the offer, but I'm not sure if staying with someone I'm supposed to be close to will help or frustrate me more." Sadness flashed in Phillip's eyes and for some reason, Logan didn't like it. So he quickly added, "I don't mind seeing you from time to time, as long as you don't push me to remember you or your family. But staying with someone that's more neutral, who didn't know me very well before the accident, might help better. That way I'll have space to figure out who the bloody hell I am and what to do about it if this is all I will be going forward. Does that make sense?"

Phillip bobbed his head. "Aye, it does. Although the older brother in me wants to keep you safe in my home, to protect you. But you're a grown male, and I need to respect that, or so my mate tells me." Phillip smiled a moment and then asked, "Have you thought of who you might stay with? Maybe someone you've met since waking up? Because Layla said the only way out of this room is for you to find a host home, of sorts."

In other words, the doctor wanted someone to be his babysitter.

Pushing aside his irritation at that thought, Logan focused on Phillip's question and instantly knew who he wanted to stay with. But there was no way Emma MacAllister would say yes.

He shook his head. "Not really. I'm open to suggestions."

"Hm, well let me ask you one thing—do you want someone to be brutally honest with you at every turn or more cautious?"

"I'd prefer honesty, I think."

Phillip nodded. "Then I can think of two choices, off the top of my head. You can stay with one of the MacKenzies—who are rather loud, like to tease, and honest to a fault, but they each have mates and children. The second option is you can stay with the

MacAllister brothers, Ian, Connor, and Jamie, who share a cottage together and are all unattached. You were never really more than acquaintances with the three lads, but they're all young males like you and would love nothing more than to be honest with you, if only to irritate their sister." He paused, searched Logan's gaze, and asked, "You've seen Emma since waking up, aye?"

He said slowly, "Aye."

When Logan said nothing else, Phillip spoke again. "Then your choice comes down to whether you want teasing and a wee bit of caution with the MacKenzies, or would you prefer the blunt honesty of young males who would love to irritate you to drive their sister mad?"

It was almost as if Phillip was trying to scare him off the MacAllisters. And yet, being surrounded by males who didn't really know much about him, and would be blunt, seemed more appealing. And not just because it might mean he'd probably see Emma more often. Or at least could ask for more information about her.

Logan hadn't forgot about his boon to kiss her, but he'd like to make the most of it, for sure.

Decision made, he stated, "The MacAllister brothers, if they'll let me stay there."

Phillip snorted. "Between Layla, Finn, and Sylvia Swift—the lads' mother—they won't be allowed to say no. Even with knowing they might be guilt-tripped into it, do you still want to stay with them?"

"Aye," he answered. "I could do without being treated delicate and special. And if I can't stand my own against them, then it's my own fault."

Phillip studied him again and unease crawled across Logan's skin. Was he behaving differently? Did his supposed brother disapprove?

It shouldn't mean anything, and yet it did, somehow.

No matter if he didn't remember Phillip or not, the resemblance between them was too uncanny to deny they were related.

Phillip's pupils flashed to slits and then became round again. "Aye, then I'll talk with Layla and the others. You won't be able to move in for a couple of days, at the earliest. But I'll make sure you have your clothes and other essentials there ahead of time." He paused and then said softly, "Reach out to me if you need to, Logan. I mean it."

He nodded and a nurse entered before he could say more. Phillip said goodbye and went to set everything up.

All during his latest vitals check, Logan could only hope he'd made the right choice with the MacAllister brothers. If they ever caught wind of his bet to kiss their sister, no doubt there'd be hell to pay.

However, something told him he couldn't let her

family scare him away. It was almost as if he knew this time he needed to be determined and strong.

Which made no bloody sense because surely if he'd kissed Emma in the past, she would've mentioned it.

EMMA WAS HELPING to care for her baby sister, Sophie, when her eldest brother, Connor, stormed into the house, bellowing her name. When he entered the living room, the frown on his face and fire flashing in his gaze put her guard up further. Something had happened.

He pointed a finger at you. "Did you set this up?"

She blinked as she stood and placed Sophie on her hip. "I haven't the faintest bloody idea of what you're talking about."

Connor crossed his arms over his chest and narrowed his eyes—the same blue all the siblings shared, along with dark hair. Whilst her eldest brother could be extremely mature when it came to business and running a restaurant, he acted like a piqued teenager when it came to his siblings sometimes.

He growled, "Oh, aye? So you didn't make it so Logan Lamont has to live with me, Ian, and Jamie for a bit?"

She frowned as she lightly jostled her sister,

hoping Connor's tone wouldn't upset her. "What are you blathering about?"

"You heard me. Finn and Dr. McFarland all but decreed he needed a place to stay, someplace with people who hadn't been close to him before he lost his memory, and said it would be at our cottage."

She raised her brows. "Aye, well, this is the first I've heard of it. Why would they do that?"

Connor's stance softened a fraction. "You truly didn't know?" She shook her head and he sighed. "I have no bloody idea, Em. I would think they'd put him with a family or something, not in a cottage of bachelors."

She snorted. "And if you had the choice, would you want to stay with a family and children of people you couldn't remember or other males closer to you in age, with no children around?"

He grunted but didn't answer. Emma rolled her eyes and switched her gaze to Sophie. Keeping her voice light and high in the way people did with bairns, she said, "Our brother is being a silly goose, isn't he, love? You'd think they asked him to give up his restaurant and join the Royal Air Force, or some such thing."

Sophie merely babbled something incomprehensible, and Emma grinned at her sister. "My thoughts exactly."

Connor shook his head. "Stop being silly, Emma. What with the restaurant and, er, other interests, I don't have time to babysit a grown male."

The other interest being his friendship with the reclusive Aimee King, a female from another clan who lived on Lochguard and was trying to heal from her long imprisonment and torture.

She often teased him about Aimee, but it wasn't the right time. So instead, Emma looked back at her brother and raised her brows. "Is that what they told you to do? To babysit Logan?"

"Er, no. But he can't remember a blasted thing, aye? He's going to need lots of help getting used to things again. Bloody hell, he doesn't even remember he's a dragon-shifter. It'll be like educating him all over again."

Without thinking, she answered, "And I'll help him. But he obviously can't live with me and Kaylee."

"Obviously, aye? I would think it'd be fine. You've rebuffed him for years. Although maybe Kaylee would take an interest."

Emma's cheeks heated. "I'm not talking about that. Besides, he's different now without his memories. I don't always know how he'll act."

Connor scrutinized her face. "He hasn't done anything to hurt you, has he, Em? Tell me now and I'll make sure he pays for it."

She sighed. "Just stop, Connor. We're fine. He's my best friend and I'm helping him, that's all."

Connor opened his mouth but she beat him to it. "And don't dare say something about a magical vagina, or what have you, as it's not like that between us, despite what you always tease."

He raised his eyebrows. "I wasn't thinking that at all. Interesting that you did, though, aye?"

Her dragon spoke up. *He's right. You want what I do.*

Hush, dragon. Not now.

Fine. But don't expect me to do so when we see Logan again. I'm looking forward to that kiss.

Ignoring her dragon, she hastily said, "Just be nice to Logan, but don't coddle him. I can easily do my work from anywhere with an internet connection, so I'll probably be spending most of my time with him at your place. You won't have to worry about 'babysitting' him, as you put it."

Connor stared a few beats and then sighed. "I'll do it for you, not him. Although if he shows the slightest disrespect toward you, I'll kick his arse out immediately."

"It won't come to that, I'm sure."

Her brother moved closer and took Sophie into his arms. He looked at their wee sister as he said, "See, this is why I'm your favorite brother, lassie. I'll do anything for my sisters."

He kissed Sophie's forehead and Emma smiled. "Although to be fair, if I'd talked with Ian, he would've convinced you anyway, Connor."

"Don't remind me of your stupid twin bond and just say thank you."

She laughed. "Thank you, big brother." Emma sobered. "Hopefully Ian will be around more soon. I miss him."

Her twin brother had been gone for weeks now, and no one knew where he was. Well, that wasn't exactly true. The clan leader and the Protectors did, but they wouldn't share Ian's location.

Connor replied, "We all miss him, Em, even if he's irritating at times. But he's doing some secret project, and you've done something similar yourself in the past. He'll be around once he's finished."

She grumbled, "I know, but I don't have to like it."

Growing up, especially after their dad's death, she and Ian had been really close and rarely apart. The dynamic had changed as they became adults, but they often confided in each other over their other siblings, and she keenly missed his presence. Especially with everything that had happened with Logan.

But she knew Ian would seek her out as soon as he could, and that would have to be good enough.

After they chatted a bit more about nothing, Connor returned Sophie to her care and went back to work at the restaurant.

And although Emma would trust her brother with her life, she was a wee bit afraid of what her brothers would do with Logan while he stayed with them. Logan had always been a more cautious and restrained individual before the incident. Whereas her brothers, well, they were loud and rather reactionary. At least Connor and Jamie were. And with Ian MIA for some secret project, who was usually the calming influence, she only hoped the bachelor cottage didn't turn into an all-out war.

Chapter Five

As Connor MacAllister introduced himself and his brother Jamie, Logan could immediately tell that the male didn't have any love for him.

Although why he glared and studied him so closely, he had no idea. According to everyone, he hadn't really known the MacAllister siblings well, apart from Emma.

Emma. He'd hoped to finally see her again in his temporary new home with her brothers, but the dark-haired lass was nowhere in sight. Despite saying she'd return the next day, the doctors had kept him from visitors to run a million tests and ensure he was healthy enough to leave the surgery. They especially kept waiting for his inner dragon—he supposedly had one—to return. But since he hadn't, they'd run even more tests.

So after being constantly poked, prodded, and

questioned, Logan wasn't exactly affable to begin with. But the macho bullshit from Connor MacAllister already grated on his nerves.

Which is why he clenched the fingers of one hand and willed himself not to punch Connor before they parted ways.

Connor grunted and finally spoke again. "We don't have an extra bedroom for you, so you'll have to sleep on the sofa."

He glanced at the battered piece of furniture, which was tilted to one side due to missing some little leg pieces on the bottom.

It was yet another way Connor was trying to get him to cry off. Too bad he wasn't giving up. At least here he'd be treated as any other male instead of a doll about to break at the first hardship.

Wanting to irritate the blighter, Logan shrugged. "No bother. Anywhere is better than a hospital bed and a room where people constantly come to check on you and document your every more. Unless you plan to do that?"

Connor snorted. "I don't have bloody time to babysit you, Lamont."

Jamie—another dark-haired, blue-eyed MacAllister—finally spoke up. "That's right, me either. I have a UK children's football tournament to help organize."

"I'll somehow find a way to dress and bathe myself," Logan bit out sarcastically. "Now, since the two of you are so busy, you can scurry off and leave me alone."

Jamie looked about ready to protest, but Connor gently pushed his youngest brother toward the front door. "Let's leave him be, Jamie. I need to get back to the restaurant." Connor looked over this shoulder. "And don't steal any of our food. You'll have to get your own."

With that, the two lads left and Logan rolled his eyes. From what everyone told him, he was older than all the MacAllister brothers. And after all the dick swinging, it certainly felt like it.

As his stomach rumbled, he headed toward the kitchen. He'd take what he wanted and deal with the repercussions later.

He hadn't done more than open the refrigerator when Emma appeared in the door leading to the back garden. He noted her flushed cheeks and the way her sleeveless top highlighted the tattoo on her arm, the one meaning she was a dragon-shifter. Then his eyes lingered on her breasts.

Breasts with already pert nipples poking through the thin top.

His cock stirred and he itched to pull her close and suck those hard little buds through her shirt.

As if noticing his gaze, Emma hugged her laptop to her chest and frowned. "Pilfering food already, I see. Connor won't like it."

If she wanted to pretend he hadn't just been

staring at her nipples, he'd play along. For now. "Aye, I got that impression. Although he won't know until later, and it's not like they're going to starve me. Once I go shopping, I'll replace it."

She rolled her eyes and moved closer to him. As she did, he noticed a faint flowery scent mixed with what had to be pure female.

He wanted to lean down and kiss her neck, where no doubt her scent was stronger.

However, her voice garnered his attention once more and he met her gaze. "Oh, he'll notice straight away since Connor labels *everything* in a unique script." She gestured toward the refrigerator. "Take a look."

She couldn't be serious. But as he turned and looked at all the things labeled "Connor" in a cursive script that would be hard to replicate, Logan shook his head. "As if writing a name will stop someone."

He reached for a yogurt and Emma snorted. Glancing over his shoulder, he raised an eyebrow. "What?"

"I wouldn't do that if I were you."

Feeling contrary, he pulled off the top with a flourish. "Oh, the horror. I should prepare for war."

She battled a smile. "You and your sarcasm. But he'll get you back, just wait and see. One thing you don't mess with when it comes to my brothers is food."

"Then what they need to do is find someone to bed and fuck senseless, and quickly."

Emma's cheeks flushed and it made her look a wee bit younger than her twenty-three years. "Why would you say something like that? They're my brothers, and that's, just, no."

Ah, so that was the cause of her distress. Apparently his old, holier-than-thou self wouldn't have teased her about her brothers getting some.

Well, too bad. He shrugged. "Why not say they need a good fuck? It's true. From what I can remember of dragon-shifters, they like sex. So if they lack a partner, it must be because of their sterling personalities."

She stood a wee bit taller. "Not everything is about sex."

"Tell that to history and all the leaders and armies who fell because of it, at least tangentially."

She raised her brows. "So does that mean you're going to go on the prowl and pull the first willing female?"

He couldn't pass up this opportunity to scan her body from head to toe and back again. "Why? Are you offering?"

He expected her to protest, or slap him, or something. But her cheeks turned even pinker.

Aye, that was interesting.

Emma readjusted her grip on her laptop and took a few steps back. "Certainly not. I have work to do. I'm here in case you need anything or have questions." He opened his mouth to tease, but Emma bit out, "But not concerning *that*."

He smiled. "And what is *that* by chance?"

Her cheeks were nearly red now, and her pupils kept flashing to slits. She squeaked a bit when she said, "You know what I'm talking about."

He enjoyed how flustered Emma became when talking about kisses or sex. "No, you need to spell it out for me. I'm not quite fully recovered, aye?"

She rolled her eyes. "Don't do that. You're clever, so don't hide it. I never understood why you always brush off just how intelligent you are."

At the mention of "always" his good humor faded. "Sorry to disappoint you, angel. But this is the first time I can remember doing it."

He spotted a spoon drying in a rack on the counter, nabbed it, and headed toward the living room.

He knew Emma had slipped up by mistake and not on purpose. After all, they'd supposedly known each other nearly their whole lives. She was bound to say things without thinking.

And yet he hated not knowing if she preferred him then or now. It shouldn't matter, and yet it did.

So he stabbed his yogurt, took a bite, and went looking for something to read so he could ignore Emma. Otherwise he might do something stupid, like argue some more, or even kiss her. He wasn't ready to claim his boon just yet. No, he wanted her burning for it first.

EMMA WAS STILL TRYING to get her blasted cheeks to cool when Logan stormed out of the kitchen.

And aye, stormed was the right word.

Surely he knew she didn't mean to mention his habits or actions from the past sometimes. She was trying, but it was still hard to think of him as a new male, one she didn't know at all.

Her dragon spoke up. *If having three brothers has taught us anything, it's that male egos are fickle things. Just be careful with his.*

I'm not going to lavish praise on him like a child.

Her beast snorted. *No, of course not. But you could always remind him of his prize to be claimed—a kiss.*

Why would I do that?

Because you want him to kiss us as much as I do.

No, you just want sex. Maybe you'd be willing to throw away a lifelong friendship for a few orgasms, but not me.

Who says it has to be only a few?

Ignoring her dragon, she hugged her laptop tighter against her chest, took a few deep breaths to cool her cheeks and relax her nipples, and decided she could change subjects with Logan and get him settled. Because if he kept stealing Connor's food, he had no idea what sort of hell awaited him later.

Stealing food often meant war growing up. Logan simply had no idea.

With her cheeks cooled down and boobs relaxed, she waltzed into the living room as if she hadn't been itching to feel his lips against her skin, or hands caressing her body.

However, the sight of Logan with a book in his hand, reading the title, was so achingly familiar that for a beat, she desperately missed her lifelong best friend.

But then she remembered that Logan's injury and lack of memory were her fault. Hers. If she'd been more considerate, it never would've come to this. She deserved the pain of missing him, and so much more.

Pushing aside her guilt, she remained silent as she sat in the comfy chair, the only piece of furniture that didn't rock or tilt to one side.

Honestly, her brothers were ridiculous when it came to decorating a home.

She'd opened her laptop and typed for a few minutes before Logan spoke again. "What are you working on?"

She glanced up, surprised to see him sans book. "You didn't find something to read?"

He shrugged. "Nothing seemed interesting."

"Given how Ian's the big reader in the family and he only reads thrillers or spy novels, that doesn't surprise me. They're all a bit over the top, although Ian says that's why he reads them."

He sat on the uneven couch and did the masculine sprawl all males seemed to do, with his legs wide and his arms splayed behind him. It took everything she had not to peek at his crotch— something she'd never been tempted to do before—as he said, "Ian is the middle brother, and your twin."

"Aye. He and I have always been close, so living apart for the first time has been a bit odd."

"Then why not live here with your brothers?"

She raised her brows. "And go crazy? Ian I could handle all the time, but all three? And without Mum's influence? No, thank you. And before you ask, Ian decided to live with Connor and Jamie instead of with me to ensure the pair don't kill each other."

When Logan did nothing but stare at her, she looked back at her screen and typed some more. She'd never get her latest software for the clan finished if she didn't try to focus.

Although as Logan ate his yogurt and tried to find a comfortable position on the lopsided sofa, she found it harder to make sense of the words and numbers on the screen.

Which was odd, given that she and Logan had never had problems with long stretches of silence before.

Her beast spoke up. *But he's different, aye? And admit it—you're curious to learn how he's changed.*

Emma tried to steal a look at Logan, only to find him watching her. No friendly or slightly annoyed look like in the past, before the incident. No, it was full of heat and desire. Even without his flashing dragon eyes, it made her lower belly flutter.

Her cheeks heated up again and she glanced back at her computer.

Logan's voice filled the room again. "Just one more question and I'll leave you alone for a bit." He waited until she looked up to continue. "What were we doing the day I was injured and lost my memory? Anytime I've asked about it, someone always changed the topic. But since you were there, you know, don't you?" She nodded. "Then tell me."

She was about to ask if he could handle it—that would be a good way to avoid answering his question —but knew it was irritating if people kept incessantly asking that question. Her eldest sister, Cat, had been on strict bedrest for almost her entire pregnancy and had quickly let them know that if she truly didn't feel well, she'd say something.

Even if the situation were different, she was going to try and trust Logan to tell her if he needed help.

Which, unfortunately, meant she'd have to answer his question. And unlike everyone else, she wasn't going to keep it from him. She had amends to make, and telling him the full truth was part of it.

Closing her laptop, she met him dead in the eye, and asked, "Do you recall what geocaching is?"

After a beat, he nodded. "Sort of like a modern-day treasure hunt which uses apps, GPS, or smartphones to track down and locate items."

"Aye. Most of them are purely for fun, where people merely seek out caches—usually it's some sort of waterproof container hidden away—to sign their name in a logbook and maybe claim a cheap prize. A few have mysteries or puzzles to solve, leading to the next one. And in rare cases, there is a competition with a prize for the first to find it."

"So I take it that's what we were doing that day? Looking for the treasure cache?"

"I was, aye. You were there in case of injury, since sometimes the locations can end up being a bit dodgy or unsafe."

"I see that worked out well," he muttered.

She didn't want to keep going, but she was determined to be honest with Logan, even if he ended up hating her after learning the full truth. "You saved me that day, Logan. You tossed me out of the way of a falling rock and took the hit yourself."

"Did I?"

Strange how no one had told him that. She bobbed her head. "You warned me repeatedly to be careful, and I brushed it aside as you being overprotective and overly cautious." She briefly explained the bloody stupid rock-climbing contest and then added, "I'm so sorry, Logan. I should've listened to you."

He stared at her a beat, and she did her best not

to fidget. However, when he spoke again, his words surprised her. "What sort of thing were you going after for this hunt?"

She blinked. "I tell you about how my recklessness nearly killed you and you want to know about the cache?"

He shrugged. "I'm alive, aren't I? Besides, now I'm curious about what you were searching for."

Since Logan had never really wanted to know the details before, a sense of excitement rushed through her. She rarely talked about her geocaching adventures with anyone. "It wasn't the usual sort, where you find a book to sign or maybe some coins or plastic toys to take as a token prize."

He raised his brows. "No? Then what were you going after?"

She bit her lip a second but decided what the hell, she'd tell him. "It was an invite-only hunt, one with a grand prize at the end. The clue on that mountain was the third phase."

"And did you find it?"

She shook her head. "Of course not. Saving you was more important."

"Could it still be there?"

She frowned. "It should be, as there are a number of further caches to find before the grand prize and the rules state you can't remove the finds or you'll be disqualified and have to pay a hefty fine."

He tilted his head. "And what's the grand prize at the end of this one?"

She whispered, "Half a million pounds."

He blinked, and then blinked some more. He eventually cleared his throat. "Who would give up that much money for a game?"

She sat up a little taller. "It's more than a game. This particular event was invite-only for those with a track record, and everyone paid an entrance fee. That helped to cover the costs. As for the remainder, I suspect this person wants to hold other competitions in the future but needs to prove their hunts are legitimate with their inaugural contest. So they're absorbing some of the prize money costs as part of a long-term goal."

Logan shook his head. "Bloody hell, that's a risk. Just how many people are looking for this massive cash prize?"

She tapped her fingers against the top of her laptop. "Thousands. It'd be more, except the search is limited to England and Scotland. Whilst it may seem that makes the contest easier with only two countries instead of the whole world, it's actually harder because the locations are all relatively close, making the competition fiercer."

"Has anyone found the prize yet?"

She shook her head, having kept track of the winner announcement page. "No. But even so, it's not as if I'm going to go after it."

"Why not?"

She finally glanced down at her hands atop her computer, twisting her fingers. "Because it was stupid and it ended up hurting you."

Logan's voice softened. "What were your reasons for joining these sort of hunts? Tell me."

Emma dared a glance at Logan and was taken aback for a second at the curiosity in his gaze. No one had ever asked that before, not even when her brother Ian had caught her in the middle of one of her first geocaching adventures.

She should brush it off. It didn't matter why she'd done it. No, all that mattered was what had happened to Logan. She'd decided to give up geocaching to avoid hurting anyone else.

But then he moved to squat next to her chair and searched her gaze. "Tell me. I'd rather not guilt-trip you into doing so, but I just might if you hold back."

She smiled slightly. "It's an odd thing to guilt-trip a person into talking about geocaching."

He shrugged one shoulder. "I'm discovering that I like to find answers, so I use whatever tools I can to get them."

That aspect about Logan hadn't changed. He'd always been curious.

Although he seemed a wee bit less cautious in his present state. She pushed aside her guilt at how much she liked the change. Instead she cleared her throat and finally answered his question. "In the early days,

I started geocaching to stem boredom. I've always been clever, and if I don't keep my mind occupied, I start going mad. However, this last one was for something grander, something not for me but others."

He searched her eyes and gently touched her thigh as he asked, "Which is?"

For a beat, all she felt was his fingers on her leg. Despite her jeans between them, a warmth radiated up toward her pussy, aching for his thumb to trail upward and stroke her.

What's wrong with me? It's Logan.

Her dragon snorted. *Aye, and he has a cock that likes females. So use it.*

"Emma?" He caressed her leg slowly and she bit her bottom lip to keep from making a sound. "Tell me, angel. I can guilt-trip you about how it hurt me, but I don't want that. I want you to tell me because you feel like it."

She stared into his brown eyes, and knew she'd tell him. Not even her mum knew what Emma wanted to do, and yet, she couldn't seem to deny the male in front of her. Before she could change her mind, she answered in a rush, "I sometimes help out pensioners and others that need some additional assistance inside the clan. And it didn't take long for me to realize they could be lonely at times, especially if their mate or other family had passed on. I want to build a senior center where they can socialize and have fun. Although over time, I thought wouldn't it be grand to also include humans too? My brother Jamie does a brilliant job with his human and dragon-shifter football matches. And whilst forming friendships between the children is key, why not do it with the elderly as well? Because change needs to take place amongst all humans, not just the young or those who mate us." She looked down at her hands. "I wanted to use the prize money to make my dreams a reality."

His hand covered one of hers and squeezed. "Then you shouldn't give up until the contest is over, and you bloody well shouldn't give it up completely if you enjoy it."

Her eyes met his again, his support doing strange things to her heart. Emma barely resisted threading her fingers through his, wanting something from him she was afraid to name. "I don't plan on giving up forever, but another contest will come along, aye? And that time I'll be more careful and strategic, to ensure no one gets hurt."

Logan moved his hand from her thigh to one of the hands in her lap and lightly stroked the back of her knuckles. The touch drew her gaze to his actions, his long fingers gently caressing hers.

Emma had never really paid attention to his hands before, but they were slightly rough with callouses in a few places. Just what did he do to get them?

She apparently didn't know as much about him as she'd thought.

His voice prevented her from asking about the rough patches on his fingers. "How about if we finish this current treasure hunt competition as a team? I have nothing else to do at the moment, and even if I can't remember my own personal life history, I seem to remember everything else. I could help you."

Her gaze snapped up to his. "You want to help me?"

He raised his brows. "Why do you say that as if I'd just asked you to sleep naked in the snow?"

She eyed him warily, but knew she had to refer to the past to make him understand. "Because you've never wanted to help me before. If anything, you tried to talk me out of it."

He shrugged. "Aye, well, I can't remember that, can I? But who knows, maybe spending time with you will help me remember a few things. We've supposedly known each other our whole lives, aye?" She nodded and Logan stood, removing his hand. Emma nearly grabbed it back, but didn't as he continued, "Why don't you confirm no one has found the prize yet, and if so, fill me in on what you've done so far. Then we'll strategize and make a plan from there, aye?"

Despite how she desperately wanted to shout yes and get to work with Logan, she shook her head. "Dr. McFarland would never let you go wandering off to who the bloody hell knows where with me in your current state."

Especially since Iris was still investigating who might've wanted to hurt them.

A determined gleam flashed in his eyes. "She declared me physically on the mend, with nothing serious to worry about. I'm sure if we let Finn know where we're going and say it's to see if it'll help jar my memory, he'll probably approve or at least be open to negotiating."

She stood and smiled at him. "Why, Logan Lamont, you're rather crafty."

He grinned and Emma's heart skipped a beat. Since when did he become so bloody handsome?

Logan replied, "All the more reason to use me to help you with your treasure hunt." He put out a hand. "So what do you say? Partners from now on, aye?"

There were so many reasons why she should brush it off and decline. After all, the last time she'd tried to find the next clue, Logan had nearly died.

And yet, Emma knew this time she would be a lot more cautious as she went. No more bravado, or silly competitions, or any other sort of distractions. She'd have to look out for Logan every step of the way; she refused for him to get hurt again. Besides, even if he was physically healed and stronger than her, without his memories, he could easily feel lost and alone.

She'd have to keep a close watch on his mental health.

Her dragon spoke up. *I say go for it. All that time alone together, who knows what might happen?*

I would focus on the contest, nothing more, dragon.

Her beast sniffed. *You say that, but I know how much his looks and even his touch affects you now. If he kissed us, you wouldn't push him away.*

Emma's eyes darted briefly to Logan's lips. No, she wouldn't.

Which scared the crap out of her. *I won't let the chance come up.*

Funny, considering he has at least one kiss to claim from us.

Fuck, she'd forgotten about that. But no matter. Emma could handle one quick peck and walk away.

Her beast laughed. *Tell yourself that. But for now, just accept his help. You've always wanted him to work alongside us.*

It was true. No one in her life truly had an interest in geocaching competitions, or the often fake treasure hunts she did merely to challenge her mind.

And now here was Logan, his hand outstretched, wanting to do exactly that.

The male in question cleared his throat. She glanced back up at his eyes and amusement danced in them. "Do you want to seal our partnership with something else?"

His gaze fell to her lips and they throbbed from the attention.

Aye, she was in trouble if he ever kissed her.

But she'd been deflecting male kisses and sexual interest for years. She could handle one more male.

Keeping it strictly businesslike, she straightened her shoulders and put out a hand. "No, a handshake will do just fine."

He snorted and took her hand. But he didn't merely shake it. No, he also ran his thumb along the back of hers, and the light touch sent a rush of heat through her body.

And judging by the glint in his eyes, he knew it.

Bloody hell, Logan Lamont was becoming too much of a temptation. And because Emma didn't want sex since it could lead to emotional attachment, it made him a danger to her plan to never get close enough to fall in love.

Love? No, she was nowhere near that. This was just a wee bit of lust, nothing more. If she played her cards right, it'd never be more than that.

She tugged her hand and Logan released it. She added, "We'll have to talk to Finn ASAP to get his permission. But before we even do that, let me check and confirm no one has found the prize yet."

He nodded and she opened her laptop. As she entered the password and waited for the secret site to load, her heart beat double-time. Not just because she wanted the prize to still be available, but also because she wanted to go searching with Logan.

She'd never really had a full partner in these endeavors before, and it'd be nice to share a big part of her life with someone.

Her dragon snorted, but Emma ignored her as she read the latest results. She clapped her hands together. "No one has found the prize yet, so there's still a chance!"

She grinned up at Logan and he smiled back. For a beat, it felt completely natural, almost as if she should always be able to share news with Logan and celebrate even the minor things with him.

Which was ridiculous. That was something partners did, mates did, and they weren't more than friends.

Standing up again, she closed her laptop and clutched it to her side. "Right, then I should share everything I have with you so that you're fully aware of what you're agreeing to."

He raised his brows. "What about your work for the clan? Can you delay it?"

Emma waved a hand in dismissal. "I'm actually ahead. I always try to be, since I never know how long I'd be away for a geocaching competition."

He rubbed his hands together. "Aye, good. Then let's get started."

She nodded toward the front door. "Everything is at my place. So I need to fetch it."

He reached out and took her hand. "I'll just come with you and see it there."

It would be easier, but everything was currently pinned to the wall in her bedroom.

Which meant Logan would have to be in her bedroom.

And with his warm skin currently against hers, she was afraid of what she might do if they were alone together behind a closed door.

Her dragon laughed. *You're the one who said you can resist him.*

And aye, I can. Just wait and see.

She tugged her hand free and motioned for Logan to follow her. "Then come on. This could take a while."

Once Logan had grabbed a few things, they went out the door and headed to the place she shared with Kaylee. She hoped her housemate was gone. Otherwise, later on, Kaylee would bombard her with questions until she got the answers she wanted. For a human, she was rather determined.

And given that not even Emma fully understood the changes between her and Logan, she wasn't going to chat with someone else about the male who walked at her side. Not yet. Maybe not ever.

Chapter Six

Logan didn't know why he'd suggested assisting Emma with her competition, but it had just felt…right. Almost as if she should always be able to ask for his help, no questions asked.

Not that it made any sense, given his lack of memories and only really knowing her for a short time, post-waking up. However, going with her would give him something to do instead of focusing on his ever-growing frustration with himself. Not to mention Logan couldn't fault Emma's reasons for wanting to win. After all, instead of going after the prize for selfish reasons, she wanted to help others.

Although why she was so bloody secretive about it, he had no clue.

It wasn't long before they reached a wee cottage, one of the older ones on the clan with a thatched roof, and Emma entered slowly. She called out, "Kaylee?"

After a beat of silence, she sagged a fraction. He couldn't help but ask, "You live with someone you don't like?"

She frowned at him. "I like Kaylee quite a bit. But she does like to chat, and I'd rather not have any distractions right now. If, and that's a big if, I do continue looking for the final prize, I don't want to waste any more time." She motioned down the hall. "Follow me."

The contrast between this cottage and her brothers' was massive, and not just because it was a lot smaller. The furniture didn't tilt, for starters, and there were little touches of art, or flowers, or even figurines. As they walked past the living room, he noticed an entire case full of fairy creatures. "You like fairies?"

She laughed. "No, but Kaylee does. Even if she knows they don't exist like dragons do, she likes to invent stories for each statue. I think she secretly writes stories in her room, but she's never shared them if she does. We're still fairly new housemates."

But then they entered what had to be Emma's bedroom, and he forgot about the fairies.

Her walls were covered in maps, pictures, scribbled notes, and various other bric-a-brac that didn't make a whole lot of sense to him.

It was more than a wee bit chaotic.

Emma snorted. "Aye, it's messy. But having everything in plain sight helps me connect the dots, so to speak. And with how big the grand prize is for this one, I didn't want to overlook the tiniest detail."

As he studied some of the notes, he said, "Explain it all to me."

She walked to one corner and pointed to the pictures and notes on the wall. "This was the location of the first find in London. Usually the first clue is fairly easy, getting harder as you go along."

"Where in London?"

She tapped a picture showing the spire-rich Palace of Westminster and the large clock tower known as Big Ben all lit up, with the River Thames in front of it. "Human Parliament. Thankfully it was in the public sections of the building as I wouldn't want to break into there, of all places."

He raised his brows. "So you've broken into places before?"

She shrugged. "Only for a clue, and never to steal. To be honest, I think the places are paid to host clues for the higher stakes competitions. No one has ever been arrested, and it would've been shared on the dark net for certain if they had been."

"Dark net?" he echoed.

"A sort of hidden side of the internet that only savvy people know how to access. I found it when I was a teenager." She waved a hand. "Easy peasy."

He had instinctively known Emma was clever, but

she was turning out to be more brilliant the more time he spent with her. "And I'm guessing you found other clues as I see other pictures that I don't think are in London."

She tapped a stone structure with two high, thin crenellated towers and a large arched entryway between them. "This is Battle Abbey near Hastings. This one I did have to break into, but I didn't get caught." She moved to a picture of a mountain near a loch, no building in site. "This is the location of the third clue, not far from here. And where I had to stop, because of you being hurt."

He stared at the picture, willing to remember what happened, but nothing came. So he focused back on Emma's wall of information. "I assume there's something important about this particular spot?"

She nodded. "Aye, you're right. I didn't connect it at first, but eventually it clicked together. See, the Palace of Westminster has been the scene of many changes in British history." She tapped the stone structure. "Battle Abbey is part of where the Battle of Hastings took place in 1066, when the Normans took over power in England from the Saxons. Another big shift or change." She tapped the mountain near the loch. "And whilst it seems unimportant or just another scenic picture, this is the site of a famous battle between the Scottish dragon-shifters and the invading Roman dragon-shifter legions. Whilst the

Scots prevailed, keeping the Romans back, it sparked a major change in how the Romans occupied Britain in the first century C.E. Mainly, they left most of the Highlands to the dragon-shifters and didn't try to invade again." She gestured to all three places. "I suspect the trend will continue, with each future destination having a pivotal role in British history, at least until the end."

He studied each location. "Is it common to have themes for this sort of thing?"

She shrugged. "Sometimes. All I know is that each location will be harder to determine, to the point it could take months for someone to find the final location and claim the prize. And given my experience, the final clue will probably have nothing to do with the previous theme, to deliberately throw a person off the trail."

"And since no one has found the final clue yet, it means you still have a chance."

Emma bit her lip. "Aye. Although if Finn tells me to stop, I will. I learned my lesson about being reckless."

He took a step closer. "Then I'll just have to convince Finn to let you continue."

She searched his gaze. "Oh, aye? And how are you going to do that, exactly?"

He brushed hair from her face and reveled in how it made her pupils flash. It took everything he had to focus on their conversation and not claim his kiss. "Tell Finn why you're doing this, your end goal. Once he hears it, I suspect he may even offer to help you."

Emma shook her head. "He has enough on his plate without adding more stress with one female's silly dream."

He cupped her cheek and leaned in. "It's not silly."

For a beat, she merely stared into his eyes. When she licked her lips, his gaze dropped to her soft, full bottom lip. The quick dart of her pink tongue sent blood rushing to his cock.

But he wasn't ready to kiss her yet. Or, more accurately, she wasn't ready for the type of kiss he wanted to claim.

She blew out a breath and stepped back. "Besides, the senior center is my idea and I should be the one to fight for it. I don't want to lay another burden on Finn's shoulders."

"And you are fighting for it, angel." He took one of her hands in his and squeezed. "But asking for help is better than giving up, aye?"

She searched his gaze a second and then sighed. "My mum always tells me I should ask for more help."

He tugged her closer. "You have my help already, no matter what. And if you need me to step up and explain it to Finn to ask his permission, I'll do it."

She lifted her chin and irritation flashed in her eyes. Good.

She growled, "This is my competition to win, not yours."

He tilted his head. "So does that mean you're going to fight for it with actions and not just words? Giving up doesn't really suit you."

Even if he couldn't remember Emma from before, the words just seemed right to him.

She tugged her fingers out of his and placed her hands on her hips. "You're trying to provoke me into saying of course I'll do it."

He winked. "Bingo. Whatever it takes."

As Emma stared up at him with her flashing dragon eyes, he couldn't resist running the back of his fingers down her cheek. She sucked in a breath, and suddenly he wanted to do something completely unrelated to her competition.

Something she might now be ready for, what with her temper riled and her inner dragon stoked.

He leaned down until his lips were a whisper away from hers. "Do I need to find other ways to encourage you?" He moved to her ear and murmured, "Maybe if you relax a wee bit, you'll be better suited to ask your favor." He nuzzled her cheek. "Maybe I can claim my kissing reward."

EMMA'S HEART raced and she tried to concentrate on Logan's words. However, his heat and scent invaded her senses, making it difficult to focus on anything but the male in front of her, nuzzling her cheek.

Her dragon hummed. *Aye, he should kiss us. And then fuck us. And make us come. That'll relax us for any sort of meeting.*

Before she could reprimand her dragon, Logan moved to rest his forehead against hers. "What will it be, angel? Do you need a kiss to relax you, or are you ready to face the clan leader now?"

It was hard to think with Logan so close. The feel of his skin against hers was like fire, and as his breath tickled her lips, she nearly closed the distance between them to press her mouth to his.

But then she remembered this wasn't her Logan, not really, and kissing the male could ruin her treasured friendship with him.

So Emma slowly stepped away and stood taller. "I'm ready to see Finn if you are."

"I will be by the time we get there."

As he turned his back, she had a feeling she knew why. But she was going to resist looking down at Logan's cock when he turned again to see if it was hard. She didn't want to know. Really, she didn't.

Because if he was aroused by her, some of Emma's barriers might fall. And she couldn't risk that.

She walked past him. "Then let's go. If, and it's a

big if, Finn gives his permission, there won't be any time to waste."

The walk from her cottage to Finn's wasn't far, and she and Logan spent it in silence. Much like back at her brothers' place, she wanted to fill it. But somehow she resisted. After all, she needed a cool head for her talk with her clan leader.

And it would distract her from the almost-kiss back in her bedroom.

By the time they arrived, she had her argument finalized and she knocked. Finn's mate, Arabella, opened the door. The dark-haired dragonwoman looked from her to Logan and back again. "If you want to see Finn, you'd better hurry. He has an appointment in twenty minutes."

Emma nodded. "Aye, that'll do."

As Arabella led them down the hall and past a room where her triplets were all at a table, coloring— or more accurately, scribbling with crayons—the dragonwoman placed a hand over her stomach. Their clan leader's mate was pregnant again. At first, Emma had been horrified at the thought of anyone having four bairns. And yet, helping to take care of her baby sister and her niece, Felicity, had helped her think that maybe someday she'd want her own child. Certainly not four, but perhaps one.

Of course, having a bairn without falling in love would take some work. But she'd find a way.

Her dragon sighed. *One day you need to realize it's worse to never fall in love.*

If you say so.

Thankfully they reached Finn's office so she didn't have to argue with her beast. And once she and Logan sat in the chairs in front of the clan leader's desk, he raised his blond eyebrows. "And what do I owe to this surprise visit? Has Logan suddenly remembered everything and wants me to punish you for hurting him?"

She blinked, knowing that Finn teased more often than not. But before she could reply, Logan growled, "Lay a finger on her and I'll do the same to you, only worse."

Finn's brows rose higher. "Would you, now?"

She placed a hand on Logan's arm, and he huffed. She murmured, "Not helping," before looking back at Finn. "I've already vowed to do whatever it takes to help Logan. That's partly why I'm here." Finn waved for her to continue. She took a deep breath and pushed on. "Logan wants me to take him back to where the incident occurred, to see if it'll jar his memories."

Finn studied her a beat. "Is that the only reason?"

She willed her cheeks not to flush. "No."

He nodded. "Honesty is wise, lass. Tell me the full truth."

She hesitated. Would Finn believe that she wasn't

being purely selfish again? How could she convince him that Logan had wanted this too?

Logan reached over, took her hand, and squeezed. After she shot him a glance and saw his nod, she looked back at Finn, whose gaze was on their hands. She tried to pull away, but Logan refused to let go.

Her dragon said smugly, *Good.*

Deciding she'd talk to Logan later about holding her hand hostage, she answered Finn's question. "You see, the reason I was there in the first place was because of this competition…" She filled in her clan leader with the details, also about what she wanted to do with the money, and then finished with, "I had planned to stop, given what happened. But Logan urged me to continue, quite adamantly. He suggested telling you and maybe asking for help since my goal —the human-dragon senior center—would help us all."

Finn looked to Logan. "You convinced her, aye?"

Logan nodded. "It seems stupid to miss this chance when Emma's gotten so far already and is clever enough to maybe win."

Finn switched his gaze back to Emma. "I already knew what you were about, lass. You might be good at secrets, but not that good. I had hoped you'd give up eventually. Especially since you snuck around and never did what you should've done—asked for help."

She muttered, "People keep mentioning that."

Finn smiled a beat before it disappeared. "But here you are, asking for assistance and involving others. I'm tempted to give you the help you need. However, answer me truthfully—how likely is it you can find and claim the prize at the end?"

Maybe some people liked to be modest, or thought it was better to dismiss their talents. However, Emma has spent her whole adult life fighting in a male-dominated industry—computer science—and she'd vowed to never belittle her talents just to make others feel better. "I'm bloody good at this, Finn. I can never guarantee anything, of course. But I'm clever, I've had loads of experience with lesser competitions, and if I have others with me? I might become unstoppable, provided we put our heads together and leave egos at the door."

Finn snorted. "That rules out a few males, then." He leaned back in his chair and steepled his fingers in front of him. After a few seconds, he nodded. "Aye, I'll allow it and provide others to help. But you aren't to run off on your own, ever, understand? I want to know where you're going and your progress along the way." She nodded and he focused on Logan. "As for you, I want daily reports. Not just on the competition, but also on your health and memory status. If there's the slightest change, I want to know about it as soon as possible."

Logan replied, "Aye, I can do that if it means I can go with Emma."

Excitement bubbled in her stomach and she couldn't help tapping her foot. She was raring to go. However, she couldn't leave just yet. "So who'll come with us?"

"Iris, for certain. However, I need to talk with a few others to determine who else."

She blurted, "But we wanted to visit the third site today."

Finn smiled. "Aye, and you will. There's quite a bit I can do in an hour, lass, even with an appointment soon. Right after lunch, go to the rear landing area and you'll meet your team." He waved toward Logan. "Since he can't shift yet, one of you will have to carry him, unless you're going to drive."

"Flying would be easier, not to mention much faster." She glanced at Logan. "What do you want to do?"

He shrugged. "As long as you're the one carrying me, I'm fine with it, aye?"

Since he still had her hand in his, he squeezed gently. Despite everything, he trusted her.

Emma decided she would do everything in her power to ensure she deserved it. "Aye, I'll be the one to do it."

Finn tapped a hand lightly on his desk. "Right, then that's decided. You'd best be off to eat and get ready. I have a few people to chat with ASAP."

It wasn't long until they were outside, heading

back toward her cottage again. Emma finally let out a squeal. "I can't believe it, but Finn said yes."

Logan tilted his head. "Aye. I'm surprised you never thought to ask before."

She shrugged. "Well, I'm a wee bit competitive and have spent years trying to prove I'm good enough. It's hard to shake off. Not to mention people like to dismiss me because I'm too young, or female, or just because I'm a MacAllister."

"As long as you remember what you said, about leaving egos at the door when it comes to yourself as well."

She bit her lip a second. "Aye, I know. It'll be hard, but I trust Iris, at least. She's another female who's had to fight tooth and nail to advance and not be dismissed because of her gender." Emma glanced over at him again. "And remember your promise, Logan. If there's any change, any at all, to your health or memory, you have to let us know."

He grunted. "As if I could forget it."

Earlier, she'd thought of reprimanding Logan for holding her hand when he felt like it. And yet, she suddenly understood the need. Taking his hand, she squeezed. "Don't forget that I probably wouldn't be doing this at all if you hadn't convinced me to have another go. That alone makes you extremely useful."

Logan tugged her a few inches closer to his side. "Is that the only way I'm useful?"

The heat in his eyes and the huskiness of his

voice made her shiver, in a good way. If he kept it up, she might actually give in to her growing weakness.

But then she remembered her dream, and what it could mean for dragon-shifters in general, to finally open her joint senior center. So she quickly released his hand and grinned. "Well, you can carry my bag. Aye, that's it—you can be my pack mule."

He growled and reached for her, but Emma laughed and raced ahead. He probably could've caught her, but never quite did.

And it scared her that she wanted him to not only catch her, but also toss her over his shoulder and cart her away like some sort of prize, with his long, rough fingers splayed over her arse.

Her dragon didn't tease her, but rather reveled smugly in the secret desire.

Fuck. Emma was most definitely in trouble.

Thankfully once they reached her cottage, she became too focused on packing what she needed and could ignore the male who kept messing with her head.

For now. If this competition took her who the bloody hell knew where, and she had to spend ample amount of time alone with him, she wasn't sure how long she could keep away from him and his addictive touch and glances.

Chapter Seven

By the time they arrived at Lochguard's rear landing area, Logan was torn between excitement at going on this geocaching chase and frustration at how Emma had purposefully avoided any of his touches once they'd reached her home again.

It shouldn't bother him so much. After all, he didn't have his bloody memories and had no idea of their past together.

However, holding her hand during their meeting with the clan leader, and again when they'd been walking toward her place, had just seemed so fucking right. As if she was somehow the missing piece to everything, as mad as that sounded.

At least he still had his kissing prize to look forward to and claim at some point.

But as they entered inside the high rock walls surrounding the landing area, he knew he wouldn't be able to claim it for a wee while given how they were going to have constant company. And when he kissed Emma, it was going to be when they were alone.

He surveyed the space. Off one side, near the stone cubbies in the wall, stood two females with dragon-shifter tattoos—one with medium-brown skin and the other dark-skinned—and a pale, slightly tanned human male with a battered fedora hat on his head, chattering away. The two females didn't look overly enthusiastic at whatever the human said.

Emma finally spoke up. "So it's to be Iris, Zoe, and Max going with us."

"Which are who?"

She pointed them out as she explained, "Zoe Watson and Iris Mahajan are two of Lochguard's Protectors, members of our clan's security team. And Max Holbrook is a human archaeologist who visits Lochguard sometimes. His field of study is primarily Romano British dragon-shifter history, although anything dragon-shifter will catch his fancy."

He eyed the human male and his slightly sloppy appearance—untucked shirt, wrinkled trousers, and a grubby hat that should've been burned years ago. Although under the clothes and disorder, there was a toned, muscled body, as if he trained regularly to protect himself from some kind of threat.

If he ever cleaned up, the human might catch Emma's fancy. And Logan didn't like that. He growled, "How's he going to be an asset to your search?"

She eyed him strangely, her pupils flashing, before she replied, "He's spent most of his life piecing together history from shards and tiny pieces of nothing; I'm sure it'll come in handy." He frowned, but Emma added before he could say anything, "Besides, if Finn ordered him to come, we can't say no."

Iris—the one with straight, black hair and medium-brown skin—rolled her eyes. "No, believe me, I tried. But Finn said Max was to come with us, end of story."

Zoe bit back a smile, but it was Max who came over and put out a hand to Logan. "Hello. I'm honored to be here and to help on this sort of quest. Who knows what we might stumble upon. As it is, the site of the third clue is extremely fascinating, and I hope is merely a preview of other places to come. Maybe I can tell you the minute-by-minute details of how the Scottish dragon-shifters drove the Roman ones back and out of the Highlands whilst we poke about the trail."

Emma smiled at the human and Logan instantly wanted to haul her closer to his side, to declare she was off limits.

The only thing stopping him was that Max didn't

seem to look at Emma with anything more than politeness in his gaze.

Emma replied, "I'm not sure we'll have the time, Max. I know you like puzzles, and the sooner we get to that old battle site, the sooner we can figure out the next clue and see where it leads."

Max rubbed his hands together. "Right, then let's get started. I can't wait to fly by dragonwing again. Lately, Iris has been too busy to take me to some of the more remote sites."

Iris sighed. "I have a job, you know. An important one."

Max opened his mouth, but Logan sensed the male would talk all day, if given the chance. So he said, "Then let's step back and let them shift, aye? The sooner they do, the sooner we can fly."

Max slapped him on the shoulder. "Right you are, old chap. Come, come, we need to turn our backs and be gentlemen."

Logan instinctively knew it wasn't a big deal to watch a dragon-shifter change forms, nude or not. Although even thinking about seeing Emma's naked body made his cock twitch. No, it was best to resist temptation.

They stood with their backs turned until the females were done and soon they were flying through the air, he and Max each being carried in the talons of a dragon's forearm. But as the wind brushed his face, there was something off about him being carried, something he couldn't place. A flicker stirred inside him, almost as if irritated, but it soon faded.

Regardless, he loved the views from up high. It calmed him in a way he hadn't felt since waking, unless he was in Emma's presence.

He only hoped this auspicious beginning boded well for the rest of the treasure hunt.

EMMA and the others managed to fly to the famous battle site quickly, deposit their live cargo safely, shift back, and toss on some clothes without issue. Due to the unstable nature of the wee mountain, they couldn't just fly and land atop it. No, they had to hike up to the ledge near the peak.

For the most part, everyone was on alert, keeping eyes and ears open for any signs of trouble. Iris had mentioned how Finn filled the rest of them in on the details. Not only that, but Iris had been the one to investigate the area right after Logan had been hit with the rock, so she was already familiar with the trail.

Now, Iris was in front of Emma on the wee path and Logan was behind her. Due to Emma's supersensitive dragon-shifter hearing, she couldn't block out Max's ramblings to poor Zoe, with both of them bringing up the rear. At least the female seemed polite with him.

Iris finally stopped and the rest of them did as well, leaving them near the spot where the accident had occurred the last time Emma had been here.

Seeing it brought back the memory of being pushed aside, and only to turn around and see Logan fall over the side and into the loch.

His mouth open under the water, him not breathing, her attempts to save him.

The seconds when she'd thought he'd died and she'd lost him forever.

Her heart raced as guilt flooded her body. Maybe she shouldn't have come back here.

Logan's hand touched her lower back and she glanced over her shoulder. He shook his head and squeezed her side, as if telling her not to worry about it.

Her dragon spoke up, *If he's not bothered, then neither should we be.*

He's only this way because he doesn't remember the before times, you know, when he repeatedly warned me to be careful.

Her beast grunted. *If he remembers, then talk to him about it. But for now, focus on what he wants, and Logan wants to help us.*

As she debated her response, Iris pointed to where some of the trail had fallen off and crumbled, leaving a wee gap. "That wasn't here before, so be even more alert. Someone's been back since the last time I was here."

Given how many were participating in the competition, Emma didn't doubt it. "The rules don't allow them to take the clue or move it, but there is some ambiguity when it comes to making it more difficult to reach it."

Iris glanced over her shoulder. "How?"

Emma shrugged. "Just that you can put obstacles in place, provided it's safe enough to still reach the clue in one piece."

Iris grunted. "I'll keep that in mind. You lot stay here whilst I scout ahead."

As they waited, Emma glanced behind her at Logan. He stared above them, at the ledge from where the rock had fallen previously, and frowned. It was on the tip of her tongue to ask if he remembered anything, but she held back.

And spent the agonizing minutes waiting for Iris by pushing down all the memories and seconds of absolute terror she'd felt when Logan hadn't been breathing.

Although the longer Logan stared up at the ledge and then down to the loch, questions burned on her tongue. Before she could blurt out any of them, Iris peeked her head from the top of the ledge above. "Just be careful jumping over that new wee gap in the trail and come on up. The rest of the way is safe."

They all did exactly that, and as Emma crested the final bit of the pathway, she took an extra-deep breath. A mixture of excitement and fear coursed through her, as it usually did right before she found a cache. Excitement at wanting to know what lay ahead, but also fear for not being able to solve the clue and ultimate failure.

And this time the failure would be that much grander, given how Finn and the others were counting on her.

Logan lightly touched her lower back yet again and whispered, "Come on. I'm trying to hold back so you can find and open the wee box, or whatever it is. But if you stand here much longer, I'm going to say fuck it, and do it myself."

She shook her head and smiled. He'd sensed her emotions and tried to distract her.

Even before losing his memory, he'd often done that.

Aye, she'd most definitely taken Logan for granted before. She was determined not to do that any longer. "No way I'm letting you do that, Mr. Lamont. If you try, I might have to kick your arse and pin you to the ground, with your hands behind your back."

He whispered for her ears only, "Is that a promise?"

Her cheeks heated, overly aware of how close

Logan stood to her, his body heat bracketing her back, his breath against her ear.

Her dragon hummed as her heart thundered inside her chest.

Iris cleared her throat, and Emma snapped back to the present. They weren't alone, and she needed to remember that.

Needing distance from the male who confused her more each minute they were together, Emma marched further toward what looked to be a hastily erected cairn. She doubted the cache would be inside the heap of stacked rocks since it would be difficult and slow going, and no one would want to waste time erecting it back up again once they'd unearthed the find.

The still intact structure confirmed the next clue wasn't inside it. She studied the rocks, though, and finally saw a faint etching on one toward the bottom. As she crouched down, she remembered the clue from her previous find:

Angels weep up high for those lost long ago to the followers of Jupiter.

"Followers of Jupiter" obviously referred to the Romans. And the "angels weep" section she had thought referred to the massive deaths on both sides during the old skirmish, but especially for the Romans, as they'd suffered the greatest casualties.

The location had been further confirmed by a pair of coordinates given on the back of the clue, which lead to a village near this mountain. However, now she saw a pair of angel wings lightly carved onto one rock, and then on one a few more down, two tears.

Directly under the stone with the tears was a tiny empty spot, as if someone had managed to take one of the pieces away from the cairn.

Emma placed her head on the ground and peered into the opening, but it was dark. Taking out her mobile phone, she turned on the front light to act as a torch, shined it inside, and smiled.

She slowly took out the long, flat container, careful not to disturb the structure. The others crowded around her as she carefully opened the lid.

Inside was a wee notebook to sign her assigned code name for the competition, as well as a laminated scrap of paper. However, unlike before, it wasn't a fully stated clue but rather a bunch of random words and numbers, ones she'd have to study, unscramble, or even decode to determine where to go next.

"Damn," she murmured. "I knew it'd have to get more difficult soon, and I was right."

Logan's voice filled her ears. "If the stakes are as high as you say, then you had to know this was coming. I'm actually quite surprised it took four clues to become challenging."

Emma shook her head. "I'm not, though. They like luring people in, giving a false sense of hope, and then suddenly only allowing the strongest and cleverest to survive. All those early phases will generate word of mouth for the next competition, aye? One where others will crave the chase and adrenaline, hoping the next time it'll just be easier." She took a picture of the clue with her phone before also writing it all down, just in case something happened. She flipped over the laminated paper, but there was nothing on the back like the last time; the words and numbers on the front side were the only clues.

Once she had everything written down, captured on her mobile, and even set the phone to send an encrypted email once they had service, Emma signed her code name and returned everything to the box.

She slipped it back inside the cairn and then lightly rubbed some dust on the stones with the etchings. It didn't completely block them—that would be against the rules—but it would make them harder to see. For good measure, she put a few stones in front of the gap. "I'm surprised no one else did that before me. It would've delayed us more than the crumbled ledge."

Max had been studying the cairn but now had an irritated look on his face. "This is a fake. Creating such things should be illegal in and of itself."

Iris drawled, "This is a contest, Max. Would you rather they deface actual ruins and such?"

He narrowed his eyes. "If I'm there, I dare them to try."

Emma blinked. She'd never seen the human male be anything but chatty or affable. It seemed he had a hidden side, one he didn't show often.

And judging by the look in his eyes, she wouldn't want to cross him.

Zoe jumped in. "No one's defacing anything right this moment. And since I hear some cars in the distance, ones I think are heading this way, we should descend the trail and get back to Lochguard to further study the clue."

It took a second for Emma to also hear the engines in the distance. "Aye, then let's go. I'd rather none of the other contestants know what my face looks like just yet. There's an advantage to anonymity."

They all headed back down, but Logan whispered to her, "I agree anonymity is great, but at least now with a group, we can rotate the faces at locations in the future, to further scramble some people's expectations."

She blinked a second. "I hadn't thought of that."

He smiled. "Aye, because you've always worked alone before." He briefly touched her arm and added, "But not any longer. You have us, so use us, aye?"

Even though she couldn't hold his gaze for more than a second since she had to watch her feet on the trail, that was long enough for something to shift inside her. She'd done so many things on her own over the years, to prove her worth, how clever she was, and how she would never need to rely on anyone for her future.

And yet that single-minded determination had probably held her back in a few areas.

Her mum's words came back to her: *Don't be afraid to ask for help from those you trust and who love you, aye? You don't have to shoulder the world, Emma. Remember that.*

The advice had never really penetrated until now. And while she wished like hell Logan had never been hurt for it to sink in, now that it had done so, Emma foolishly wished for more than she'd ever hoped for before.

Namely, to truly find a male who stood by her side but didn't try to take over, or think her foolish for dreaming big.

Someone to help her hold up the world and keep her from being crushed under it.

Her dragon said softly, *I say we've already found him.*

No, this isn't Logan, not really. Once his memories return, he'll go back to scolding me all the time.

Will he? Since he's lost his memories, you've changed as well. That will probably stick, aye?

It would, and that made Emma worry about the future of her friendship with Logan Lamont.

However, they were soon at the area where she could shift again. Once she was in the air, with Logan gently gripped in the talons of her left forearm, she did her best to ignore the male. Focusing on the competition, especially given her days-long delay, was the most important thing. Only if she won could she then help her clan and all the dragon-shifters in Scotland.

That had to be her top priority and nothing else.

Chapter Eight

Hours later, long after dark, Logan was alone with Emma inside the building that served as both a library and archives for Lochguard. The other three team members had some jobs and errands to run, and Emma had said they could meet again in the morning to see if any of them had made any sort of breakthrough with regards to the clues.

However, Logan had refused to leave. He rather liked watching Emma's face as she frowned, or growled, or sighed as she tried to put the words into some type of meaning.

He looked down at the list of words again, wondering if anything new would pop out:

Craig
Ford

Moray
Two
Reverse
Archer
Messenger

A STRING of numbers written in numerals was listed below the words, but they'd all agreed to focus on the words first and worry about the rest later, just in case the numbers were a red herring.

Emma had earlier worked out how the first three words referred to the Battle of Stirling Bridge in Scotland. While many knew of the infamous William Wallace thanks to the movie *Braveheart*, few people really knew about the other male who'd led the charge on that date, Andrew Moray. Apparently they'd camped near Abbey Craig before the skirmish. And after the Scots had attacked the English on the bridge and won the battle, the English had destroyed the structure in its wake, making the Scots later have to ford the River Forth to pursue them.

That took care of the words Craig, Ford, and Moray.

However, the remaining words Emma hadn't been able to make sense of yet: Two, Reverse, Archer, and Messenger.

The word "archer" snagged his attention for

some reason. So Logan reached for and studied the photocopied map of the area where the Battle of Stirling Bridge had taken place. Using symbols, it marked the locations of all the military forces, with the archers on the hill marked with little bows.

The sight of the bows niggled at his brain. The clue before this one had referenced the Roman god, Jupiter. Wasn't there another god who was some sort of messenger with arrows?

Without a word, Logan slid Emma's laptop in front of him. She looked up and he said, "I need to research something. Give me a moment."

"As long as research isn't a code word for porn, go ahead."

He rolled his eyes. "As if I'd do that here. Mrs. Mahajan would tug me out by the ear."

The dragonwoman was Iris's mother, who had warned them all that if they damaged any of her books or documents, there'd be hell to pay. She didn't mince words, and Logan rather liked her despite her furtive, concerned glances, which she'd given when she thought he wasn't looking.

And since she'd smiled so warmly at him at first, Logan had a feeling he'd been to this building many times before.

But he already had a headache and didn't want a worse one, so he pushed aside any wonderings about his past to focus on his hunch.

A quick search brought up his Roman god-related answer: Cupid carried a bow and arrow. And while famous for love and matchmaking, sometimes it was mischievous in nature. Also, Cupid's father was Mercury, the messenger of the gods. That related to two more words on the list: Messenger and Archer.

He pulled the map back in front of him. What if a message were supposedly shot from the archer positions, a sort of matchmaking as it would unite the contestant with the cache?

Although the meaning behind "two" and "reverse" still eluded him.

Emma's voice broke his concentration. "You're frowning. Did you end up at a dead end again?"

He shook his head. "I don't think so." He explained his findings and then asked, "But what about the words two and reverse?"

She tapped her chin. "Hmm. Aye, well, sometimes the words will only make sense once you're there and either find the cache or try to pinpoint its location." She gestured to her other list, with a random column of numbers. "This could help once we get there as well. Or some of it could just be there to mislead a person. Either way, we need to visit this old battle site near Stirling to determine if your idea about shooting a message is correct. Maybe Max can even bring one of his replica bows with him to test it out. Who knew his eclectic hobby of collecting and mastering ancient weaponry would come in handy?" She stood. "I should go pack supplies and let the others know about our plans straight away. We can leave at first light."

Logan stood and reached for her hand, halting her exit. "What you need is some rest, and first light is only a handful of hours away. Sleep, and then we can leave closer to noon."

She frowned up at him. "But every second counts."

"Aye, I know it does. But I'd rather you not drop me out of the sky because you doze off whilst flying."

She straightened her shoulders. "I never doze when flying." He arched an eyebrow. "Almost never. But I'd certainly never drop you."

He squeezed her hand. "Regardless, one of the best ways to sharpen your mind is with proper rest. What if we have to stay awake for twenty-four hours to find what we need? Sleep and we'll leave a little before noon."

She grumbled, "I sometimes hate when you're rational."

He tugged her closer. "Only sometimes."

Her lips twitched. "On occasion it helps. Such as when it keeps me out of trouble. Like when—"

She paused a beat as she realized what she'd nearly said. "Sorry. I know how much you hate when someone references the past."

He grunted. "At first, that was true. But I'm curious about this story. Tell me what happened, Emma." She hesitated and Logan tugged her against him, placing his hands at her waist to keep her in place, doing his best not to notice her warm body against his front. "I won't let you go until you do."

She tried to take a step back, but he tightened his hold. She huffed. "It's not fair that you're stronger than me."

He grinned. "At this point, I'll use every advantage I can get, angel."

Emma searched his eyes a beat before finally nodding. "Aye, I'll tell you, but only on the way home. I'd rather not risk someone overhearing this here. It's a wee bit embarrassing, after all."

He couldn't resist stroking her waist with his thumbs. Leaning down, he murmured, "Just know that if you try to run, I'll catch you, toss you over my shoulder, and keep you captive until you talk."

She sucked in her breath and Logan's eyes moved to her lips. His own throbbed a bit, wanting to feel her softness against his mouth.

But now wasn't the time to claim his kissing prize. No, he wanted to hear her tale more. So he met her gaze again and waited. She finally sighed. "I won't run off. Now, come on. I'm starving as well, and I'll need to see if Connor has any food that's still warm for us at the restaurant."

They tidied up, collected their belongings, and headed into the early nighttime air. Once they were far enough away from any building, Logan asked, "So tell me about this one time I managed to keep you out of trouble, aye? And promise to tell me all of it, no matter if I acted like an arsehole or not."

She raised her brows. "Why do you think you did?"

He shrugged one shoulder. "I don't know, do I? But it's past time for me to hear a few bits and see if it helps trigger anything or not. I promise I'm more than strong enough."

"Of course you are. You've always been strong when it mattered."

He puzzled over her words, but Logan decided to wait in silence, not wanting to distract her. For once, he was eager to hear something about his pre-amnesiac self. Maybe it'd give him a better insight into what his relationship with Emma had been before. But no matter what it revealed, he knew he was going to keep trying to win her over. He just needed some more information to better form his strategy.

EMMA WASN'T sure why she was nervous to recount a tale from the past. But it was almost as if she wanted to impress amnesiac Logan, and the story wouldn't put her in a flattering light at all.

Her dragon snorted. *Everyone does stupid stuff when they're young. Even if he can't remember his own youth, he's clever enough to realize that.*

Aye, you say that, but...

You're afraid he'll suddenly remember everything. And you don't want that.

She resisted biting her lip. *Which makes me a horrible person.*

Her beast sighed. *I still say Logan will end up being a combination of his before and after self. It may not be so bad.*

And yet, the thought of Logan going back to the slightly aloof, scolding version made her heart twist. She rather liked the more forthright version of him.

Even if she was far from being in love with him, it'd hurt all the same to lose the male she was wanting more by the day. The one who might be able to coax his way into her knickers and end her self-imposed celibacy.

She'd never even thought about doing that before.

Emma mentally growled. *This is why I stay away from males.*

Her dragon sniffed. *You're being ridiculous. Even with everything Mum went through, she gave love a second chance. That should tell you something. Maybe you should just ask her about it.*

Aye, maybe she should.

But then Logan cleared his throat, garnering her attention. He asked, "And what is your dragon going on about now?"

"Do you want to know that or the story?"

"The story."

"Aye, well, then let me begin." She kept her eyes trained ahead, so it'd be easier to share. "Even though we all knew about the English dragon clan in the Lake District, Stonefire, growing up, I never heard someone speak about them from experience until I was in my teens. Relations hadn't been good for most of my life at that point, and given what I remember of Lochguard's former leader, it wasn't hard to see why.

"But Brodie's younger sister, Jade, is my friend. Her older brother was and still is a Protector, and back then she'd heard how he'd met with another of the Protectors from Stonefire to investigate a disappearance. At any rate, Jade went on about how things were changing on Stonefire, and that both Protectors had thought it'd be good to meet up every once in a while, just to share information about dragon hunters or other such common enemies.

"It all sounds so amazing, and I thought it'd be brilliant if I could go and make friends on Stonefire too and try to prove to both clan leaders that it was time to end the isolation and show everyone just how easy it would be."

She kicked a rock along the pathway, doing her best to keep her shame and memories at bay. After hitting the wee stone again, she continued, "As you might've guessed, it wasn't that simple to do. But I was young, and a bit cocky after recently discovering the dark net and some of the harder places to crack on the internet, and thought I could do this too."

She paused, remembered how she thought she could do anything, if only she tried hard enough.

Oh, how naïve she'd been. But she was getting ahead of herself, took a slow breath, and carried on. "I did find some Stonefire clan members online, ones who were clever with computers like I was. One was a male a bit older than me, and I thought what if he and I could work together, form a friendship, and use it to prove how we could be allies again? I knew I was young, and if someone found out that I snuck away to meet an English dragon-shifter that I'd get into a lot of trouble. However, I was so determined to do this and so I set up a secret meeting.

"Of course I was so excited about it, I had to tell someone but only someone I trusted. You were my friend and my most trusted confidant, and had always encouraged me with computers before when others tried to steer me away, so I thought you'd help me with this too."

He smiled faintly. "I'm guessing I didn't."

She shook her head. "No. To be honest, you said I was daft for even considering it. Did I know anything about this male? Was he even truly from Stonefire, let alone a dragon-shifter? Was he really in his twenties as he'd claimed? What did he want to do with a sixteen-year-old girl? And so you threatened to tell my mother if I went through with it. I argued, of course. But we agreed—if I could find out who exactly this person was, learn everything about him, and ensure it was as altruistic as he claimed it would be, you'd help me meet him."

For a moment, she remembered how hopeful she'd been. How she, Emma MacAllister, would do something to help her clan in a way that mattered.

Pushing aside the disappointment of what truly happened, she pushed on. "It took some digging, and pushed all my covert investigative skills to the test, but I eventually learned he was a dragonman in his fifties, one who had been jailed before for raping a teenage human girl, and he didn't actually live on Stonefire but had managed to run off and hide on his own. The DDA was looking for him, as was Stonefire. He wasn't a good male."

She looked back at Logan, but she couldn't read his expression, but definitely no recognition showed in his eyes. No sudden return of memory meant she had to keep sharing. "I wanted to forget the whole thing since my ego was bruised and battered. But it was you, Logan, who convinced me that he could try to lure someone else and end up hurting them. So even if it was embarrassing, I needed to report him to the DDA."

"And you did."

She nodded. "Anonymously at first. But they wanted details and a chance to talk to me about how I'd found him. Guilt weighed heavily on me, afraid some other female would be hurt because of my cowardice. So I eventually told them who I was, leaving out a few of the illegal parts of my story, and they caught him. But…"

Logan took her hand and squeezed. His touch gave her the strength to finish. "Lochguard's old clan leader, Dougal, was furious. For what exactly, I don't know since he never said. However, I think he didn't like a teenage girl snitching on another dragon-shifter to the humans, and saw it as a betrayal to our kind. Regardless, he said I wasn't allowed near a computer again until I turned twenty-one."

"Which meant he took away the thing you were good at, the one thing which meant so much to you."

She sighed. "Aye. All my plans for the future, for a job, for anything vanished."

He rubbed his thumb against her knuckles, the warm touch helping to soothe her a fraction. "But obviously that punishment was rescinded at some point given your job now. So, what happened?"

She smiled. "Finn. As soon as he took over the clan leader position, he reversed the decision. Since the old clan leader had smeared my name to anyone who'd listen for the first few months after it happened, Finn knew all about it. And he not only gave me my future back, he said that if I wanted it, I could work with the Protectors once my training was finished and I passed all the necessary tests."

Logan pulled her a little closer to his side. "It

sounds like you did brilliantly, putting yourself out there to protect future victims. Why would that be embarrassing?"

Her cheeks heated. The next part was the part she was dreading.

And yet, Logan had been nothing but courteous, polite, and even supportive with the story thus far. She didn't want to keep it from him.

After taking a deep breath, the words rushed forth. "You should've hated me at that point, and yet you supported me and made sure I didn't make a fool of myself. Even after the fact, you growled at anyone who tried to belittle me for what I did."

He raised an eyebrow. "That sounds like a good thing, aye?"

"Perhaps. But a few weeks before you did so much to help and support me, I'd hurt you. You see, you'd kissed me. And confused and scared as I was, I did what I always do when taken by surprise—I brushed it off with a laugh.

"However, the moment I laughed, pain flashed in your eyes and your gaze turned cold. I'd hurt you without really meaning to, and yet I wasn't strong enough to tell you the reason why I acted the way I did. Instead, I just pretended I didn't notice your reaction."

Not for the first time, she wished she could've slapped some sense into her sixteen-year-old self. Hurting Logan back then and pretending she hadn't noticed was one of the things she still regretted to this day.

He asked quietly, "Are you strong enough to tell me about it now?"

Emma's first instinct was to distract him and keep her secret fear safe. That way she could keep on as she had, always brushing males away to never get close enough to get hurt.

However, keeping it locked up hadn't helped her, not really. The guilt she carried for Logan's injuries and amnesia weighed her down; she didn't need to be in love to feel pain. Besides, if she was going to tell anyone, it should be Logan.

Taking a deep breath, she finally bobbed her head. "I think so." She paused, gathered her courage, and said the words she hadn't told anyone before. "My dad was murdered when I was young, and my mother spiraled into a deep depression at his loss. At times, I wasn't even sure if my mum wanted to keep living." She stared at her feet. "The next few years were difficult as my mum learned to survive without her true mate and love of her life. That constant struggle, and witnessing her heartbreak, left an impression on me, to the point I vowed I never wanted to fall in love and risk myself in the same way. If I could do that, then I'd never end up as miserable as my mum had been."

She glanced at Logan, and she still couldn't read his expression. At one point, she could read him like a book. The loss of it made her heart twist a bit. Maybe she did miss bits of old Logan.

Her dragon spoke up. *Tell him the rest. He deserves to know.*

Aye, I know. Even if I wish he could forget it forever.

That isn't fair to him.

With a sigh, she finally said, "We were friends for years, long before my dad was killed. Over time, we grew impossibly close. And once we were teenagers and I started noticing your shoulders, and your lips, and even your arse, it confused me and bloody well terrified me. I didn't want to be attracted to any male because it could possibly lead to love and hurt. And then that night, there you were, my best friend—an impossibly handsome one to boot—who kissed me and muddled everything I'd convinced myself I wanted. For a second, I wanted you to kiss me again. But then I remembered everything my mum went through, the years of pain and struggle, and I pushed you away to protect myself."

Eventually she'd gone back to seeing him as a friend. Although sometimes late at night, right before she fell asleep, she'd wondered how her life would've ended up if she hadn't pushed him away.

No other male had ever tempted her even the slightest bit to risk her heart.

But she'd made bloody well sure Logan would never try again, hadn't she?

He was silent a beat before asking, "You truly never told me this before?"

She shook her head. "After the whole catfishing incident, we soon fell back into being just friends. I never knew why you did so, but I was grateful since I'd missed you when we'd stopped talking to each other." Emma bit her lip and finally met Logan's gaze. This time she saw curiosity and she answered his unspoken question, "And no, we never spoke of the kiss itself again."

He still had a hold of her hand and so he pulled her to a stop to stare down at her. "So every time you've responded to my touches recently, was it merely because of a wish fulfillment with the male I was?"

"No, no I don't think so." His gaze was skeptical, so she pushed on. "Your touches and almost kisses made me see you in a way I hadn't thought about for years." Well, hadn't thought about *much*. "I rather like how honest you've been since losing your memory. I know that's a horrid thing to say, but I want to be truthful with you." When he didn't say anything, she added, "I do miss who you were before, but I also like who you are now. I only wish I knew what the future held."

He grunted. "So do I." He glanced to the fork in the pathway a few feet away and Logan released her hand. She instantly missed his firm touch.

He took a step backward. "I'll leave you to find

some food and get some rest. I'll see you at half eleven tomorrow, for the trip to Stirling."

She wanted to press Logan, to know what he thought of her words, but before she could do that, he walked off in silence.

Had some of his memories come back? Was he mad about her being a coward and pushing him away because his kiss had scared her?

Emma wished she knew what the bloody hell he was thinking.

Her dragon spoke up. *Let him think on it a bit. It can't be easy for him to hear some of his past, especially if he still can't remember anything.*

Emma wondered if she'd made a mistake sharing a crucial part of their history together or not. But the deed was done, and she couldn't take it back.

How she was going to get any sleep this night, she had no idea. But regardless of how things changed, or didn't, with Logan, she had bigger things to worry about. Finn had put his faith in her once again and she wasn't about to let him down, no matter what.

Chapter Nine

The next day, Logan watched as Max scouted the top of the hill near Stirling Bridge, looking for the best place to start testing his theory of a message being at a bow shot's length away.

Emma and Iris were further afield, ready to watch where the arrows landed before they could begin their search. Or to maybe see if the two remaining words from the clue made more sense after they knew the bow's general range: Reverse and Two.

Zoe stood near him, keeping an eye on the surroundings in case anyone else showed up.

All of it meant Logan had plenty of time with his thoughts. Something he was already tired of after Emma's revelations the night before.

His memories hadn't returned, although what she'd told him had seemed familiar in some way.

Almost as if it were hidden behind a thick piece of ice, hazy and unclear for the moment but it might eventually reveal itself once the ice thawed.

That hazy feeling wasn't what really bothered him, though. No. Emma revealing that they'd kissed before and she'd pretended not to like it made him pretty bloody uncertain about everything between them since waking up without his memories. He couldn't push away the feeling she yearned for the best friend she'd had and not the male he was currently. Maybe he'd get his memories back, maybe he wouldn't. And if he kissed her and coaxed her into his bed, he didn't want to constantly question why she'd let him.

Something stirred in his mind, much like last night, but then settled. It wasn't the first time he wondered if his inner dragon was slowly coming back. After all, everyone said he had one.

And if the dragon came back, it might mean all his memories returned as well. Of course that meant he might also go back to the way he was before the incident, and Logan wasn't sure he wished to.

If his old self had been satisfied with being friend zoned with Emma, he must've been crazy, a coward, or both. Every time Logan saw his black-haired angel, he wanted to strip her naked and worship every inch of her body. Even now, his gaze drifted off to Emma chatting with Iris. As the breeze blew her hair around her face, he itched to feel how soft it was.

When she smiled at something the other dragonwoman said, he nearly growled and stormed over, wanting to be the cause of it.

So no, the thought of going back to being merely friends didn't really sit well with him. She'd explained her fears of becoming attached and he could understand that, given what she'd seen with her mum. However, maybe with time, he could change her mind. He doubted his pre-amnesiac self had ever tried to do that, fool that he seemed to be.

Zoe's voice brought him back to the present. "Max is about to start."

They were off to the side, safe from being hit. As Logan watched Max ready his bow and draw the string back, he noticed the male's determined face. It was such a contrast to his usual flippant, chatty demeanor.

Which sort of made Logan think there was more to the human male than he let on.

They'd agreed to have Max shoot five arrows. The first one he'd send it as far as he could. Then the human would aim closer and closer until he was as near as he could be without shooting straight down. Max released each arrow with ease, making it look effortless when Logan somehow knew it wasn't that simple.

Once the human was done, Max moved to the closest arrow while Iris and Emma checked out the furthest.

Logan's search area, in the middle ground, wasn't that remarkable. Some grass and rocks, as well as a few quickly covered up holes here and there, showed that someone had probably been here before them to dig around. But given what Emma had explained of the rules, about how they would be able to locate the cache without disturbing the local area too much, he didn't bother searching every covered hole; they should be able to dig or shift something in plain sight. And the more closely he studied his section, the less he found worthy of examining. To be honest, Logan leaned toward ruling out his section and maybe the whole area in front of Abbey Craig facing the river.

Logan studied the full area around them and that's when he noticed how behind the Abbey Craig rise there were much taller areas called the Ochil Hills, if he remembered right. What if Max reversed his aim, the other way? That would use one of the other clue words: Reverse.

He called Max's phone and asked the human if he could try, and he nodded. Max turned to glance behind him at the hills. "That might just be the ticket, old fellow. It'd be much easier to hide a clue on the hills or in a small cave, or even a crevice. Clever idea indeed. It'll be a bit of a challenge to get the arrows to stick, given the rock. However, the hills nearest have a lot of grass and soil, which will be easy enough. I'll start there and see how far up I can go."

Zoe ran over to let the other females know the

plan while Max readied himself to shoot from the higher position. He again shot methodically, yet quickly, trying to spread the arrows to cover the full range. Or, at least the fullest range he could manage as one person. But it would give them a starting point and narrow down where to search.

Max lowered his bow and signaled he'd finished. Iris, Emma, and Zoe reached Logan a beat later. Emma asked, "What made you think of hitting behind the rise? It would've been ages before I thought of reversing the arrow's target into the hills."

He shrugged one shoulder. "Aye, well, it's just a theory. It'd be easier to hide something out of sight there, as well as make the clue's location look more natural. I assume that's the aim, to hide from the others what you've found."

They made their way to the lower areas of the hills and spread out to see what they could discover without hiking or needing to climb up higher.

It was a slow, arduous process. Nothing was in easy reach near the foot of the hills. However, his gut said they were close. Since getting Max to repeatedly go back and release arrows would take forever, he did a quick search on his phone to see if anything of significance was in these hills. *Bingo*. There were a few car parks and a popular trail on Dumyat Hill, which led to a few memorials and a fire beacon.

He explained it to the others and they decided it was worth checking out. So they made it up to the trail and kept an eye out for a clue. Even if they climbed a bit higher than where Max had been able to hit with his arrows, it seemed relevant still. After all, a fully trained archer probably had more strength than a modern-day archaeologist.

By the time they neared the summit, Logan first noticed a bright, white memorial badge to the Argyll and Sutherland Highlanders. But nearer the top ridge, there was a metal beacon fire stand. And before that, were two older memorials to the Argyll and Sutherland Highlanders, made of metal plaques and rock.

Two, just like the last, unused clue word.

Emma met his gaze, and they nodded at one another. She stated, "I don't know how they want to count, from the new one to the older ones, or in reverse. But let's spread out and check the area whilst it's still empty. No doubt tourists will be making the hike soon enough, once they finish lunch."

Logan went to the beacon and noticed how there was a weathered badge—he guessed, given the deterioration—there as well. He didn't know if that would count or not toward the clue, but he'd try including it first. Using the beacon as a start, he went to the old metal plaque on concrete. Between it and the stone badge were lots of rocks, as well as a wee patch of grass. He looked closely, feeling his way. Eventually his fingers caught on something sharp. He cursed and pulled his finger away, and saw he's sliced it. But he soon dismissed the pain as he noticed a metal ledge, of a sort, sticking out from the rocks.

Carefully, he looked under the metal piece and felt beneath it. There were a few rocks that easily rolled away. Then his hand brushed against something plastic, and his heart raced. This could be what they were searching for.

He said over his shoulder, "Emma, come here. I think I found something."

They were all surrounding him by the time Logan slowly slid out the dark plastic box. The top was scratched slightly, and he swore there was some dried blood on it. But he ignored that, opened the container, and offered the contents to Emma.

Inside was a wee notebook, like before, and another laminated paper. However, instead of words there were just loads of numbers.

Emma hummed. "Well, now that's interesting as it's the first clue containing only numbers. And no, I don't know what they mean right off the bat. But let me jot them down and snap a few photos so we can leave. I don't want to give away the location so easily to someone else."

Zoe spoke up. "Max and I will start heading down the trail. That way if we meet someone, we can distract them for a bit, giving you time to catch up to us."

Max nodded. "I can easily tell them about the history of Stirling Bridge. I may not be as familiar with that time period as with anything Roman, but after some research last night, I know enough to stall."

The pair left and Iris scanned down below. Logan asked, "Do you see anything?"

The female shook her head. "No, but I get the feeling we're being watched." She glanced at Emma. "Do they do that sometimes with these sort of competitions? Have people monitor the participants to ensure they're following the rules?"

Emma slid the box back into place. And as she placed some rocks in front of the opening, she replied, "Aye, sometimes. Although it could also be a competitor who was stuck and is looking for a hint." She stood. "Which is why we should head down the other way, where the trail splits. That way if they see Zoe and Max, they won't be able to place all our faces together. Aye, it's possible they have binoculars and watched the summit, but I doubt they'd get a good enough look at our features from so far away unless they have some high-tech gadgets."

Logan grunted. "Let's just get out of here and head back to Lochguard. I don't want to give anyone else bloody hints. And I want to start looking at the next clue as soon as possible."

As they walked, Emma smiled up at him. "Getting into the spirit of things, aye?"

He smiled back. "Maybe. I have to admit I had a small thrill of excitement when I suggested Max firing arrows behind him. And then finding the cache hidden in that wee space? Bloody brilliant."

Emma laughed but then her eyes zeroed in on his cut fingers. "Why didn't you say you'd hurt yourself?"

She took his hand and any sting he still felt from the cut vanished at Emma's touch. As she cradled her hand in his, he wished she'd kiss his palm to make him feel better.

But then she clucked her tongue and frowned up at him. "We need to clean this. I can't believe you didn't mention it, Logan. You're supposed to help with medical emergencies, and that doesn't exclude your own."

He raised his brow. "A cut isn't an emergency."

She growled, and all he could think of was how he wanted her growling when naked as well. "Still, you know what I mean."

He lowered his voice so Iris wouldn't hear. "But it's more fun to have you tend to my wounds, aye? Then I can feel your fingers caressing my skin. Maybe I should get hurt more often, just so I can have more of your touch, angel."

He'd expected Emma to blush. Instead, she rolled her eyes. "Stop being ridiculous. If you kept it up, getting injured just to catch my attention, you'd soon be at the surgery again, covered in bandages and no one could touch you then."

He chuckled. "I wouldn't want to become a mummy. But a cut or two? That might be enough."

He leaned closer. "Although as long as both of our lips are fine, I could still claim my kiss reward."

She glanced at his lips. "You aren't going to do that now, are you? We're out in the middle of nowhere, with too many eyes on us."

He didn't like how she wanted to keep their kiss hidden, like a dirty secret. Still, he didn't want to interrupt his teasing and flirting. "No, not right here and now. But I think I should claim it tonight, after we have dinner."

She smiled at him. "Why, Logan Lamont, is that your roundabout way of asking me on a date?"

"If it wasn't clear, let me try again." He moved his mouth next to her ear. "Eat dinner with me, angel. Let me hold your hand, stroke the skin of your wrist, and once your heart races and your cheeks flush, I'll claim my kiss then."

As he moved his face away, he casually brushed his nose against her cheek and Emma sucked in a breath.

He couldn't wait to get her alone. She'd said she had reasons to protect herself and her heart, aye. However, if he could soften her a wee bit toward him, and she responded as he hoped, he might be able to use her attraction to slowly wear down her defenses as he proved himself to her.

Since she hadn't yet given her answer, he lightly nudged her shoulder with his own. "So? Is that a yes?"

Clearing her throat, she finally met his gaze again. Her pupils flashed a few times to slits and back before replying, "Aye, I'll have dinner with you. But you have to ask me to kiss you before you do it. That's my rule."

He frowned. "That wasn't part of our original agreement."

"Maybe not, but I don't want to be surprised."

He studied her face, trying to judge what she was about. However, even if he couldn't read her expression, he had a feeling she wanted to prepare herself so that she wouldn't respond to his kiss. "As long as you promise to participate and not stand there with your eyes squeezed shut and jaw clenched." He covertly brushed his hand against hers. "This might be the only time you allow me to kiss you, and I want to make the most of it."

She frowned a beat, but then her expression cleared. Good. She didn't much like his mention of one kiss. That boded well for his pursuit.

"Fine, I agree. Although dinner will have to be at the restaurant. I can't cook, and I don't want to have my brothers hovering if we eat at their place."

He raised an eyebrow. "But doesn't Connor spend most evenings at the restaurant? If anyone would hover, I think it'd be him."

"Aye, he usually would. However, Connor will be in the kitchen with the supper rush. If I ask Mum to keep him busy and distracted, she will."

Logan smiled slowly. "So you can have me all to yourself."

"You and a room full of people." She bit her lip, as if to prevent a smile, and then added, "We can kiss on the way home, for privacy's sake."

"Like a sweet first date?"

Her reply was so low he nearly didn't hear it. "Aye."

Interesting. Was Emma coming round to the idea she could give him a chance and not constantly think of him destroying her at some unknown date in the future?

He didn't get to ask further, though, because they'd reached the bottom of the hill and quickly rushed to the rendezvous point with the others.

And as Emma carried him back up into the air, that unknown force inside him stirred a wee bit more. It seemed that flying helped rouse whatever it was, but not enough if it was indeed his inner dragon slowly coming round.

Even if he didn't understand it, his mind felt lonely, and empty, as if he were missing a huge chunk of himself. More so than his memories, it seemed. It was as if his entire being yearned for that faint awareness that never fully emerged.

However, once they arrived at Lochguard and Emma went to work getting everyone copies of the numbers from the cache, he pushed the wondering aside. Until he had to get ready for his date, he'd try to help Emma with the clue. He didn't think he'd get as lucky as before and figure it out with hunches, but he wasn't about to give up. There was only one more cache after this clue, and no matter what happened, he wanted to see Emma's face when they won.

And aye, he wanted to win—both the competition and Emma MacAllister.

Chapter Ten

E mma had technically been on dates before. However, they'd all been part of her grand scheme to appear as if she were looking for her true mate while not really doing so. She hadn't cared how the date ended, or if she bumbled through—usually on purpose—to drive suitors away.

Her dinner with Logan, though, was different. She not only knew he would kiss her at some point in the evening, but she also didn't want to muck it up on purpose. Part of her wanted it to go brilliantly, and yet another part of her was scared to death of what could happen if things went well.

Just as she finished pinning her hair back, there was a knock on the front door. Glancing at the clock, she noted it was too early for it to be Logan. And since Kaylee was busy watching Arabella and Finn's triplets and couldn't answer the door, Emma went to do it and blinked at finding her mother there. "Mum? What are you doing here? I have plans, like I told you before."

Her mother nodded. "Aye, I know. But I wanted to have a wee chat with you first."

In the past, her mum's "wee chats" had usually been about how she should be less reckless, or to check and ensure she was being careful sexually—she'd never told her mother she was still a virgin—or to be nicer to her brothers. "Can't it wait?"

"No, Emma. Now, let's hurry, aye? I don't want you to be late for your dinner with Logan."

She guided her mother to the living room and they sat together on the sofa. Her mother turned toward her, searched Emma's face with blue eyes the same shade as her own, and then took one of her hands.

Her dragon sighed. *That's not a good sign.*

Ignoring her beast, she focused on her mum's words. "You're a clever lass, and I'm sure you've known how Logan has fancied you for years, aye?" She nodded slowly and her mum continued, "So what made you change your mind about him now? If you're only going to push him away, spare the lad. He's gone through enough as it is."

She blinked. "Why would you think I'd go on a date with him to push him away?"

Her mother raised her dark eyebrows. "I'm not stupid, Emma. You've gone on more dates than just about any female inside Lochguard, and yet never with the same male more than once. Nearly every single time ended awkwardly, or with food in the male's lap, or some other wee calamity. I knew something was going on after about the first five or so times it happened in a row."

Her dragon spoke up. *I told you Mum would've noticed at some point.*

Hush, dragon.

Emma shifted in her seat a little. "I'm surprised you didn't say anything about this before now."

Her mother shrugged. "You're an adult, and it wasn't anything that would hurt you. I figured you were either truly trying to find your true mate, or appear that way, and would eventually sort it all out. Although I'm curious: Why *were* you doing it? Surely not merely to provide amusing tales to the elderly you also snuck around to help on the clan."

She blinked. Her mother may be quieter than most, and didn't like confrontation, but she was bloody observant, more than Emma had ever given her credit for.

Her dragon said, *Just tell her. You wanted to ask her about her time after Dad was gone. Now's the time to do it.*

Emma could brush off her beast and say she didn't have enough time for a heartfelt chat. But in truth she did, and to avoid it now would be to deliberately run away from sharing her pain and hearing the full truth about her mum's. Especially since Emma still couldn't believe her mother had risked her heart again by falling in love with Jake and mating the human.

Taking a deep breath, she forged ahead before she could change her mind. "I was afraid that I'd fall in love, so I did everything I could to prevent it from happening."

Her mum frowned. "Why would you fear love, lass?"

Searching her mother's eyes, ones so similar to her own, she wished there was a way to avoid bringing up a painful time to her mum. But she couldn't discuss this without doing so. "Because of how it hurt you, once Dad was gone."

Her mother's face softened. "Oh, lass."

"I remember how happy you were with Dad, and how he made us all laugh. I thought I was the luckiest girl in the world to have parents who loved each other so much." She looked toward her lap. "But then Dad was murdered, and the world turned upside down. I was still young and didn't quite fully understand how Dad would never come back. But you, aye, well, I saw with my own eyes how you suffered. How you closed in on yourself, how you struggled to even eat, let alone do anything else. Cat always said you loved Dad so very much, and the loss pained you more than even us. We all were hurting, aye, but you most of all. And during that time, before Cat convinced all of us to get you out of bed, is when I decided that I never wanted to fall in love and suffer like that. And the only way to protect my heart was to never give myself a chance."

The room fell silent and Emma finally gathered the courage to look into her mother's eyes. At the unshed tears there, she felt horrible. However, before she could apologize for bringing up her mother's worst days, her mum cleared her throat and said, "It was a dark time for me, aye, it was. But it seems I didn't handle the time after it very well either."

Emma squeezed her mum's hand still in hers. "You were a brilliant mum, once you finally came out of your room. Don't think you weren't."

Her mother smiled sadly. "I was adequate, at best, for the first few years after your dad died. But whilst Jamie had always needed extra care in the years that followed your dad's murder, you were always so happy and full of smiles. I somehow missed this hidden, hurting part of you, Emma. And I wish I hadn't. Because, aye, love can cause pain. I won't say it never will. However, it can also be the most glorious thing in your life, helping you to become a better person. When you find the one individual who knows you better than anyone and accepts you, flaws and all, it all becomes worth it." She squeezed her hand again. "But knowing what I know now, I wouldn't change meeting your father and becoming his mate for anything. Arthur was my first love and he not only made me incredibly happy, he also gifted me with the five of you."

She searched her mother's eyes. "But you have to say that, aye? It's not as if you'd tell me you'd wished I was never born."

Her mother raised her brows. "Emma Lucia MacAllister, don't you ever think for a second that's what I wanted. Understood?"

At the unusual vehemence in her mother's tone, she nodded. "Aye."

"Good. Now, let me see if I've pieced this together then. You sabotaged all those dates because you didn't want to give males a chance to worm their way into your heart, aye?" She nodded. "Then what do you intend to do with Logan?"

She bit her lip and hesitated a second. Emma hadn't decided what she wanted to do with Logan. "It's complicated."

Her mother tilted her head. "Because of his lack of memories?"

"More than that, Mum. His personality is a wee bit different as well. And it's entirely possible that this version of Logan will vanish when his memories return."

"And you're not sure you want that."

She clenched the fingers of her free hand into her skirt. "I know it's awful, and of course I want him to remember who he is and get his dragon back. It's just so bloody confusing."

"Do you want to hear my honest opinion?" She bobbed her head and her mum continued, "I think this is a part of Logan he's mostly hidden from the world but has always been there. He was far more determined about you until the relationship between you two suddenly became strained years ago. Whatever happened, he grew cautious after that, and then once his older brother went missing, he became even more so."

His brother Phillip had run off years ago to win back his love, Yasmin MacFie, before she entered into an arranged mating with a dragonman in Iran. The pair of them had been so afraid of the former Iranian dragon clan leader, they'd gone into hiding for years, only reappearing when Yasmin was pregnant and in desperate need of medical attention.

And now that her mother had mentioned it, Emma remembered how Logan had focused more on his studies and work than socializing after the loss of his brother, even around her. First, she'd tried to push Logan away after his declaration in their teens, and then his brother and other best friend had vanished.

Her throat choked with emotion. She'd been a silly teenager and hadn't really thought of more than keeping Logan at arm's length. She'd done her best to be his friend again after his defense of her and then his brother's disappearance.

However, in their own ways, both she and Phillip

had abandoned Logan. Was it any wonder he'd become so cautious? "So it's possible he won't completely retreat once his memories and dragon return?"

Her mother shook her head. "I can't claim to know for certain, lass. But if you go on this date tonight, if you let him in, then be sure you're not toying with him. If you want something, you have to go after it. So even if Logan retreats back into himself once his memories return, you'd have to work on bringing him out again. Trust me, I know it's not easy to put yourself on the line. After all, I went to America unsure if Jake felt the way I did. But you know what? He did, and now I'm happier than I've been since your father died. I never would've had that second chance if I hadn't gone after what I wanted, risks be damned. So just remember that, aye? If you end up wanting more from Logan than friendship, fight for it."

Jake Swift was her stepfather, and one of the nicest males in the world. He made her mother extremely happy in more ways than Emma could ever count.

And it was true—her mother had fought for him, drugging her dragon silent just so she could fly halfway around the world to see Jake at least one more time. It should've shown Emma how love could hurt but also reappear again to heal. But she'd been too busy focusing on geocaching treasure hunts and maintaining the status quo regarding her fears to really acknowledge or notice.

Not that she'd be able to just instantly change her view and fears. They didn't work on demand, unfortunately. So she said, "All I can say is that I won't try to push him away. But it's far too early for anything else."

"Aye, well at least you know he's not your true mate, so you don't have to worry like Cat when she kissed Lachlan, triggered the mate-claim frenzy, and had to make hasty decisions. You have time, lass, to better know him and figure things out. But just remember you can always talk to me, aye? Even if I have Sophie now, you were my youngest daughter for more than twenty years and I'll always have a soft spot for my wee girl."

Her eyes heated with tears, and Emma blinked them back. "Don't make me cry, Mum."

Her mother laughed. "Sorry, love." She hugged Emma a few beats and then released her. "Now, off with you. I'll arrive at the restaurant before you two, and keep Connor occupied."

"Thanks, Mum."

After murmuring her goodbyes and gathering what she needed, Emma headed toward where she would meet Logan before they headed over to the restaurant together. As she walked, her heart raced faster.

Her dragon spoke up. *Don't be so afraid. It's not as if you have to mate him tomorrow.*

Aye, I know that. But it's still strange. I've never tried to have a real date before. I'm not sure what to do.

Just don't spill soup in his lap if you can help it.

Emma laughed at one of her regular tricks. *No, I won't do that. Or water, or anything else to drive him away. I'm still nervous, though.*

I say it's because you want to kiss him and you'll be focusing on that the whole time.

That's what you want, dragon.

Her beast sniffed. *And you too, even if you pretend not to.*

More like Emma was nervous about where kissing could eventually lead. But she'd cross revealing her virginity, if it came to it.

As she saw Logan waiting up ahead, dressed smartly in his button-up shirt and trousers, she let herself examine his tall, lean form, broad shoulders, and nicely rounded bum. Aye, he was a braw, handsome male.

Now she just had to treat him as not just her friend, fight not to run away, and somehow be charming.

More easily said than done for a female often referred to as the wee harridan by many of Lochguard's gossips.

Chapter Eleven

Logan had spent the last few hours before meeting up with Emma trying to find any sort of pattern within the numbers from the clue. He'd still ended up with nothing more than a handful of coordinates that didn't seem to relate to one another, but it'd given him something to do instead of wondering if he'd ever get his memory or dragon back.

However, as he spotted Emma walking down the path toward him, wearing a dress that hugged her breasts before flaring out at the waist, his mouth went dry.

He had no idea if he'd ever seen her in a dress pre-amnesia, but he knew for certain he hadn't since waking up. It hugged her slight curves, and even gave him a peek at her cleavage. Add in her dark hair piled on top of her head, highlighting her long, graceful neck, and his cock started to harden.

Given that he didn't have a jacket or anything to hide it, he did his best to think of anything to calm his dick. Such as the latest threats from her brothers, one of Max's lectures about Roman jewelry techniques, or even the early signs of Alzheimer's. By the time she reached him, he'd just managed to get himself under control. "You look bonnie, angel. I'm torn between drinking you in slowly or finding a shirt to toss over your head to hide your skin from every other male."

The corner of Emma's mouth kicked up. "Considering how just about everyone has seen me naked at some point right before I shift, I think your jealousy is a wee bit over the top."

He growled. "Nudity for shifting is one thing. But displaying your breasts to the world, hinting at what's beneath, will drive everyone mad to claim you."

She snorted. "I don't care about everyone else." Emma moved closer and whispered into his ear, "Does my dress drive you mad?"

He wondered a second if Emma was actually flirting back with him. But rather than dwell on it, he focused on her and murmured, "At this rate, you're going to have to stand in front of me at the restaurant to hide from everyone else just how much you affect me, angel."

Her gaze darted down to his dick and blood

rushed south again, eradicating his earlier efforts to keep himself under control. He groaned. "Don't do that. You're only making it worse."

She laughed. "I should have just enough time to distract you before we get there, don't worry. Somehow I don't think you want to accidentally run into my eldest brother with a hard cock, aye?"

Mention of her brother helped tamp down his arousal a fraction, but only a little. "I thought your mum was going to keep him away?"

"Most likely, but Connor can be rather stubborn."

Logan drawled, "He wouldn't be the only MacAllister to share that trait."

She lightly hit his arm. "Be nice, aye?"

He placed a hand on her lower back and heard her heart rate tick up. "Maybe I should ratchet up your arousal as well, and then see how you feel walking into a restaurant full of dragon-shifters with supersensitive senses of smell. They'll know you're as randy as me."

"Logan," she half-heartedly admonished.

Slowly caressing her back in circles, he loved how she leaned into him. "We could skip the supper all together and just find a quiet spot to ourselves."

At his words, she stiffened underneath his fingers. "No, no, we can't do that. Come on, I'm more than a wee bit peckish."

Something had spooked her, although Logan had no idea what.

He'd find out eventually, but as they headed toward The Dragon's Delight, Logan focused merely on the fact he had an evening with Emma and at the end, he'd finally be able to claim his kiss with her.

So far, so good, Emma thought. She'd somehow flirted back with Logan and then her nervousness had faded a fraction.

It was bloody hard work not trying to sabotage a date on purpose.

Her dragon snorted. *By now, you know everything you shouldn't do to scare him off. But just kiss the male and I guarantee he'll be putty in our hands. We could even lose our virginity tonight.*

Not so fast, dragon. I'm not sure I want to do that until his memory, dragon, or both return.

Her beast sniffed. *It's a stalling technique. But I'll humor you for now. Not forever, as I've been incredibly patient. However, I want some cock, and I want it now.*

Despite her best efforts, her cheeks heated. And damn him, Logan studied her and asked, "What's your dragon saying now, angel?"

"It's not nice or proper to ask that."

Amusement flashed in his eyes. "I remember that much but I'm asking anyway. Because anything that turns your cheeks that red must be worth hearing about."

Thankfully they were nearly to her family's restaurant, so she had a ready excuse to deflect. Taking a deep breath, she shook her head. "No, it's not something to spout about in public." She smiled up at him. "You'll just have to spend the evening wondering about it. Maybe I'll even share later on."

Before he could do more than frown, she took charge and opened the door. However, Logan placed a hand on her back, held the door with his hand, and gently pushed.

She allowed it, mostly because his touch and the way he lightly made circles on her back made her forget how to speak.

The person working the front entrance was, thankfully, not her younger brother, Jamie, who often still helped out at the restaurant when needed. No, it was Miles, one of the teenagers. The male smiled at her, but before he could say anything, Logan growled, "We have a reservation."

The younger male frowned but nodded. "Aye, I know."

"Then show us to our table."

Emma frowned up at Logan. "Be nice, aye? You don't want to anger anyone related to your food."

Not that Logan seemed to care if someone would spit in his dinner. He growled, "Our table," as his hand moved from her back to her waist before bringing her against his side.

Her dragon chuckled. *It seems even without a dragon, he's a wee bit possessive.*

Logan has never been possessive in his life.

Well, he is now. And I rather like it.

Emma knew her dragon turned randy when a male took charge at times, saying it was a nice change from Emma always getting her way. *Not this again. It's not as if I'm going to listen to him if he orders me to strip in the middle of the room.*

Of course not. But I wouldn't mind a male so desperate he'd pin us against the wall and fuck us senseless.

Since her cheeks would most assuredly heat again if her dragon didn't shut it, she threatened, *I'll toss you in a mental maze if you don't behave, aye?*

Fine. But once we're alone with him, don't expect me to just watch and say nothing. I plan to enjoy that kiss.

Between her dragon behaving and the short walk to the table off to the side near a window, Emma managed to calm her racing heart a little. If things kept going as they had so far, then between her dragon and Logan, Emma would lose her virginity without even realizing it.

Okay, she'd realize it. Maybe. Unless she did drive Logan mad and he made her lose her head first.

They sat down, the host offered menus and the special, and left them. Since Emma knew everything on the menu—plus what wasn't, but what her brother could make on request—she studied Logan as he read all the offerings.

He really was handsome with his deep-brown eyes, strong jaw, and blond hair a touch too long. In fact, she itched to brush the random strands off his forehead. There was something almost normal and mundane about sitting down with him to eat. And yet, once he put down the menu and asked, "Did you solve the new problem for our wee project yet?" hinting at the geocaching contest, she knew this was better than mundane. He might, just might, end up being a male who didn't dismiss who she was, one who she might even risk her heart with.

Pushing that thought aside, she kept her voice low and her words deliberately vague as she answered, "No, not yet. Sometimes putting things aside for an evening or two and coming back to them is the best strategy, even if I'm impatient to get going."

She fiddled with the fork on the table and Logan reached across, took her hand, and moved it to the side where he could keep it in his and lightly stroke her knuckles.

Even though the touch was barely there, each slightly rough caress of his fingers made her heart thunder louder at the same time heat spread through her body, ending between her thighs.

Bloody hell, she needed to get a grip on her

hormones or everyone really would know how much she wanted to strip Logan and ride him.

Wait, no. She didn't want that. Did she?

Her dragon laughed, but Emma ignored her to focus on Logan's deep voice. "Just remember you're not alone this time, angel. You have a team, so it may get solved quicker than you think."

It was still difficult to remember she wasn't working on her own. "Aye, I know. But I'm a wee bit competitive, aye? So even when it comes to my own friends or teammates, I'll still keep trying to finish something before everyone else does."

The corner of his mouth ticked up. "Are you competitive in every situation then, angel?"

The heat in Logan's eyes nearly made her fan herself. He was talking about sex, of course. "You'll just have to wait and see."

Bloody hell. Had she really just insinuated they'd be naked together?

Given Logan's smug smile, she reckoned so. "I look forward to it, angel."

She frowned. "I still don't know why you keep calling me that."

"Don't you remember? I said an angel was standing over me when I first woke up."

She raised her brows. "I wasn't even standing at first, if I recall."

He lifted her hand and brought it closer to his lips, to the point his breath danced across her skin.

"Does it matter? I still think of you as a bonnie, dark-haired angel, here to watch over me. Although I do like how you're a wee bit corruptible, aye? No prim and proper angel types for me."

She laughed. "Prim and proper aren't words anyone would ever use to describe me."

A third voice butted into their conversation. "Certainly not, despite all my offers to help with that wee problem."

Emma resisted a sigh, steeled herself, and looked up at Meg Boyd, her grandfather's paramour; girlfriend wasn't quite the right word for the threesome of Meg, Emma's granddad, and another male named Cal. "Hello, Meg."

Instead of the usual exasperated expression Meg had when looking at her, Emma nearly blinked at the approval in the older dragonwoman's eyes. "At least you've finally settled on a sensible laddie. Logan will set you on the straight and narrow, especially once his memories return."

Logan never released Emma's hand but did lower it back to the table. "*If* they come back, Meg, is it?"

Och, that's right. She's forgotten Logan hadn't reacquainted himself with Meg, lucky devil. But before Emma could do the introductions, Meg nodded. "Aye, Meg Boyd. If you ever have questions about the clan, come see me. I know everything."

Logan smiled blandly. "I'll keep that in mind."

Meg frowned—the expression of oncoming

doom, Emma privately called it—and decided she'd best get Meg away before she lectured Logan for an hour about why she did, in fact, know just about everything that happened on Lochguard. "Is my granddad waiting for you, Meg? Or Cal?"

The older dragonwoman waved a hand in dismissal. "They'll keep a bit longer. Maybe I should sit and answer a few of Logan's questions, aye? He's been a bit reclusive since waking up."

She jumped in before Logan could. "He's been a bit busy, Meg."

Meg's look turned curious. "Wooing you, you mean? Will there be another mating ceremony in the near future? Just imagine, one so soon after your mother's. But hopefully yours will be a proper dragon-shifter one, and not that silly blended type with human traditions."

Emma had more patience than her other siblings when it came to Meg, probably due to her volunteer work with the elderly clan members, and merely murmured, "Her mate is human, Meg."

"Aye, I know." She sniffed. Meg and Jake didn't get along at all, mostly because Jake stood up to the older dragonwoman like few did. "As I said, you have a proper dragonman, as you should. Your sister's mate is okay for a human, but I still think a lusty dragonman in the bedroom is better than anything a human can do. And believe me, I've sampled both myself."

Not wanting to hear about Meg's sexual exploits —because she *would* go into explicit detail, if given the chance—Emma said, "Well, aye, I'll believe you. But if there's to be any wooing, we need a wee bit of privacy, aye?"

Meg nodded, as if the idea had been her own. "Aye, aye, a fine plan." She patted where Logan still held Emma's hand in his. "I'll be hoping for the best. Now, go on and do whatever you young people do. Just enjoy it whilst you can. Age does bring a few restrictions when it comes to acrobatics. Don't pass up the chance and take advantage of it whilst you still can."

With words she'd never wanted to hear from Meg, the dragonwoman finally left and headed toward where both her males waited for her at the door.

Logan chuckled and Emma's gaze shot to his. "You're not angry with her?"

He shook his head. "No, although I'll admit I'm not sure how much I can take of her beyond a few minutes."

She smiled. "You're not the only one. Although be prepared because she'll tell everyone who'll listen about us being here tonight."

His gaze turned sizzling. "Let her. That means the other males will stay away."

Oh, dear. His gravelly voice and fiery look suddenly made her clothes too tight and confining.

Almost as if she wanted to strip right then and there to ease the feeling.

Her dragon snorted. *Hurry up and eat then so we can strip in front of him in private.*

Thankfully the server came up and took their orders. And as she answered a few questions for Logan about his past, talked of her work, and shared some of the craziness of her family when she and her siblings had been younger, the night flew by without a single mishap.

She also stopped being nervous about what this date could mean for her future and simply enjoyed Logan's innuendos, heated looks, and how he'd often stared at her neck, or lips, or even her small chest.

By the time they finished and Logan offered her a hand up, she nearly jumped at the feel of his skin against hers once more.

And at Logan's whisper of "Let's find somewhere quiet where I can finally claim my kiss," her heart beat double-time and her breasts swelled as she imagined how it'd go.

It was time to find out if Logan was as good as his promises. And Emma couldn't wait to find out.

Chapter Twelve

While Logan had enjoyed himself during supper, chatting with Emma and teasing her, now that he had her walking away from the restaurant, meaning he'd be finally kissing her sweet lips soon, it took everything he had not to scoop her up into his arms and race toward a secluded spot.

Given how she'd fallen quiet as well, he had a feeling Emma was thinking about the kiss as much as he was.

He'd scouted out a few secluded places on his walk to meet the female, and spotted the wee building not too far from the great hall. It'd been unlocked, and had only a sturdy-looking table, a sink, and few random items inside. Since it was still dark, he opened the door and swept Emma inside.

Pulling her up against him, he murmured, "You asked for a warning, so here it is. Tell me I can kiss you, angel." He caressed her cheek. "I've been thinking of nothing else since you licked the icing from your lips during dessert."

Her pupils flashed from round to slits and back again. "I didn't even realize I'd done that."

He ran his finger from her cheek, down her neck, and back up again. "So you're just naturally a flirty angel, then, aye?"

She smiled. "No one's ever called me a flirty angel before."

"Sexy angel, more like. But I thought I'd ease you into it." He moved his head closer to hers. "You still haven't said I can kiss you, Emma."

For a beat, she said nothing. Then she laid her hands on his chest. Not to push away, but to slowly stroke him, the heat of her fingers through the material nearly making him moan. "That depends. Will you stop if I tell you to?"

Unease flickered through him, but he did his best not to show it. "Aye, of course. But why are you worried about that?"

She bit her lip a second, then shook her head. "It doesn't matter." She lifted her head up. "Kiss me, Logan." She lightly dug her nails into his chest. "This time, I promise I won't laugh."

Even though he wanted to prod a bit more about why stopping mattered, as soon as she told him to kiss her, he lost all reason and brought his lips down to hers.

The second her flesh met his, heat raged through him at the same time something stirred in his mind.

But he didn't care about that and instead hauled her closer against him as he nibbled and stroked her bottom lip with his tongue, pleading for her to open.

With a moan, Emma did, and he plundered her mouth. Groaning at her taste, and heat, and the way she clung to him, he used every stroke, and caress, and nibble to let her know how much he wanted her. More than air, more than even memories, he wanted to claim Emma MacAllister as his own.

When she moaned and kissed him back just as fiercely, waging a battle against his tongue as if she was dying of hunger for his taste, Logan moved her back toward the table and managed to lift her to it. Without a word, she parted her thighs and he stepped between them, pressing his hard cock to the sweet, wet center he wanted to explore for hours with his tongue, his fingers, and most definitely his dick. She wasn't wearing anything beneath her dress, either. *Bloody hell.* His sexy angel indeed, already drenched and begging for him.

Fuck, he wanted to taste her sweet honey on his lips.

Something moved in his mind again, but then Emma rubbed against his trouser-clad erection, making him even harder. As he ground back, loving her gasps and mewls, a pounding desire to open his fly and claim her right here and now surged through him. The friction wasn't nearly enough. No, he desperately wanted to feel her heat, her tightness, her lovely pussy surrounding and grasping him as she lost her mind.

But then his hand found her breast, and the feel of her hard nipple against his palm distracted him. No, her cunt could wait a few minutes. He needed to see her tits and sweet nipples first.

Given her low neckline, it was easy to pull it down and expose her. Emma's dark pink buds made his mouth water and he didn't waste time taking one into his mouth to suck, and lightly bite, and gently tug with his teeth. She dug her nails into his scalp and arched into his touch, his name a whisper on her lips.

A growl went through his mind, but he didn't pay attention. No, he moved to her other breast, sweetly torturing her other hard nipple, loving how when he tugged with his teeth, she moved her hips even closer to him, as if needing more, much more.

Emma's breathy voice garnered his attention. "Logan, I can't take much more. Please."

He released her and stared at her face, loving the heat in her gaze and flush on her cheeks. With a smile, he moved a hand to her thigh and stopped short of touching her pussy, still amazed that she didn't have on anything underneath her dress. "Maybe I should torture you a wee bit more, until you fully beg." He lightly ran a finger through her short curls and brushed her clit with the lightest possible touch. When he did it again, she clung to his biceps and dug in her nails.

Logan lightly traced her opening, loving how wet and swollen she was for him. He purred, "Aye, I think I can torture you slowly by tasting you first and teasing you with my tongue."

He dropped to his knees, waiting to see if Emma would tell him to stop. But she didn't, thank fuck, her pupils flashing rapidly as her upper chest turned pink.

Logan ran his hands up her thighs, slowly sliding the skirt of her dress up, inch by inch, loving how her breathing turned ragged. His thumbs met the crease where her thigh met her cunt, and he stopped, keeping his gaze trained on Emma. "Tell me you want my tongue."

She hesitated and nodded.

He stilled his fingers. "Tell me plainly, Emma. I want to hear it."

Her cheeks turned even pinker, making him think no male had ever gone down on her before.

Fools, all of them. Already he could smell her arousal and he could barely keep himself from devouring her right then and there.

But he wanted her consent. If he was going to pursue her—and he was—then he wanted no ambiguity between them.

Emma cleared her throat. "Aye, I want it."

Pressing her legs wider, he spread her lower lips and murmured, "That's my angel," before staring down at her. She was glistening, pink, and perfect, and he couldn't believe his former self had never tried to win this female over.

A snarl went through his mind, making Logan pause. But Emma's sweet pussy was too close, her scent driving him mad, and he needed to feel her against his tongue, and he forgot about anything else.

He leaned down and lightly licked her slit up to her clit and back again. As her salty, musky taste filled his mouth, his cock turned to stone and he couldn't hold back and see out his torture. No, he licked, and lapped, and teased her pussy with his teeth, careful to avoid her clit, wanting her squirming and desperate before he let her come.

Her nails dug into his scalp and she tried to move her hips so his tongue would touch her hard, little bud.

Instead, he fucked her cunt with his tongue, groaning at how tight she was. The snarling in his head increased and a crack sounded.

But he was so lost in teasing Emma, and bringing her closer to the edge, he didn't care. He finally moved his mouth to her clit, lightly suckling her at the same time as he thrust one of his fingers inside her.

"Oh, Logan. Please. Just a little harder. Just like that. Aaah."

As Emma screamed, he reveled in her squeezing his finger. He continued to torture her clit, wanting to draw out the pleasure, loving every moan and sigh as she fell apart.

The entire time the cracking in his mind grew louder.

When she finally relaxed, he moved away and rose to take her mouth with his own. He'd barely slipped his tongue between her lips when her hand moved to his still-clad cock. As she stroked him, the cracking sound in his head turned deafening.

The sound of shattering crashed through his brain, a flood of memories rushed forth, followed by the unmistakable sound of his dragon.

Fuck her. I want to fuck her, finally. Pin her hands behind her and do it. Now.

Logan stepped away, gripping his head in his hands, trying to make sense of the bombardment of images, the repeated forceful and lusty demands of the second personality in his head, and he stumbled backward.

It overwhelmed him and he finally slumped to the floor in front of the door right before he blacked out.

EMMA HAD LONG AGO LEARNED to pleasure herself, but it didn't compare in the slightest to Logan making her orgasm with his mouth.

Then he kissed her, making her taste herself on his lips, and she burned, wanting more. For the first time in her life, she didn't care about possibly risking her heart in the long run with sex, or that she risked being destroyed in the future if it didn't work out.

So she'd reached down tentatively to stroke Logan's cock and suggest more.

But that was when he moved away from her, gripping his head, and crying out in pain.

It happened so fast that she'd barely hopped down from the table when he slumped to the ground, propped against the door, unconscious.

She kneeled next to him and caressed his cheek. "Logan? Och, no. Logan, are you okay? Talk to me."

When he didn't respond, her dragon said, *I think his dragon came back. I saw his pupils flash once before he shut his eyes.*

As she gently readjusted his position, sliding him to the floor away from the door, a mixture of fear and hope raced through her. On the one hand, she wanted Logan to have all his memories back. She missed their shared history, private comments, and all the small things she'd taken for granted.

On the other, she didn't know how he'd act if he no longer had amnesia and was afraid he'd retreat again.

But her musings barely lasted a few seconds. Once Logan was comfortably on the floor, she tugged up her neckline, and went to her bag she'd left forgotten on the table. Taking out her mobile phone, she dialed the surgery.

As soon as someone said they'd come, she opened the door—both to let the doctor find them but to also air out what had happened since dragon-shifters had keen senses of smell—and knelt next to Logan. As she stroked his forehead, she did her best not to panic. If he had his memories and acted a wee bit different, then she'd just have to fight, as her mother had said.

Although the worst-case scenarios ran through her mind. Maybe he'd be embarrassed at what they'd done. Maybe he wanted to go back to his goal of leaving for Edinburgh as soon as he could for his doctor's studies. Maybe Logan even wanted nothing to do with her until he recovered and sorted everything out.

Or, maybe his dragon and memories hadn't returned and this was a flare up related to his injury. And the injury was her fault.

She swallowed and blinked, not wanting to cry. Logan would be okay. She couldn't imagine her life without him.

For too long, she'd taken him for granted. And in the end, it might be too late after all.

No. She wouldn't start thinking the worst. Logan would make it through. He just had to.

She whispered, "Don't you dare give up, do you hear? I won't have it. You'll wake up, in whatever state, and I'll be there. From here on out, I'm not turning away from you, Logan Lamont. So don't you dare bother running away."

Logan lay still, his chest rising and falling, unable to respond.

Emma didn't know how long she sat there, stroking his forehead, before Dr. McFarland found them. She'd come with a pair of sturdy male nurses. And as they maneuvered Logan onto a stretcher, the doctor took her aside and asked what had happened.

Embarrassing as it was, Emma explained in low tones what had transpired. Dr. McFarland nodded and murmured, "Lust and desire is one way to bring a dragon back, aye. Randy beasts they are."

Her cheeks heated and the other female's eyes softened. "Don't worry, Emma. I'll only tell those who need to know. What happens between you and Logan is private, aye?" She nodded and the doctor continued, "If you remember anything else, make sure to share it."

The two nurses had Logan on the stretcher and as they carried him toward the surgery, Emma started to follow but Dr. McFarland laid a hand on her arm. "It's best for you to go home, Emma. I'll let you know when you can come see him." She opened her mouth to argue, but the doctor continued, "I promise to keep you informed. But if he regained anything, or even both his dragon and his memories today, then he might be confused or even angry. Once things calm down, I'll let you know."

Staring at Logan's retreating form on the stretcher, she swallowed back the emotion in her throat. She nodded. "Just tell him I want to see him as soon as possible."

Dr. McFarland took in Emma's mussed hair and wrinkled dress, and smiled. "Aye, I know you do."

With one more squeeze on her arm, Dr. McFarland left to follow the nurses.

Once they were out of sight, Emma sighed and headed home. Maybe she should go see her Mum, who always knew the right thing to say to her children to help them. But in the moment, Emma just wanted to hide in her room and think about what had transpired with Logan.

And maybe come up with a few plans of what to do if Logan was different yet again. Aye, that would help her avoid thinking about how things could all turn to shite soon enough.

Her dragon spoke up. *And the clue. That would be a good distraction too, aye?*

I suppose. Although the rush isn't there, like usual.

Still, the end goal is a noble one. Even Logan's Great-Aunt Mary would benefit from such a fine senior center, aye?

Fine, I'll attempt it once my mind settles a wee bit. But if Logan asks for me, that's more important.

Her beast grunted, probably still hopeful for some sex in the near future.

But rather than focus on all the negative what-ifs, Emma went home, focused on her work and the clue, and did her best not to think of Logan every minute and how she might have finally found a male to risk her heart with. One who might not want it in the end, though, once he remembered the pain of her repeatedly pushing him away in the past.

Chapter Thirteen

I ris Mahajan had been taking a break from her Protector duties to study the list of numbers from the latest geocaching clue when Faye MacKenzie popped her wild, curly-haired head into her office and said, "You have a rather special visitor, Iris."

She frowned. "Who?"

"Antony Holbrook."

Her dragon spoke up. *Good. I was wondering how long it'd be before he showed up again.*

Calm down, dragon. He's not here to see us merely because he wishes it.

You don't know it. I'd still like to strip him and show him a thing or two. He may be older, and more experienced, but I'm sure I could still surprise him.

Not wanting to think of Antony naked and get distracted, Iris replied to Faye, "Did he mention what he wanted?"

The other female raised an eyebrow. "You've met the male, aye? Do you think he's going to tell me anything if he doesn't want to, even if I press him?"

Rolling her eyes, Iris finally stood. "And here I thought you were in charge here, aye?"

Faye stuck out her tongue. "I debated bringing my cousin Freya here and letting her sit on him until he answered, but I think he may be the one person in the world who can resist her cute baby dragon form and big eyes."

Iris snorted. Freya Stewart was their clan leader's daughter and the only toddler they were aware of who could shift between dragon and human with ease at such a young age. She already had most of the clan wrapped around her wee fingers. "In another year she might be heavy enough in her dragon form to pin someone like Holbrook in place, though, without killing him. Something to keep in mind."

Faye turned and they walked down the hallway. "I don't know. He's a bit mysterious, aye? I'm sure he'd have some sort of technique to free himself." Faye was one of the co-leaders of the Protectors, and despite her bubbly nature, far more clever and observant than many people realized. "I'm curious why he's asking for you instead of me or Grant."

Remembering the last time she'd met him, when Antony had helped her to capture a Lochguard dragon illegally selling dragon's blood, she knew why.

The male bloody well liked torturing her, or teasing her, or just being annoying.

But she wasn't about to tell Faye that. No, the female would probably then try to get the pair of them to work together on purpose. Not to cause Iris pain, but rather to matchmake.

As if she wanted a mate. She had far too many investigations and projects ongoing with Lochguard to think of something like that.

Her dragon chuckled. *You don't have to mate him to fuck him. I still say we give it a go.*

She drawled to her beast, *Right, because that won't backfire on us later. I don't need him using anything else to taunt us.*

Her beast sniffed. *I'm almost positive he's some sort of spy. If he wanted to taunt us, or hurt us, he probably has tools we can only dream of.*

Yet another reason to stay away from him as much as possible.

Before her dragon could answer, they reached the room used for non-clan visitors. Faye stopped to the side of the door. "He wants to see you alone." Faye waved. "Have fun and see me and Grant when you're done, aye?"

She sighed, turned the knob, and walked inside.

Iris immediately blinked. Every time she'd seen him before, Antony Holbrook had always worn some sort of nondescript suit.

Oh, aye, he was still tall, with broad shoulders, a

lean waist, and brown hair with gray at the temples. But this time, he wore a light-blue buttoned-up shirt, open at the collar and revealing a light dusting of chest hair. It looked dark, but was probably salt and pepper, dark with bits of light mixed in to match his hair. The thought made her want to open a few more buttons on his top to find out, and then maybe run her fingers through it.

Bloody hell. She curled her fingers into a fist. She was not going to think of undressing the male.

Her dragon laughed. *All he has to do is flick open a few buttons on his shirt and you'll be drooling all over the floor, admit it.*

Shut it, dragon.

Antony smiled slowly and walked toward her, only one button undone on his shirt and no hint of him going to open more. His deep, cultured voice rolled over her. "Good to know you like what you see, my dear. Although that sort of thing isn't why I'm here."

Iris's cheeks heated at being caught staring. She quickly cleared her throat and focused on the smug tilt of his lips.

Firm-looking lips that probably knew what they were about.

She barely resisted shaking her head when she finally replied, "My name is Iris, not 'my dear' as I told you before."

His smile widened. "Do you really want to quibble over that, or discuss why I came here to see you?"

Antony's slightly more proper, and decidedly south of England accent, should irritate her.

Too bad it made him seem a wee bit dirtier somehow.

At her dragon's laughter, she clenched her jaw a beat before replying, "Just tell me why you're here. I have plenty to do, despite what you may think."

Antony crossed his arms over his chest—his rather broad chest—and nodded. "I imagine so, given what I've heard." Before she could ask for details, he added, "A number of dragon hunters from across the world have teamed up to claim the £500,000 prize Emma MacAllister is also after."

She blinked, hating how this male always seemed to surprise her when few others ever did. "How do you know about that?"

He raised an eyebrow. "Trust me, my dear, I know things you can't even begin to imagine. But the point is, we need Miss MacAllister to get to the final clue as soon as possible. The group we've been tracking visited the Dumyat Summit the day before your team did. My colleague trailing them was found dead and buried in the woods not far from there, which means we've lost their trail. It's imperative we know where they're headed so we can catch them. I have a few people working to solve the clue, but Miss MacAllister is much better at this sort of thing and will probably figure it out faster than them."

Iris had always been quick to follow thoughts and with her initial surprise gone, she had no problem now. "But why would you wait until the final stage to apprehend them?"

"Excellent question, my dear. All I can say is that the person hosting this event is someone of interest. The grand prize may or may not have a few breadcrumbs to lead us to their location. However, we need to at least try, given how evasive the buggers are, which means we need someone to win." He shrugged one shoulder. "Making an arrest or disappearing a competitor without a word will most likely halt the entire thing, and we can't have that." He took another step toward her and studied her face. "So tell me if you've figured out the latest clue yet."

Her curiosity burned to ask about this mysterious person Antony wanted to find. However, she'd learned from their first interaction that he only shared what he wished, no more, no less. It was far better to focus on what she could control.

So Iris raised her brows. "We're supposed to just trust you without question, aye? Would you do the same?"

He winked, reached into his jeans pocket, and handed her an envelope. She couldn't tell if Antony deliberately brushed her fingers with his or not, but his warm skin against her sent a rush of heat throughout her body.

Yanking the missive closer, she pushed away the tingly feeling; it wasn't as if she'd act on it.

Opening the envelope, she scanned the note, which was from the DDA Director, Rosalind Abbott:

ANTONY HOLBROOK IS WORKING with my office. The phoenix is in flight again. Trust him.

THE SECOND SENTENCE might seem like nonsense to most, but "the phoenix is in flight" was a coded phrase, meaning they had a clue about Simon Bourne's location.

And since Bourne was the leader of the British dragon hunters, and a male who had quietly gone underground a number of years ago, any link to him was definitely a high priority for both the DDA and the dragon-shifters.

The seal on the bottom of the note, as well as the series of numbers the DDA Director used with every message to the Protectors, meant Antony might be telling the truth.

Of course, given how she suspected he was a spy, it could be a fake. "Do I have time to confirm this?"

He took out his mobile phone. "Need to use mine?"

As if she'd use anything of his. The male probably had it bloody bugged. "Wait here."

Before he could say a word, Iris went into the hall and down a few doors to the IT section of the Protector building. Since Emma and Ian MacAllister were both working on side projects for the department, she went to one of the males covering their posts and asked him to check their encrypted messaging system. It was something they'd set up when Abbott took over, to have a secondary verification that the DDA Director had approved the message. Since the last three numbers of the chain always changed, it was easy enough to check.

The dragonman nodded. "Aye, it's legit." He tapped the screen. "Her office logged it here."

After thanking the male, she mentally cursed and headed back toward the room with Antony Holbrook. Barring some great emergency, she'd have to work with him until whatever mission he had was complete.

Her dragon cackled. *Good. Then maybe we'll get a chance to shag him at least once.*

No shagging is going to take place, aye? None.

Her beast sniffed. *We'll see about that.*

Ignoring her dragon, Iris took a deep breath and charged into the room. Once she shut the door, she crossed her arms over her chest. "All right, what do you propose we do?"

Thankfully he didn't comment about her abrupt departure and got straight to the point. "We need to gather the whole Lochguard team together and work on the clue."

"That may be a problem." As she explained how one of the team members, Logan, was currently unconscious, she finally added, "And I'm a bit unsure if Emma's in any state of mind to concentrate."

"If she's conscious, bring her and the others here. We need to work together, me included now."

She frowned. "You? Why? Do you have experience with treasure hunts?"

That smug smile crossed his face. "I may. I have experience with a lot of things, my dear. It comes with age."

Her dragon hummed. *I bet it does. He probably knows how to make a female come three times with only his tongue.*

Dragon, shut it.

Why? A quick fuck will most definitely settle our nerves.

Behave or it's a mental maze for you.

Her beast grunted. *You'll give in eventually, just wait and see.*

Her dragon settled down and she noticed Antony watching her. She swore his gaze turned blazing for a beat, but then it vanished, returning to his ever half-amused look. Before she could think of it, she blurted, "We'd better get started, old man, before you have to take a nap to keep up."

She nearly covered her mouth with her hand, as if she could erase the outburst, but restrained herself. She couldn't take it back.

What was wrong with her? She never insulted or even teased people like that. Her job required forming relationships and gathering information, not pissing off everyone.

She waited to see if he'd turn angry. However, Antony surprised her by chuckling. "This old man could probably run circles around you. Some day, I may just have to show you." He leaned forward a fraction and turned momentarily—and deliberately —Scottish, "Aye?"

For a beat, they merely stared at one another. Iris's cheeks heated again as she imagined Antony chasing her through the woods before catching her and pinning her against a tree, restraining her hands and quickly fucking her like his life depended on it.

But then she remembered that she didn't have time to trade barbs with the human. If there was even the smallest chance they could find a hint of Simon Bourne's location, she'd take it. After all, while the dragons had managed to bring down the Dragon Knights, the hunters were still too big of a threat, one where her clan still couldn't move around without constantly looking over their shoulders.

And Iris wanted to change that.

So she took out her mobile phone and stated, "I'll text the others. Sit down and wait for us."

She left before he could say a word. Distance helped her regain her equilibrium. And by the time she entered the room again with the blasted male, she was in work mode and was able to ignore most of his shite to focus on what needed to be done.

Chapter Fourteen

Logan opened his eyes to see the bloody white, boring ceiling of the surgery again.

He'd barely frowned up at the blasted thing when a now-familiar voice spoke up. *Good. We can finally talk again. Not even trying to reach you in our dreams seemed to help.*

Logan at once knew everything about his inner dragon and also wasn't sure what to say. It was as if he didn't quite know who he was anymore. Aye, he remembered his brother, and his great-aunt, and even his coworkers. And yet, any memory of them was tinged with a new lens, as if he didn't quite know how to act with them.

And then an image of Emma, her legs spread as he lapped her pussy, flashed into his mind. Sitting upright, he remembered. They'd been on a date, she'd kissed him, and then things had gone further, as in Emma digging her nails into his scalp and calling out his name as she came.

He should be happy, thrilled even, that she'd finally seen him as more than a friend.

However, it'd been the Logan he'd been briefly, the one with no hesitations or caution, that had seemed to catch her fancy.

And his spirits sank. Could he be that male? Running a hand through his hair, he blew out a breath. He just didn't bloody know.

His dragon spoke up. *Don't doom things before they happen. You have a tendency to do that.*

Not that I want to, dragon. But if Emma only wants us when I'm more forthright and borderline possessive, I'm not sure I can do that.

We were that way once before, remember?

Aye, before Emma had laughed at his kiss. His misjudging the moment had struck a blow to his ego.

Then the memory of her telling him *why* she'd done it came back—she'd been afraid to open her heart and get hurt, all because of what had happened to her mum after her dad's murder.

The fact she hadn't been able to tell him that, her best friend, made him scowl. Maybe she hadn't trusted him as much as he'd thought.

His dragon said, *If you push her away now, it will be the last time and only confirm her fears. Don't fuck it up.*

Rubbing both of his hands through his hair, he

growled and then hit the mattress with his palms. *Give me a moment to sort myself out, aye?*

Logan rarely lost his temper with his beast, and his dragon knew it. So he bit out, *Aye, I will. But this conversation isn't over.*

He put his head in his hands and tried to sort through everything that had happened during his bout of amnesia. Emma was the main focus, and her geocaching contest.

Thinking back, it had been a wee bit fun solving and exploring things with her. When he didn't act like a mother hen, afraid she'd get injured by every little thing, she blossomed a bit more.

Of course, now knowing that someone might've been intentionally trying to kill her when he'd pushed her out of the way of that rock didn't ease his need for a bit of caution.

He didn't want to give up the contest, yet he had a feeling it would only get more dangerous from here on out. The question was: Did he keep helping Emma to protect her? Or fall on his old ways and try to convince her to quit?

Although flashes of her face, full of joy and excitement when they'd found the clues, made him want to see her that way again.

What a bloody tangle.

As he went back and forth about what to do, Logan didn't notice how much time passed before Dr.

McFarland entered the room. She smiled. "Awake at last, I see."

He sighed and met her gaze. "Aye, Layla. Both of us, and fully too."

Her eyes widened a fraction and then she went into her doctor mode, checking his vitals and asking a few questions only he'd know if Logan had all his memories.

Once she finished, she crossed her arms and studied him a beat. He raised his brows. "What?"

"I have a message for you, but I'm trying to decide if you're well enough for it, aye?" She bit her bottom lip and then added, "It has to do with Emma."

Swinging his legs off the bed, Logan stood and growled, "Then tell me."

Layla smiled a second, telling him it wasn't bad news. "You do know that I'm the best female inside Lochguard at ignoring male gruffness and dominance on the clan, aye? So calm down and ask me a wee bit more rational like."

Layla was correct—doctors had to be good at resisting dominance, growls, and any other manner of bullshit that, usually, male dragon-shifters tended to display when ill or injured. "Then please tell me the message, aye? I need to see Emma."

She searched his eyes. "Aye, I know what you two were up to right before you passed out. Although this is more about the treasure hunt."

"She didn't go out on her own again, did she?" He looked around for his clothes. "Where are my trousers and shoes? The female bloody well knows how she works better with a team and I need to remind her of that."

Layla snorted, garnering his attention. "She *is* working with a team. Calm down, Logan. After what happened with your injury, no one is letting her go off alone."

His scowled deepened. "Then what's your message? Don't try my patience, Layla. I'm still trying to sort out what happened, my dragon is a wee bit grumpy, and I still don't know where my trousers are."

His beast grunted. *I'm not the grumpy one.*

The dragonwoman shook her head. "I'll have Holly bring your clothes. As for the message, you need to promise me you won't hie off without me saying you're fit to do so. If you won't promise, I won't tell you. And none of your growls or scowls will change my mind."

He resisted clenching his fingers into fists and did his best to calm his voice. "Aye, aye, I'll wait for your approval. Now, what's going on?"

She studied him a moment, must've seen he meant it, because she nodded. "Emma, Iris, Max, and Zoe are all working together on the latest clue inside the Protector building. If you're still interested, and able, she wants you to join them when you can."

The fact Emma wasn't sure if he'd come made anger churn in his belly. Maybe he still had some figuring out to do, still had to think of who he was now, but if she thought he'd give up so easily after finally being able to taste her sweet pussy and having her cry out his name as she came, then she was in for a big surprise. "I'll go." Layla raised her brows and he grunted. "Provided you clear me first."

"Just a few more questions, aye? And you have to vow to come back to see me tomorrow."

He suffered through Layla's questions, resisting the urge to snap at her, and made the bloody vow.

It was hard to concentrate, let alone be patient, when all he craved was seeing Emma again, almost as if she were the key to figuring out who he was anymore.

And once he finally rushed toward the Protector building, he debated if he could kiss her straight away or if he'd need to wait until they were alone.

Either way, he was done dancing around her. She'd given herself to him once, and he was determined to win her for good.

EMMA ROLLED her shoulders and then lightly slapped her cheeks, trying to wake herself up a wee bit.

They'd been looking at the clue from so many angles, and yet all they knew so far was how using all the numbers didn't make sense for coordinates. Aye, they matched up, mostly, but they were random locations all over England, ones that didn't seem to have any sort of connection.

Despite the frustration, the only good thing was it had distracted her from thinking about Logan.

Aye, well, most of the time.

He'd been unconscious for two days. She'd wanted to visit him, but Dr. McFarland had wanted only a small group of staff around him until he woke up. Amnesia, especially the kind that involved silent dragons, was unpredictable. Not much had been studied on the subject, but from what the doctor knew, some people woke up confused and violent.

Her dragon yawned and said, *Maybe we should go home for a wee while. Antony and Max should be back soon, to share what they'd found in the archives, if anything.*

Learning Max had a brother had been somewhat shocking, but the resemblance was uncanny and undeniable despite their being roughly a decade apart in age. The pair often worked on their own, not that they'd ever said why.

At any rate, everyone checked in twice a day, with a promise to let them know if there was any big breakthrough. She replied to her beast, *After they report their progress or lack of, we'll go home and sleep a bit. I'd love to put these bloody numbers aside for a few days to let it simmer in my subconscious, but Antony won't allow it.*

No, in fact the male was rather fond of barking

orders. Iris was the only one who didn't mind telling him to "*haud yer wheesht*" and argue with his rather dictatorial style.

Emma, on the other hand, didn't care enough to battle the male. She wasn't at the top end of the dominance scale for the clan, but not near the bottom either. She spoke up if it merited it but didn't see the point of arguing just to argue.

With a sigh, she decided she'd best work on her latest guess, about the numbers being some sort of code, until the Holbrook brothers returned. Just as she tried to see any sort of pattern within the numbers of the clue, the door banged open and smacked loudly against the wall.

She, Iris, and Zoe all jumped and swung their gazes to the intruder.

It was Logan.

Not only that, his eyes were fixated on her, full of anger, determination, and a wee bit of possession.

She should maybe be annoyed at his look given how they'd been on exactly one date, and yet it made her hopeful that part of the Logan she'd liked during his bout of amnesia was still there. "What's the matter? Did you forget your manners?"

He stalked toward her, as if she were his prey, and growled, "Come with me."

She frowned. "But I—"

Logan took her hand and lightly tugged her to her feet before he replied, "Right now, we need to talk. And I'm not above tossing you over my shoulder and carrying you off."

The image of him manhandling her should irritate her. It would if it were one of her brothers.

But Logan was most definitely not one of her brothers. And she swallowed at the image of him carting her off, his hand on her arse, claiming her for all to see.

Before she could stop herself, she stated, "Then do it."

His pupils flashed to slits a beat before he leaned down, put his shoulder into her middle, and hefted her up. Once his hand landed possessively on her arse, Emma barely resisted a groan.

It seemed some of newish Logan was still around.

Her dragon spoke up. *Aye, he is. Maybe we'll lose our virginity now.*

Iris stood, eyes narrowed, and growled, "Put her down, Lamont, before I have to make you release her."

Emma ran a hand down his back and felt him stiffen under her. Oh, aye, he was just as affected as she was. "No, it's fine, Iris. I'm too tired to focus on the clue right now anyway."

With a grunt, Logan didn't wait for a reply and carried her out of the room and down the hallway. She noted a few looks as he exited the building, but Emma didn't really pay them much attention.

No, Logan's warm hand rubbing circles on her arse made her wet and so close to begging for him.

Her dragon hummed. *Aye, aye, that's exactly what we should do. It won't take much to convince him either, with his dragon back.*

For a split second, she actually considered the idea.

Reason returned to her brain, but before she had a chance to say anything, she heard a familiar voice that made her groan in a bad way—it was her twin brother, Ian. "What the bloody hell are you doing to my sister?"

Emma managed to get a glimpse at her brother, older by minutes, and double blinked. Ian was usually the calm one of her siblings, but apparently his anger flared at seeing his sister being carted around like a piece of meat.

Not that Emma minded if Logan was the one doing the carting.

Before she could say so, Logan stopped, tightened his grip on Emma and grunted. "She and I need to have a wee chat."

"Then put her down. She's not your female to claim."

"That's what you think."

She sighed as her dragon murmured, *My, my this will be fun.*

Not wanting the two males to come to blows, she

placed her hands on Logan's back, pushed up, and wriggled her hips. "Let me down, Logan."

He slowly slid her down the front of his body, pulling her close against his firm wall of muscle, and as their eyes met, her mouth went dry at the heat she saw there.

Aye, amnesiac Logan's forthrightness combined with old Logan's desiring her was a potent combination.

But Ian growled, reminding her why she was on the ground again. Emma turned toward her twin, both grateful to see him again after weeks without, and annoyed because he was being overprotective. "I'm fine, Ian. I need to talk with Logan right now. I'll come find you later."

Her brother narrowed his blue eyes the same shade as her own. "I don't trust him with you."

Emma rolled her eyes. "You may be slightly older, but we were born on the same day. So stop acting like you have heaps more experience than me and just listen to me when I say I'm fine, aye?"

Ian searched her eyes a few beats, but he must've seen the truth because he sighed. "Are you sure? He just woke up and I don't exactly trust him."

Logan's arm tightened around her waist, bringing her back to his front, and it took all the resolve she had to ignore his hard body pressed against hers. "Logan won't hurt me."

The male behind her growled, but Ian ignored

him. "I hope not." He looked at Logan a second and then back at her. "If this means what I think it does, then he'll need to attend a family dinner before any of us will give him a chance."

She was about to say they'd known Logan for years, but Ian glared once more at Logan and walked away.

That was Ian in a nutshell—he rarely showed anger, but when he did, her twin was quick to calm.

Logan's hot breath danced across her ear. "Do I need to cart you off again or will you come willingly?"

As much as Emma wanted him to toss her over his shoulder again—she'd enjoyed the possessive display more than she'd ever dreamed—she restrained herself. "Aye, I'll come with you willingly."

He released his grip on her waist, took one of her hands, and carted her off toward a wee copse of trees. Only when they reached the center, to stand in a small, empty clearing, did he stop, although he didn't let go of her hand.

Emma stared into his brown eyes, watching his pupils flash, and her heart raced. Part of her burned to kiss him again, but she knew they should have a proper chat about his memories being back and what that might mean for the pair of them.

However, just as she opened her mouth, Logan closed the distance between them and kissed her.

Chapter Fifteen

Logan knew he should've talked with Emma first, or maybe asked if she wanted to kiss him again.

However, after having her earlier, tasting her mouth, her breasts, and even her pussy, he was addicted. So much so that he couldn't hold back like he had for years—long, frustrating years—and he claimed her lips again.

And as Emma leaned into him, looped her arms around his neck, and opened her sweet mouth for his tongue, he forgot about everything but this female. How she stroked her tongue with his, how her nails dug into his scalp, how her sweet breasts pressed against his chest, her hard nipples making his mouth water for another taste.

Then he let his hands roam, sliding down her back, across her hips, and then gripping her arse. As soon as her front made contact with his, both of them moaned at his cock pressing against her.

His dragon hummed. *Aye, that's it. But strip her, and fuck her here, now, to let her know she's ours.*

But she's not our true mate.

No. But that doesn't matter. She wants us and no other male should touch her.

He agreed with his dragon but focused back on the sweet female in his arms, somehow getting them both on the ground, her lying under him on the grass. As her legs cradled his hips, he moaned and broke the kiss. "I've waited so bloody long, Emma. Tell me I can have you and then I'll talk as much as you want." He arched his hips against her pussy. "I want to be inside you, Emma. More than anything."

Emma instantly stilled beneath him, her gaze turning a wee bit…scared? Of him?

Doing his best to keep his confusion hidden, Logan stroked her cheek with his fingers. "What's wrong? Tell me."

She pushed against his chest and he sat up. Only once she moved a few feet from him—he somehow held back from hauling her to his side once more— did she answer. "Aye, your cock more than let me know you want me, Logan. But we can't just pretend you never had amnesia, or that it hasn't changed you a wee bit."

He studied her face, but all traces of fear and apprehension had vanished. That was one of the good things about knowing her his whole life and remembering it—he could read her body language better than most people. "You're trying to change the subject, angel. Don't bother. Just tell me what happened a few moments ago. One second you were kissing me back as if you'd never get enough, and the next you looked as if I were about to hurt you. Why?"

He nearly frowned at calling Emma angel, and how it felt right but distant at the same time. Bloody amnesia and melding of memories.

But she finally bit her lower lip and replied, "If you remember everything, then you know why, Logan." She raised her chin a fraction. "So do you remember the last few days?"

"Of course I do. But given how you let me lap up the sweet honey between your thighs, I thought we were past the fear bit."

She looked down and plucked at the grass. Just what the bloody hell made her so nervous?

Her voice was low, nearly a whisper, when she answered, "There may be a wee bit more to it."

As he watched her nervously destroying the grass next to her, combined with her averted gaze, dread pooled in the pit of his stomach. "Did a male hurt you at some point?"

Her eyes shot back up, full of surprise. "No, no, that's not it."

He let out a sigh of relief. One less male he'd

have to kill then. "You're not one to hold back and beat around the bush, Emma. If you want to forget what happened between us, say it now. But know that I won't try again. This is it. After all, a male can only have his heart trampled so many times before he gives up."

He mentally cursed. Logan hadn't meant to share his heart. But his memories had revealed how much he cared for her, always talked with her, laughed with her, and felt more at ease than with anyone else in his life. Combined with the last wee while when he'd been able to kiss and taste her, Logan wanted her as his mate, always by his side.

His to hold, to treasure, to even love.

But to do that, he needed to discover the root of her fear. Just as he was about to push, she let out a long sigh and went back to pulling up grass at her side. "I'm a virgin, and I have no bloody idea what I'm supposed to do. Well, beyond the obvious, of course. Still, it's a bit intimidating, aye? Watching a video and doing it yourself are two different things."

He blinked, and then blinked some more. "How is that possible? You've gone on more dates than anyone I know."

She glared and he knew he'd fucked up. He hadn't meant to imply she was easy or sleeping around. His jealousy had obviously skewed reality.

A quick apology wouldn't be enough, his gut said. The only way to figure out how to convince her of his regret was to see what she said and form a plan accordingly. Only then could he try to correct course and prove himself to her.

And maybe, just maybe, if he were lucky, she'd let him be the first to claim her.

Maybe even the last.

Not wanting to get ahead of himself, he watched the female he'd known forever and waited for his chance.

EMMA KNEW what the clan thought of her. Flirty, forthright Emma MacAllister, the lass who didn't take life too seriously and had a way with the lads.

It was an image she'd cultivated on purpose so no one would look too closely and ask about her plethora of doomed dates. Or how she preferred to spend her free time helping and chatting with the older clan members instead of spending time with those her own age.

However, she'd hoped that Logan of all people wouldn't have made assumptions. She'd never really talked about her dates beyond her usual spiel of wanting to find her true mate—which she hadn't wanted to do—to spare Logan's feelings.

Her dragon murmured, *You did kiss many of them, and it no doubt got back to Logan. You can't blame him for the image you wanted everyone to believe.*

Logically, Emma knew that. And yet her heart still hurt from him thinking the worst of her after sharing her deepest fears.

"Emma? If you're keen on trimming the grass, maybe you should move to a new spot or it may never grow back."

Looking down, she noticed how much she'd yanked up. Brushing her hands, she intertwined her fingers and laid her hands in her lap.

"Lass?"

Lass, not angel, like he'd been calling her. Despite her disappointment at his assumptions, she rather missed the endearment.

And now she was delaying the inevitable. She took a deep breath and met Logan's gaze again. The uncertainty there lessened her irritation a fraction, but not completely. "I may have kissed a few males, but I've never had sex with anybody."

He nodded. "Because of your fear."

She swallowed. "Aye." She now plucked at her trousers. "Tell me the truth, Logan. What did you really think of me before you lost your memory?"

With a sigh, he ran his hands through his hair. His soft, slightly too long hair that she wanted to feel against her fingers again.

But then she remembered she was a wee bit mad at him and pushed that thought aside.

He finally answered, "Mostly I kept trying to convince myself it was time to move on, given how much attention you paid to nearly every male around our age except for me. It's why I finally accepted a post in Edinburgh, with the medical school. I could complete my doctor studies and put distance between us. That's the only way I thought I could forget you."

Just hearing how he'd wanted to forget her did something to Emma's heart. She didn't like it, not at all.

Not that she'd had the right to anything in the before times.

She studied him, seeing vulnerability in his gaze. He probably thought she was going to push him away again.

Her dragon said softly, *Talk with him, clear the air, and see what happens.*

Aye, she owed him that. So she blurted the first thing that came to mind, "Even when I hurt you and laughed at you, you still wanted me all that time after?"

He smiled wryly. "Fool that I was, aye, I did. Although between my cautious self, especially once my brother ran away, and your drive to protect your heart, we never would've had a chance before." She was about to reply, but he continued, "But now it's different. Losing my memories changed everything, gave me a chance to act without all the excuses clogging my brain, and I'm not going to hold back any longer. I want you, Emma. I'll be an arse sometimes, I'm sure. And you may retreat, still thinking I'll crush your heart and leave you reeling." He scooted a few inches closer and his pupils flashed a few times before he added, "But it's rare to love your best friend and desire her more than any other female in the world. We could be good together, angel. I'm not saying we have to plan the future out just yet, but will you at least give us a chance?"

It took a second for her to digest his words, and she focused on the most important bit—he loved her.

And that old fear, the one where she'd end up alone and dying inside from losing the love of her life, rushed back, making her chest tighten to the point she could barely breathe. It'd been hard enough when Logan had lost his memories. Emma couldn't imagine what would happen if she let herself love him and lost him forever.

Logan took her hand and gently squeezed. "You don't need to declare any sort of feelings right now, aye? And I need to prove I mean what I say with actions since they're stronger than words. But don't run away now, or we may both regret it forever. All I'm asking is for a chance. And if it means no sex for a while, I'll listen. I won't like it, and I'll kiss you as often as possible, but I'll acknowledge what you want, what you need, and be patient. I'm rather good at that." He smiled. "Mostly."

Her heart raced inside her chest. As she stared into his familiar brown eyes, ones that meant so much more to her than even last month, Emma tried to find the words and strength to say aye, she wanted a chance with him.

And yet, she couldn't find her voice. No, memories of her mother's struggles, how she might've given up on life if not for her children, crushed her. What if that happened to her? Could she manage to pick up the pieces or would she drown in her loss and sorrow?

Her dragon spoke up. *We're not making a decision that will seal our fate for good. Besides, I rather want this new combination Logan to be the first one to claim us. His single-minded focus will come in handy for sex.*

Her cheeks flushed as images of Logan making her come with his mouth flooded her mind. She could only imagine how much more thorough he'd be if she were completely naked.

And never before had another male made her as hot and needy as him. Not only that, but he understood her more than almost anyone. Despite all her faults, he loved her.

Saying yes didn't mean they'd be mated with three bairns the next day, after all.

Swallowing past the tightness in her throat, Emma finally found her voice. "I want to try with you, Logan." She moved a little closer to him and placed her free hand on his chest. "And even if I don't know what the future holds, I want my first time to be with you."

His pupils flashed rapidly between slits and

round. His voice was extra gravelly when he finally said, "It's taking everything I have not to scoop you up and carry you to a bed right now."

She ran her hand up his chest, traced the side of his neck, and finally cupped his jaw. Leaning close, she gathered her courage and said, "For now, just kiss me."

Unlike when they'd been teenagers and Logan had been cautious, in the present day his lips crushed against hers as he hauled her against his body. She didn't hesitate to open her mouth, press herself against him, and forget about her fears for at least a wee while.

MAYBE LOGAN SHOULD'VE BEEN GENTLER, TAKEN his time, and eased Emma into their kiss.

But he didn't want any doubt between them. Just because she was a virgin—a fact his dragon rather liked since it meant they'd be her first—didn't mean he couldn't devour her mouth as if he were starving.

Because he most definitely was starving for the angel in his arms.

He licked, and nipped, and explored every inch of her mouth, registering her moans and groans. He might've known everything about her as a friend, but Logan was determined to learn everything she liked when it came to sex and desire as well.

Such as when he gently tugged her hair, Emma moaned and pressed her breasts against him. Or when he nipped her neck and soothed it with his tongue, she cried out his name. And when he finally cupped her breast and lightly squeezed, she dug her nails into his shoulders and asked for more.

His dragon growled, *Just strip her and take her here. She wants us, and we've waited too long.*

Logan was tempted. The scent of her arousal and moans had turned his cock into granite.

And yet, he wasn't about to take her virginity in the dirt, where anyone could find them.

He took her lips in one more possessive kiss, until he could barely breathe, and pulled away to stare into her lust-filled eyes. He brushed hair from her face and smiled. "Definitely no laughing this time, aye?"

She shook her head. "No, definitely not." Emma cupped his cheek and he leaned into her touch, the soft touch he'd dreamed about for so long. "I hope you remember my explanation. It wasn't that I didn't want you then, but I was young and terrified."

He moved her hand until he could kiss her palm. "I remember everything from my bout of amnesia, even if it's a wee bit strange to have memories swirling and impulses conflicting with one another."

She smiled. "I, for one, am glad some of them stayed around. I can be quite a handful, aye? And a truly cautious male wouldn't stand a chance."

He raised an eyebrow. "Don't make it so I have to toss you over my shoulder on a regular basis."

Her pupils flashed and she smiled slowly. "Is that a threat?"

He groaned as his cock throbbed, the memory of her sweet arse beneath his hand still fresh. "At this rate, I'm going to start beating my chest and dragging you about like a caveman."

She kissed the corner of his mouth. "No dragging, although carting and carrying me around might not be so bad. My dragon likes a display of strength now and then."

Logan was about to suggest he cart her off to a bed right now when someone cleared their throat loudly, from somewhere amidst the trees. He scanned but didn't see who it was. Before he could ask, Iris's voice filled the space. "I didn't want to interrupt you, but his mighty highness Antony demands your presence. And aye, he used demand. I told him where to shove it, but his brother said it was important, something about the clue. You two need to come straight away."

With a sigh, Logan slowly stood and helped Emma up. "We'll be there shortly, Iris."

Footsteps sounded away and he frowned down at his dragonwoman. "Please tell me that once this bloody geocaching contest is finished, we can take a wee break from treasure hunting? I'd rather like to spend some time with you without worrying about constant interruptions."

She patted his chest. "After this one, I have no desire for more. No, then you can help with my senior center plans, if you have time with your studies." She squeezed his hand in hers. "I don't want you to give them up. Although I'm a wee bit selfish and hope you'll take the mentor route and stay on Lochguard."

Dragon-shifters training to be doctors had two options: mentoring from an established doctor on the clan with regular interviews and exams on-site at the medical school, or solely attending the school and learning from a hospital there. Logan had been doing the former for a year or so before changing his mind. "I'll keep studying with Layla, aye, of course I will."

She searched his eyes. "Are you sure? I can wait if you want to go to Edinburgh."

He used his free hand to trace the bridge of her nose and then down to her lips, unable to keep his hands off the female he'd restrained himself around for too many years. "I only wanted to go to Edinburgh to put distance between us. With that no longer being the case, I'd rather stay and learn from Layla. She's a rather good teacher." Emma opened her mouth to protest, but he added, "Besides, I need to be nearby to help you with your project when I can. At least with that I suspect an architect, supplier, or government official won't come looking for us in a clearing and disturb a rather heated snogging session, aye? Although that would make for quite the report."

He winked and she laughed, and the sound washed away most of his irritation at Iris's interruption. Most, but not all.

She finally caught her breath and said, "I hope not, as I'd rather not have my backside described in detail, forever ensconced in an official document."

He growled, pulled her close, and put his free hand on said backside. After a quick squeeze, he murmured, "No, this arse is for me and me alone, angel."

For a few beats, they stared at one another, breathing heavily, and all he wanted to do was kiss her and finally worship every inch of her naked body.

He willed himself to step back, to be the sensible one. But he couldn't seem to let her go, almost as if he were afraid he'd lose her.

However, Emma was the one to step back and squeezed his hand in hers. She grinned. "You'll just have to wait a wee bit longer for a full body inspection." She sobered a fraction. "Besides, too much is at stake with this contest. Once it's sorted, I'll be yours for however long you like, I promise." She tugged his hand. "Come on. Let's find out what they discovered. Because the sooner we finish this hunt, the sooner you might get me all to yourself for more than a handful of minutes at a time."

With that prize dangled in front of him, Logan picked up their pace. And as he studied her in the new light of her finally being his, Logan vowed to finish this bloody treasure hunt as soon as possible so he could finally, after what seemed like a lifetime, have Emma in his bed.

Chapter Sixteen

E mma tried to focus her mind on what Max and
Antony might've found. But during the entire
walk toward the Protector building, she stared at
Logan from the corner of her eye, smiling. It was
weird to think her best friend was also the sexiest
male alive to her, and yet it was true. He was tall and
leanly muscled, with deep-brown eyes and wide
shoulders that would feel delicious while holding her
close.

Shoulders that felt wonderful beneath her when
he'd carted her off over them.

It made her wonder what else he might be, er,
firm and controlling with.

Her dragon grunted. *This news had better be bloody
important. Because we could've been naked and moaning in bed
right about now.*

Emma willed her cheeks not to blush. *Hush,*

dragon. I'm trying to forget about his tongue, and cock, and hard body against ours or I'll never be able to focus on the clue, or what happens next.

Her beast sniffed. *I'd be fine giving it up.*

Maybe you are, but I'm not. Besides, the DDA wants our help with this. We need to help dragon-shifters in general, and most especially the clan, aye?

Her dragon grumbled but stayed silent. Which was good, because as they entered the meeting room where the others stood around a table, Emma noticed Max's triumphant expression. As soon as they shut the door, Antony didn't waste a moment to say, "We've cracked the codes used for the clue."

Emma raised her brows. "Codes, as in plural?"

Antony nodded. "Yes. I know the first thing we all tried was the basic A1Z26 code, but none of the clusters made words, and none of the possible anagrams made any sense. Not to mention some of the numbers went far above the limit of twenty-six."

The A1Z26 cipher was something even schoolchildren toyed with. Each letter was represented by a number: A was one and it went sequentially until it ended with Z being twenty-six. "What was the other code or codes you figured out?"

Max jumped in. "Well, one of the random cluster of letters was actually an acrostic cipher for the title of an ancient dragon-shifter text."

Even if she wasn't an expert, she'd come across a few ciphers during her past hunts. An acrostic cipher was where each letter stood for a word, like "man" translating into "**M**eet **A**t **N**ine" or some such thing.

Emma started to put it all together. "And the remaining numbers, the ones above twenty-six, were for a book cipher."

Max nodded, but Logan asked, "What's that?"

Emma explained, "At the most basic, one number represents a page and another number denotes a word on that page. Sometimes a number will denote a paragraph instead, or another merely a letter. Whilst there are a number of limited possibilities, it'll eventually spell out a word or phrase. Does all of that make sense?"

He nodded just as Iris asked, "What's the ancient dragon-shifter text title? You haven't said yet, Max."

Max held up an old book in his hands. "This is an outdated translation of the early Romano-Dragon agreement signed by Queen Alviva and the Romans. It allowed English and Welsh dragon-shifters to remain in control of their lands despite the Roman invasion of Britain."

Zoe frowned. "Why do you need an outdated translation of that?"

Max answered, "Because of how the code spelled out the title: *Alviva's Accord* instead of *Alviva's Treaty*. They're the same document, but various translations have used different words." He waved the book in his hands. "This is the only one in English to use 'accord' in the title."

Antony crossed his arms over his chest and spoke again. "To save us a lot of time—and a lecture from my brother—let me summarize: the remaining numbers gave us the next location, which is Venta Belgarum. That's modern-day Winchester."

Emma tried to remember what she knew of the city in England. But thankfully Iris spoke up. "That's not far from Clan Skyhunter."

Antony raised his brows. "Very good, my dear. One of the most powerful dragon-shifter sites in Roman Britain wasn't far from Winchester, and that's where Queen Alviva lived for a while; over time, the dragons moved their location to Skyhunter's current location. But all we need to focus on for this competition is the riddle in the rest of the clue."

Iris muttered, "Of course there's a bloody riddle."

Emma did her best not to smile—this was a treasure hunt after all, so riddles were commonplace —just as Logan grunted. "What is it?"

Max read it aloud and Emma focused on the human. "Round and round we go, hosting traitors and kings, also possessing the power to heal and murder. The tunnel of secrets will reveal nearly all, but tease and hold fast the truth." He looked up. "And no, I'm not entirely sure what it means. My specialty is Roman history, but Winchester was a key historical site for many centuries after the Romans left."

Logan spoke up. "Have you asked Alistair Boyd

to take a look at it? He's the history teacher here and spends a lot of time in the archives. He might have an idea of where to start looking."

Iris glared at Antony a second before replying, "I tried to convince his mighty highness here we should talk to him or my mum, but he refused."

Antony shrugged. "Forgive me, but Boyd's mother is the worst gossip in possibly all of the United Kingdom. I won't risk it."

Emma blinked. How did Antony Holbrook know so much about Meg Boyd?

Of course Iris was the first to say anything back, raising her dark brows as she asked, "And what about my mum? She's read nearly every book in the history section of the library. I still don't understand why you refuse to approach her."

Zoe surprised everyone by saying, "It may make her a target, Iris. If we do find the end prize, it might drive the losers to search and take what they think is theirs by any means necessary. I wouldn't dismiss torture, or worse, for that much cash."

Iris opened her mouth but Antony beat her to it. "Miss Watson is correct. The fewer people involved in this, the better. Besides, I already set up an appointment with someone we can trust, someone who has faced worse than an irritated fortune seeker and can handle themselves." He paused dramatically and Emma growled with impatience, along with just about everyone else. And still Antony waited a beat.

She was starting to see why Iris called him "mighty highness." The male was used to always getting his way, no doubt, like some sort of nobility of old.

Antony finally stood and stated, "We're off to Clan Skyhunter. That's all I'll say for the moment. And before you ask a multitude of questions, yes, we have permission. I handled the DDA, and Finn said yes for you lot. We leave in an hour. Oh, and we're all driving. So plan accordingly."

Emma frowned but the bloody human and his brother were gone before she could say a word. She finally muttered, "Flying would be faster, even if we had to do it in legs to take breaks and avoid notice."

Logan placed a hand on her lower back. He murmured for her ears only, "I know you hate riding in cars, but it'll be safer. Especially if the DDA director is worried about Bourne's resurfacing."

"Maybe," she muttered, knowing that the dragon hunter leader might have some sort of rocket weapon to hit dragons out of the sky. "But I'm allowed to be a wee bit grumpy. Sitting still inside a car for that many hours will drive me mad."

He smiled and whispered, "Aye, well, since you don't know how to drive, you can nap most of the time." He moved his lips even closer to her ear, his hot breath dancing against her skin. "Or maybe even sleep in my arms. I promise to behave in front of the others, unless you want to put on a show in the back seat."

Her cheeks heated and a mixture of desire and embarrassment coursed through her.

Not wanting to think about how she might want people to watch her and Logan have sex, Emma focused on the embarrassment side of things. "Not for my first time. So behave, or I'll ensure you sit next to Max the entire ride."

He groaned and she bit back a laugh. Max was a nice male, but far too enthusiastic about his archaeological digs. And Emma knew Logan didn't care much about that sort of thing, preferring science and medicine over interpreting bits of rubble in the ground.

After Iris declared they'd meet up in the car park near the Protector building in fifty minutes, Emma maneuvered Logan out of the room. Once they were back in the fresh air, she yanked his hand to take him to the side, out of view, and leaned up against him. "Let me give you something to think about until we finish this, aye?"

His pupils flashed but Logan didn't move. Clearly he wanted her to control the situation.

So she stood on her tiptoes and pressed her lips to his. At the touch, Logan groaned, pulled her close, and seamed her lips, asking for permission. She opened and reveled in his possessive licks, and nibbles, and full-on dominance of her mouth. Gone was the hesitant lad, replaced with a grown male who knew what he wanted.

But Emma wasn't about to let him control everything, so she tangled with his tongue and finally managed to taste his mouth. There was something about his taste, a combination of male and pure Logan, that made her dig her nails in his shoulders and rub against him.

Her dragon hummed, encouraging her. However, all too soon Logan broke the kiss and laid his forehead against hers, taking a second to catch his breath. "You don't know how much I want to bloody keep kissing you, and not just your mouth. But I'm not going to claim you for the first time against a wall, angel. And we need to get ready for the morning."

Disappointment rushed through her, even if she knew he was being logical. Sounding more like a pout than she intended, she murmured, "I wouldn't mind being fucked against a wall." She stroked the side of his neck with her thumb. "Are you sure I can't change your mind?"

She licked his neck and Logan groaned, his grip tightening on her waist. "Fuck, Emma. You make this so bloody hard to be noble and wait."

Nuzzling his cheek, she smiled. "When I make a decision, I get impatient to see it through."

Logan lifted her head, kissed her gently, and stroked her lower lip with his thumb. Each light caress sent heat rushing through her body. It took everything she had to focus on his words. "Not tonight, angel. I want enough time to worship you properly." He moved to her ear, licked the outer rim, and added, "But just know that I'll be thinking of every way I want you when we finally have a wee bit of time to ourselves. You should do the same and make sure to tell me a fantasy or two once you're fully debauched and no longer a virgin."

Leave it to Logan to use fancier words, like debauched, and make it sound so wicked. "I'll hold you to that."

He chuckled, leaned back, and caressed her cheek with the back of his knuckles. "Aye, now with that sorted, we should head home and pack. If there's special treasure hunting gear I need, let me know."

She snorted, but as they walked away from the Protector building, hand in hand, she teased him about what not to bring and it all felt so normal and perfect. One second, he'd been kissing the crap out of her, and the next, they were joking about unusually large packs filled with useless stuff.

Oh, aye, her heart was going to be at risk, big time, if it continued like this.

But Emma refused to doom everything before it started. And so she focused on the moment and tried not to think of finally having sex with Logan.

Well, at least not every second, at any rate.

Chapter Seventeen

Each moment during the long drive from the Scottish Highlands down to almost the bottom of England had felt like torture to Logan. Aye, he'd had Emma to himself in the back seat of one of the cars, but her warm, soft body against his for hours on end caused all sorts of torment, made even worse when he finally dozed off and had vivid dreams of how he wanted to take her the first time.

Coffee on their arrival didn't help, and the longer they waited for Skyhunter's clan leaders to meet them, the more he clenched and unclenched his fingers in impatience.

His dragon spoke up. *Calm down. Skyhunter is still trying to heal from the sociopathic dictator that ruled them previously.*

I'm surprised you're so bloody patient. You want Emma as much as I do.

Aye, but this is important to her. Just think of how she'll reward us later, after we help make her dream a reality.

He mentally snorted. *Dragon halves aren't usually the long-term thinkers.*

Maybe not. But after being forced into silence for a bit, I have a new respect for the future.

He sobered a bit. *I know, and I wish I'd remembered how to reach you. But you're back, and if Emma keeps her promise not to go chasing after another cache anytime soon, we'll all be safe and can even be a wee bit boring for a while.*

The female in question sidled up to him, holding out a blueberry muffin—one of his favorites. She smiled and offered it. "Here's the last one. I thought maybe some sugar would get you to smile."

He snorted, took the muffin, and kissed her briefly. Leaning to her ear, he whispered, "I'd rather eat you till my heart's content, but I suppose the muffin will have to do."

Her breath hitched and he smiled. After nipping her ear, he leaned back, loving the blush on her cheeks. He offered the muffin. "I know you like the top part the best, so have a bite whilst you still can."

As Emma snagged a piece of the muffin top with her fingers and ate it, he marveled at how something so normal—them sharing food and offering what the other liked—had taken on a whole other meaning. No longer chaste friends, he could tease her with sexual innuendos while sharing.

And he rather liked it.

Emma licked the crumbs from her lips, rather thoroughly, and he groaned. Amusement danced in her eyes. "It's only fair to tease you back."

Just as he wanted to tell her a much better way to tease him—such as with her tongue on his cock—the door opened and a tall dragon-shifter pair in their thirties strode in. Both were pale-skinned, but the female was blonde with a warm smile on her face whereas the male had dark hair and what looked like a perpetual frown.

It was Honoria Wakeham and Asher King, the co-leaders of Clan Skyhunter, who also happened to be mated to each other.

Logan had only seen them briefly once before, back when they'd visited Lochguard for a multi-clan gathering over the summer, and so he didn't know them well. However, they were one of Lochguard's allies and Finn trusted them, which meant so did he.

Although the human male he didn't trust completely, Antony Holbrook, strode in behind them with another male on his heels. One with dark brown skin and a shaved head whom Logan didn't recognize. Given his dark, flashing eyes, he was most definitely a dragon-shifter.

Once everyone was in the room and the door closed, Honoria was the first to speak. "Welcome to Clan Skyhunter. We haven't had many people here from other clans in recent years, so it's a rather special event." She paused to glance at Antony. "Even if Mr. Holbrook has been a bit vague on why he's here."

The last part had been drawled, and Logan snorted. It seemed Honoria was another person unwilling to bend to Antony's will just because, although in a less feisty manner than Iris.

Honoria continued, her gaze on each of them in turn. "Regardless, if you need help, I hope you'll reach out to us, or our Protectors. Feel free to stay as long as you like. Although I do hope you'll join the clan for our first celebration in years to honor our guests. All of us are rather looking forward to it, truth be told. Right, Ash?"

Asher grunted and shrugged. "Yes, it'll be a nice break for everyone."

Honoria rolled her eyes and smiled back at everyone else. "He's happy, I promise. Now, I'll leave you all to do what needs to be done. Once you're finished with your meeting, some of our Protectors will show you to where you'll be staying. Ash and I will check on each of you later on."

With that, the pair nodded and left the room. Logan didn't know a whole lot about Skyhunter and its leaders, but he'd believed Honoria's words. Skyhunter would be a safe place for them until they figured out the bloody riddle and found the prize.

His dragon spoke up. *Besides, I think we should stay*

with Emma in one cottage. We won't be interrupted, and it'll be a special memory for her.

We'll see. Right now, we need to focus on the clue, aye? And I'll need all the blood flowing to my brain I can get to do it.

His beast grumbled but fell silent a beat before Antony gestured toward the male with him and spoke. "This is Christopher. And no, don't ask for a surname or other details. A friend of mine is letting us borrow him and his knowledge." Antony snapped his fingers at his brother. "Give me the clue, Max."

Max took it out—they'd decided to keep everything on paper to avoid any sort of hacking—and passed it over.

Christopher read it quickly and grunted. He spoke in English, but it was accented, although Logan couldn't place it. "The use of round, plus traitors and kings, makes me think of the Great Hall in Winchester, the only standing portion left of Winchester Castle."

Logan blinked. "That was quick."

Christopher shrugged. "I have an eidetic memory, so it's easy to recall what I need. Besides, British history and customs are my specialty. This is child's play for me."

Zoe asked, "But what of the rest of the clue? The full thing reads: Round and round we go, hosting traitors and kings, also possessing the power to heal and murder. The tunnel of secrets will reveal nearly all, but tease and hold fast the truth."

Christopher didn't miss a beat. "Visit the Great Hall and pay attention to the gardens. If you can't figure out the rest, then you lot are stupider than I thought."

Everyone blinked at that. Antony cleared his throat. "Excuse Christopher. He's a brilliant genius but his social skills are, shall we say, a bit rough." Christopher looked about to protest, but Antony added, "Don't worry, you'll get a glowing report from me to your superior. If there's nothing else you wish to share, you may go."

Christopher raised his brows, stared at Zoe, and stated, "The gardens," before leaving.

Emma drawled, "So, we need to visit the gardens I take it?"

Iris rolled her eyes. "Obviously. However, I already rung the Great Hall and it's closed for a private event today. The earliest we can visit is tomorrow. I suggest we all rest and prepare for what's to come."

Once plans were made to meet at 9:00 a.m. so they would arrive shortly after the Great Hall opened at ten, Logan put a hand around Emma's waist and waited for the others to leave. Once they were alone, he faced her. "My dragon had an idea, angel." He paused a beat, but decided he was done being cautious and blurted, "We should share a cottage here. That way we can finally be alone."

The corner of her mouth ticked up. "To do what, I wonder?"

He ran his hand from her waist down to her arse and rubbed one of her cheeks in slow circles. "Whatever you wish, angel. But I know I'd like to find a bed and do some exploring of our own before hieing off to Winchester in the morning."

She snorted. "Your charm is a wee bit corny."

Despite her easygoing outward appearance, her muscles had tightened a fraction under his touch. "We don't have to go the whole way, angel. But even if I merely get to sleep with you in my arms, it'll help soothe both man and beast."

Her pupils flashed a few times and then she stepped closer, until only a few inches remained between them. "We'll start there and see where it leads. But aye, let's share a cottage. All those hours in the car without me being able to kiss you was torture."

He waggled his eyebrows. "You could've kissed me anytime you wanted, and I wouldn't have protested."

She shook her head. "Right under Zoe and Iris's watchful gaze the entire time. Maybe you're ready to give anyone a show, but I'm not there yet."

"Yet?" Logan nuzzled her cheek and nipped her earlobe. "I like the sound of that. I've always wanted to claim my female and have people watch us." Another nibble. "Although definitely not until after I've had you a few times all to myself, aye?"

"Logan," she breathed out.

He tightened his grip on her arse cheek. "I think someone is adventurous for more than merely treasure hunting. If so, tell me the word and I'll take you to a place I've heard of just outside Inverness, where we can satisfy your curiosity."

He kissed her jaw and she moaned. "Where has this side of you been all these years?"

"Mostly hidden, but always under the surface. Much like you, I think. If you hadn't been afraid of getting close to someone, and of sex in general, I think you would've realized these curiosities about yourself sooner."

His dragon spoke up. *Stop teasing her and just get her to our cottage here. I want her naked, and under me. Hurry up.*

He chuckled and relayed his dragon's words before adding, "And given your flashing eyes, I'd say your dragon is about the same." He offered his arm. "Shall we?"

Looping her arm through his, she leaned against him and laid her head on his shoulder. "Aye. I think it's more than past time for us to be alone."

And once they shown to their cottage, Logan followed Emma inside, scooped her into his arms, and went upstairs to where they'd been told the bedroom was situated.

After all these years, it was finally time to claim Emma as his own. Even if she didn't say she loved him yet, he didn't care. All he needed was a chance with her and he'd find a way to make it work. There was no bloody way he was giving her up again, if he could help it.

Chapter Eighteen

E mma did her best to focus on Logan's beating heart under her hand on his chest, the solidness of his muscles, and the spicy scent of him mixed with some sort of wood. Because if she didn't distract herself, she'd let her nerves get the better of her.

Her dragon spoke up. *Don't worry about it. He's not only wanted us forever, he can be rather naughty at times with his whispers. I'm looking forward to it. Once our virginity and initial soreness is gone, there's so much we can try.*

Just the thought of Logan tugging her nipples with his teeth or the hot, wet feel of his tongue licking between her thighs made her skin burn and her lower belly flutter.

Aye, she wanted him, more than anything.

She replied to her dragon, *Be patient the first time,*

aye? I know you want a turn, but the first go is mine and mine alone.

Her beast harrumphed. *Just don't take too long. Me and his dragon need to fight it out a wee bit for control.*

She mentally laughed. *That will be entertaining. He and I are close on the dominance scale, so anything goes.*

Her dragon sniffed. *I'll win, just wait and see.*

Logan's voice filled her ear. "Is your dragon going to let me have you for a bit anytime soon?"

It was then that she noticed he stood near a bed, and she blinked. "Oh, we're here."

He chuckled. "Aye, we are." He slowly set her feet down, turned her away from him, and pulled her back up against his front. As Logan nuzzled her neck, his hot breath danced across her skin as he said, "I think I need to make sure I have your full attention first, aye?" His hand roamed from her waist, up her ribcage, and finally he cupped her breast. She leaned into his firm touch, and he added, "It's time to learn exactly what you like, angel. So don't hold back. I want to hear your groans, and moans, and sighs. They'll tell me exactly what to do. Only then can I figure out how much to push you."

The thought of Logan pushing her sexual boundaries—ones she didn't exactly know yet—made her clench her thighs together. A few months ago, she never would've guessed this side of him. And now? Well, she was eager to see what he wanted.

But not yet. No, she had to get her bloody virginity out of the way first.

To distract from thoughts of Logan taking her to some forbidden house of kink, Emma was about to tease him but then he lightly pinched her nipple and Emma arched her back. When he did it again, the mixture of pleasure and pain shot straight between her thighs.

She definitely liked that, for starters.

Logan kissed and nibbled the side of her neck as he tweaked her nipple again. "Och, you're so responsive, angel. I can't wait to see what you're like when naked."

Finally able to put two words together, she teased, "Then let's find out."

Before she could lose her nerve, Emma walked forward and he released her. Once she was a few feet away, she kept her eyes on Logan, and swiftly tugged her top off. His gaze shot straight to her bra, a lacy thing that didn't quite hide her already hard and throbbing nipples.

Nipples that ached for his touch again.

Damn, she could already see how Logan Lamont could become an addiction.

Not wanting to go down the road of where that could lead, she instead watched as he strode forward with a determined glint in his eye. He was going to take control already.

She stepped back. "Not yet, Logan. I want to be naked first."

He growled, "Then you should bloody well hurry up or I'm going to tear your clothes off."

The image of Logan extending a talon and slicing her bra, trousers, and underwear off made her pussy even wetter.

There was something about him being a wee bit impatient and possessive that she rather liked in the bedroom.

Not that she was going to give in so easily. This encounter would set the tone for any future ones. And given how bloody long she'd waited for sex, she wanted to be able to occasionally take control and explore him too.

So never taking her gaze from his, she kicked off her shoes, undid her trousers, and slide them slowly down her legs. Standing up, she noted Logan's flashing pupils and heated look, and every bit of her that could warm and throb did so.

How the bloody hell had she managed to push him away so easily before? No male had ever viewed her this way, as if he'd die if he didn't see all of her skin.

Her dragon spoke up. *Forget the past right now. Get on it with it. I want his cock, and I want it soon.*

Emma slid down one bra strap, and then the other. Pausing, she hesitated a second before stating, "Take off your shirt before I go any further."

She resisted blinking as Logan tore off not only his shirt, but his trousers and boxers as well, until he stood naked, his cock hard and jutting out from his body.

Seeing a dragonman with a flaccid penis when shifting was entirely different from seeing one aroused. Logan was much thicker and longer than she'd thought, and she wondered if it'd hurt. She wasn't naive and knew dragons liked to fuck. A lot. But still, were all dragonmen that big when aroused?

Logan's gravelly voice caught her attention. "Come now, angel, stop your torture and show me all of you. If you keep staring at my cock like that, this isn't going to last long."

She finally met his gaze again, took a deep breath, and shed her undergarments. It took everything she had not to cross her arms in front of her chest or put a hand in front of her pussy.

Logan took one step, and then the other, each step making her heart pound harder. When he finally reached her, he pulled her until they were skin to skin. The feel of his hot, hard body against hers made Emma suck in a breath.

As he laid a possessive hand over her arse cheek, he said, "You're so bloody beautiful, Emma. I want to lick every inch of your body, but if I'm not inside you soon, I just might die."

Her nervousness faded somewhat, and she

smiled. "I don't think death by aching cock is a thing."

He snorted, pressed her even closer, and she couldn't ignore his hot and heavy arousal pressing against her belly. "I'd rather not find out."

He lightly gripped her chin and tilted her head back. For a beat, he stared at her, his gaze alone making her even wetter.

She was about to growl about him taking too long when claimed her lips in a quick, rough kiss, and then scooped her up again. "Come on. It's about time you lost your virginity to a male who loves you."

There it was again—the mention of love. It made her heart race, yet at the same time a wave of unease crashed over her.

Her dragon growled, *Don't focus on that but on the upcoming orgasm from a male's touch. His tongue was delicious, but I want more, much more.*

Logan laid her on the bed, crawled over her until his upper body touched hers while his lower body was off to the side, and he kissed her.

As his lips touched hers, all doubts and thoughts unrelated to his demanding kiss fled her mind. Each nip, and lick, and swipe loosened her tension and made her sink into the mattress a bit more.

Strange how his kiss could calm her when she'd spent so many years afraid of doing exactly this.

She threaded her fingers through his hair, arched her back until her nipples brushed against his chest hair, and ached to feel Logan everywhere. As if reading her mind, he ran a hand down her belly and lightly brushed her clit. She jumped at the touch and Logan chuckled. "It's not going to take much to make you come, is it?"

He stroked her slowly, back and forth, and she gritted her teeth. "Stop teasing me already."

"Ah, but I need to make sure you're nice and wet for me, angel. It'll make it better for you the first time."

She wondered how he knew that, and a surge of jealousy rushed through her. But before the rational side of her brain could say he was a nurse, after all, he pushed one finger inside her cunt and she moaned at the delicious fullness.

Especially as he curled it upward and slowly moved back and forth, hitting some spot that made her cry out. Not to stop, but to move faster, harder, to drive her mad, to help her crash over the edge instead of hovering.

But when he stilled his finger to kiss her slowly and lick inside her mouth, thoughts filtered through her lust haze, some of her wariness returning. If she was that full with a finger, what the bloody hell would his cock do? If only she'd given in to her curiosity and bought a dildo at some point. But no, she hadn't wanted to lose her virginity that way.

Her reluctance seemed bloody stupid now.

Her dragon huffed. *Don't you fucking make excuses. I*

want him, and we're going to have him. I've waited too long for sex.

Logan leaned down and took one of her nipples into her mouth, her worries forgotten again. Between his licks, and suckles, and tugs, she moaned and groaned and made all sorts of noise, but none of them were actual words. Regardless, he seemed to know what they meant because he soon suckled and nibbled hard, like she wanted.

Then he moved his finger between her thighs again as he tortured her other nipple with his lips and teeth.

She gripped his head, wanting to keep him in place. As he tugged her hard, she arched upward. Bloody hell, Logan was good at this.

And her dragonman kept at it. Licking, and tugging, and pinching until she was so wet she had to be dripping onto the sheets.

Not to mention the pressure was building. She was close, so close, and murmured it to Logan.

Just when she thought she couldn't take any more, Logan rubbed her clit in fast circles and in the next instant, spots danced before her eyes and pleasure exploded, rushing through every inch of her body.

She dug her nails into Logan's skin, his sweet torture by finger making the wave go on and on until she finally slumped against the mattress, her breathing harsh and her skin hot, oh so hot.

Finally releasing her nipple, he moved to kiss her lips. A slow, tender kiss that ended with him nuzzling her cheek. "Ready for the rest?"

Emma could barely move after the best orgasm of her life, although somehow she made her mouth work. "I hope I don't have to do much more than lie here because I'm still recovering from whatever magic you just did."

A pleased look filled Logan's eyes. He kissed her again. "I suspect you'll be moving again shortly, angel."

Logan rolled away from her, and she instinctively reached for him to no avail. He plucked something from his bag that someone from Skyhunter had brought to their rooms, tore open the package, and she noticed the condom rolling down his cock.

She smiled. "You were optimistic, aye?"

Condom on, he crawled back onto the bed until he hovered over her on his hands and knees. "I have about twenty of them packed, so aye, I'm optimistic, angel." He kissed her. "Now it's time to make you mine."

The possessiveness in his voice should've irritated her. But in this moment, with Logan staring at her, the scent of her arousal mixed with his own, she wanted him. Desperately. "Then stop stalling and do it already."

Laughing, Logan moved between her thighs, rubbed the head of his cock through her folds, and she arched into him. "There's my lusty angel, impatient for my cock." He positioned his dick at her entrance. "If you say stop, I'll stop. But I hope like hell you don't."

Cupping his cheek with one of her hands, she looked Logan in the eye, his familiar brown filled with a mixture of heat and tenderness. And in that moment, Emma knew she'd made the right choice to wait for this male right here, right now, no matter how many years it had taken her to realize it.

She wanted her sexy, somewhat growly best friend and no one else. "Make me yours, Logan. Please."

At the please, he growled—of course—and took her lips again. His tongue tangling with hers distracted her at first, but as he inched his dick inside her, she did her best not to tense. He was so bloody big and stretched her almost painfully.

Logan finally thrust to the hilt, her virginity dying with barely a pinch, and then he released her mouth and laid his cheek against hers. "All right?"

She did her best to sound nonchalant despite the somewhat uncomfortable fullness of him. "I suppose."

He moved to look into her eyes and then frowned. "Why do you look both wary and disappointed? There's more to it, angel. I'm not done yet."

She ran her hands over his marvelously broad

back. "It's just that according to books, it's one of two things when it comes to losing your virginity—so ecstatic you never notice, or such a huge, pain filled thing that almost kills the mood. And yet, it's neither."

He raised an eyebrow. "Given how you were shouting my name a few minutes ago, I thought you were rather enjoying it all."

Oh, crap. She didn't want him to think she was putting him down.

Taking his face in her hands, she pulled it down and bit his bottom lip. She murmured, "Coming by my own hand doesn't compare in the slightest to what you can do with one finger."

His gaze turned proud and a wee bit heated again. After pulling his hips back a fraction, he thrust forward, and Emma gasped. "I guess I need to work harder on making this bloody fantastic for you then, aye?"

She smiled, wriggling her hips, and loved how Logan groaned. Even with him caging her in and his cock inside her, she still had her own sort of power over him like this. "I wouldn't complain about that, not at all."

He laughed. "As much as I like being able to laugh with you even when I'm balls-deep inside you, I think you need to see just how good this can be." He retreated a bit father this time and thrust back.

Emma dug her nails into his back. "Fuck, yes. Show me the rest, Logan. Please."

He stroked her hip, down to her leg, and curled one around his hip. "By the end, you'll see fireworks again, angel. I promise."

Her dragon roared. *Stop talking already and let him get to it. I want a turn, and you're taking so bloody long.*

Emma didn't agree. Logan had made this time memorable in his own way—heat, laughter, and an all-around sense of it being right, despite the sort of awkwardness of her not really knowing what she was doing.

Her beast grunted, portending a tantrum, so Emma decided she'd better get Logan moving again, no matter what. "Then I think you need to show me the rest, and quickly."

His pupils flashed and with a growl, he moved his hips slowly. The first few thrusts were sort of strange to her, but the more he moved, the more the slow ache from before built inside her until she was clinging to his shoulders and making those undefinable noises again.

She tried to keep her eyes open, wanting to see Logan's face as he came, but she couldn't. The more he moved and angled to hit her clit with his thrust, the harder it was to think of anything but the building storm.

All too soon she called out his name as euphoria

raced through her, filling every cell of her body, and she temporarily forgot where or who she was.

Only when Logan stilled and growled in her ear did she finally come back down to earth. His entire body weight lay atop her, but she clutched him closer, loving the heat and solidity of him.

Right here, right now, it was perfect. She felt safe, wanted, and blissful.

But as the minutes ticked by and her breathing calmed, she fought back the panic, the wondering if this would all collapse one day and leave her in pieces.

Because despite her best attempts, she had a feeling she was falling for him. It'd been coming on for a while, since his amnesia. But with his memories back and the way he worshiped her in bed, it was getting harder to ignore.

The panic clawed out slowly and it took everything she had not to push him away, both physically and emotionally. She could fight this, she could.

Maybe.

LOGAN HAD BARELY CALMED down from the most intense orgasm of his life—it seemed being with the female he loved made it that much better—when Emma tensed under him.

Pulling back, he saw her eyes tightly shut, her jaw clenched, and she looked to be mumbling something to herself.

Not exactly what a bloke wanted to see after taking a female's virginity.

He pulled out of her, sat up against the wall, quickly took off his condom, and slowly drew her into his lap. He wrapped his arms around her, and as he murmured and soothed nonsense, Emma finally relaxed and laid her head against his chest. A glance told him she was better—her eyes were open at least—and so he asked, "What happened, angel? Did I hurt you?"

He'd tried to be gentle, at least until the end.

Before he could try and analyze all he'd done, she answered softly, so softly a regular human wouldn't have been able to hear it. "No."

He stroked her hair. "Then what happened? And don't you bloody dare say nothing."

She bit her lip a second and then answered, "It's going to make me sound crazy."

He drawled, "Your entire family is crazy, Emma. This isn't news to me."

As he had intended, she looked up with a glare and lightly smacked his chest. "Be nice, Logan."

"I'm still waiting."

She stared, and he stared back, raising his brows to emphasize how he wasn't going to be distracted. Emma finally sighed. "You're bloody stubborn now."

He waited and she grunted. "Aye, fine, I'll tell you. But don't you dare laugh, or it's a quick reach to twist your bollocks a bit."

"I'll do my best, although I'd be able to stop you and pin you under me before you got ahold of my balls, angel."

She looked as if she was going to test him, but then shook her head. "I'm trying to distract you again, so let me just get this out and maybe it'll be less awkward." She paused, took the deepest breath he'd seen, and blurted, "It was nice, Logan. Quite nice. But then after I was melting into the bed, my bones turned to jelly from another orgasm, I felt safe and warm for a moment."

"Aye," he said cautiously.

She searched his gaze before continuing, "And then I thought about it all disappearing, you leaving or dying. Of how I'd only just found how wonderful and sexy and nearly perfect you are, and then lose you. And it crippled me a bit." She looked down at where her fingers stroked his chest and murmured, "I know it's irrational, but my dad's death devastated my mum. I keep thinking that's going to happen to me too."

Logan placed a finger under her chin and lifted until she met his gaze again. The uncertainty there tore his heart in half. "Let's look at it this way. Your mum is lovely, and extremely kind and gentle. However, would she ever go off on a sort of treasure hunt, climbing rocks, and exploring new places just for the hope of a find?"

"No, but—"

"And would she have risked her passion and future livelihood like you did when you confessed to that arsehole luring you on the internet, which made the old clan leader take away computers from you, all so you could protect some unknown future victim?"

"I don't know, that's never come up—"

"And unless you're extremely good at hiding it from me, of all people, you don't suffer from depression like your mum, either. Aye?"

"No, I don't, but—"

He stroked her cheek, putting every bit of conviction into his words he could muster. "No buts, Emma. You are your own person and different from your mother. Who we are with regards to families, memories, and even friends, colors our experiences, aye. But we're each our own person too, no two people ever being exactly the same. You agree, aye?" She nodded and he continued, "And if something happened to me—and I was lucky enough to have you as my own at the time—then I know you'd eventually find a way to get past it and rebuild. That's just who you are—always fighting for what you want and not giving up, no matter how difficult it could be." He smiled. "Although don't make too many contingency plans about my demise as I have no desire to leave your side, if I can help it."

Silently, Emma searched his eyes a few beats and he wondered if he finally gotten through to her.

Logan understood irrational fears and decided whether he truly wanted to convince Emma, he needed to lay a bit of himself bare. Taking a deep breath, he blurted, "I have my own fears too, angel. I first lost my parents as a teen, and even Phillip vanished for years without a word. For a while, I thought I was fated for people I love to leave or abandon me." Logan included Emma in that bit, back when they were younger, but didn't mention it. He cupped her cheek. "But whilst I'll always worry about you finding some sod more handsome or devoted than me, I'll fight for you. I'll fight for *us*. I want it more than anything, and that has to be enough, even if there's a possibility you'll leave me too. So I guess my question is—will you let the fear continue to control your life? Or will you do your best to kick its arse and fight tooth and nail for the future you want?"

Logan's heart raced as he waited for Emma's answer. They'd come so far—hell, he'd come so far—in a short time. But if she were to doom them before they ever had a chance, he wasn't sure what he could do to change her mind.

No, he wasn't giving up easily. However, Emma would have to fight as well, or it was a lost cause in the end. Because no matter how he might wish it differently, Logan couldn't magically make certain memories or fears disappear from Emma at will.

After what seemed like hours, she said softly, "I want to try and do that, kick this fear's arse. But understand that I've had this for a long time now, and it won't go away overnight."

He stroked her cheek with his thumb. "I know, angel." He kissed her gently, loving how when he pulled away, she pressed her lips to his again for another beat. He added, "I'll be doing my bloody best to prove I want to be here. Because now I've had you once, I want you again and again. I'd say until I got my fill, but I don't think that would ever happen."

Emma's pupil's flashed to slits and back. She smiled. "My dragon said she wants to get started on trying."

Logan's beast, which had been patient, spoke up again finally. *I agree. I want to tame her dragon and show her who's in control. Let me fuck her. Now.*

He replied to Emma, "My dragon is wanting a go. Yours too?" She nodded, and he grinned. "Then we should let them get to it. Mine is rather determined to dominate yours."

Her pupils flashed even faster. "No, my dragon is going to win."

They both laughed and then let their dragons take over. The ensuing battle went back and forth, ending in a declared draw.

One that both the human and dragon halves said deserved a rematch as soon as possible.

But as Logan fell asleep with Emma cuddled in his arms, he focused on having the female he loved finally in his bed and how the next day he was going to try his hardest to win this bloody geocaching competition. Because the sooner they did, the sooner they could go home and maybe start a life together.

Chapter Nineteen

The next day Emma stared up at the giant round table on the wall inside the Winchester Great Hall. It was divided into sections with paint, sort of like a pie cut into pieces, except for the large flower painted in the center. It was a replica of King Arthur's round table, one that dated back to the late medieval period, or so the helpful guide in her hands stated. She murmured to Logan at her side, "Well, the round and round we go part makes sense, aye?"

His hand squeezed her waist. "Aye. And kings, too, given how many had lived at the castle before it was destroyed."

The Great Hall was the only remaining bit of the old Winchester Castle. Although its use hadn't completely faded away once it was the only structure left standing.

The traitor reference in the clue was a bit more obscure to everyday people, but not only had an earl been beheaded here, apparently some humans had led a rebellion and were tried and convicted in this hall as well.

However, while all of that helped confirm they were in the right spot, what they needed to focus their energies on the most was the recreated thirteenth-century garden outside. It wasn't large, though, and they'd decided it was better for Emma and Logan to pretend to be on a date inside the hall to keep watch while Iris and Zoe scoured the garden. The guidebook had said it contained a variety of plants and herbs, ones that could heal or murder, depending on the variety.

From what they could tell, the clue should be in the tunnel arbor, the one constructed of wood with vines growing up and over it.

No doubt something was tucked into the vines. Even if it were small, that would only add to the challenge. And she itched to see if she could spot it first.

Not that she could. And for Emma to stand here pretending to be interested in an old table, or the stained glass windows above it, while waiting for the others to find the clue was, well, it was difficult.

As if sensing her tension, Logan moved his mouth to her ear and whispered, "It had to be this way, angel. You vetoed me pretending to be on a date with Iris or Zoe."

She'd actually said it would be better for Antony and Iris to pretend to be on a date. But Antony had said no, he couldn't be seen in public with them.

And neither woman nor beast had wanted any other female draping themselves all over Logan.

Her beast grunted. *Of course not. I have a score to settle with his dragon.*

Aye, I know. If not for me being sore, I would've let you try again this morning.

Making him wait is part of my tactic. I'd rather pounce when his beast isn't expecting it. Then I'll win.

Emma couldn't help but smile. *We'll see dragon, we'll see.*

It was then that she saw Iris enter from the garden, tapping her leg as she walked, signaling that they'd found something.

However, the plan was for her and Logan to leave last. So despite her every instinct wanting to race after Iris, she leaned against Logan's side, shared tidbits from the guidebook, and tried her best not to let her irritation show in her voice.

All this bloody careful planning and patience was exactly why she'd never be a good spy or even Protector.

Nearly an hour later, they finally exited the Great Hall and headed to their car. They'd each come in their own, again not wanting to seem as if they were a group.

By the time Logan pulled into the car park of a chain supermarket, Emma didn't waste time exiting the car and heading down an alley and then another, toward where they were going to meet the others at some address Antony had given them.

Aye, they could've gone back to Skyhunter, but just in case they needed to meet with one of Antony's acquaintances again, they were staying in Winchester a bit longer. After all, it was easier for someone to meet them on the sly in a city of more than forty thousand people than for someone to drive all the way up to a dragon clan's land.

When they finally reached the right address, Emma looked at the boarded-up building with the For Sale sign on it, and wondered if it was merely a cover. Given everything she'd learned of Antony Holbrook, the male was full of secrets.

Logan placed a hand on her lower back, looked each way, and then went to the door. After waiting a beat, a lock clicked, and they entered.

The entry way appeared as shabby at the outside. However, once they turned a corner and entered the only door in the hallway, Emma blinked.

A large room, one that had to take up most of the space inside the building, was modern and filled with not only furniture, but also high-tech equipment. The various consoles, and stations with headphones, and even radar blipping on the far side said this was no accidental address Antony had given them.

"Just what is he up to?" she murmured.

Antony's voice garnered her attention. "If I told you, then I'm afraid I'd have to kill you, Miss MacAllister. And since I'd rather not do so, come join us at the table and let's go over what Iris and Miss Watson found."

It was then that Emma noticed Iris, and the dragonwoman kept looking around the room, to Antony, and then back to their surroundings.

No doubt she was eager to find out what was going on, and if there was anyone on Lochguard who could ferret out the human's secrets, Emma would bet it was Iris.

But none of that mattered right now. She let Logan lead her to the large table off to one side, where everyone else from their team was gathered.

Done with patience, Emma blurted, "So what did you find?"

Zoe answered, "A wee flash drive. Antony already pulled up the information, avoiding some trap or something, and we wrote it all out before it erased."

Emma wanted to grumble as she should've been the one to dodge the trap and bring up the clue but knew it wouldn't accomplish anything. As if sensing her irritation, Logan squeezed her waist before asking, "Then what did it say, exactly?"

The others, apart from her and Logan, all looked

at Max. It was only then that she noticed the male had his arms crossed over his chest and a deep frown on his face. "I know where the final clue is."

"Already?" Emma leaned forward. "Then where?"

For the first time since meeting Antony, his voice held a twinge of impatience. "My brother seems to think he can keep it secret and just guide us there, wearing blindfolds of all things."

Max glared at his brother. "It took me ten years to find this bloody place, and if we're not careful, *she* will follow us and steal it from me."

Antony brushed off an invisible piece of lint from his sleeve. "Yes, yes, that dragonwoman archaeologist rival of yours. But as I said, if she tries to poach it from you, I will have her visa and DDA permissions revoked and she'll be forced to go back to Australia."

Emma eyed Antony warily. "You have that sort of power?"

The human shrugged. "That isn't important." He looked back at his brother. "I'm asking nicely, Max. Don't make me go the harder route."

As the two brothers stared at each other, Emma started to wonder if Max had a secret life that he kept from everyone else. The chatty, genial human seemed to have vanished completely.

Before she could think too much about it, Max finally grunted. "Fine. But I'm going to keep you to your word about that she-devil, if she follows us."

Antony nodded and Max took out a wee notebook from a pocket inside his jacket. After thumbing through it, he opened it to a certain page and laid it open on the table. "This is where we need to go. Everything in the clue references the legendary coronation site of Queen Alviva, the secret site where she also held court every year for the heads of the dragon clans to pay homage."

She frowned. "You mean Dragon's Court? I thought it was merely a myth children were taught at school."

Max shook his head. "Everyone thinks it's only a tall tale these days, but I've found clues, little details, in old Roman mosaics and records. The location of Dragon's Court was secret for a reason—Alviva didn't wish for humans to attack them at one of the gatherings and try to bend all the dragons in England and Wales to their whims. I was only able to piece it all together because apparently Alviva had invited a human Roman general there once, to share her bed clandestinely, and he must've talked to others about it at some point."

Queen Alviva going off for secret meetings with a lover sounded so much more interesting than the mere regal peacekeeper she'd been made out to be when Emma had learned about her in school.

Logan asked, "Then if this location is so secretive, how did the competition organizers know to put the final cache there?"

Max grunted. "I have no concrete evidence, but only a guess. About three years ago, one of my interns was found dead after staying late on one of my dig sites. It was ruled a suicide despite how I said he never would've killed himself. Regardless, all of his notes had also been stolen, which the police dismissed, saying he probably destroyed them." Max shook his head. "But this intern never would've done that; he believed any document, no matter how trivial, could be important later on." He tapped the notebook. "Someone wants this site and must've believed my intern knew where it was even if he didn't. Although I don't know *why* they'd want this location. There shouldn't be any treasure there. I've only discovered a few murals inside the cave network and the occasional brooch or shard of pottery. The earth didn't look disturbed, either, when I first set foot in it a few months ago, as if someone had been digging around."

Zoe asked, "Have you unearthed every inch of Dragon's Court yet?"

Max frowned. "No, but I highly doubt there's a mysterious treasure sitting there, waiting to be dug up. Dragon's Court wasn't even a residence."

Iris jumped in. "And yet, the queen met her lover there. Who knows if he later used it himself to hide something, or learned of something Alviva wanted to keep secret from everyone. Besides, if I remember right, didn't Alviva have a twin sister she was close to?"

Max nodded. "Edwina. Little is known about her, though, apart from how she aided her sister when she could."

Emma said, "Maybe Alviva hid something from even her sister. Who knows, just because you haven't found something yet doesn't mean it doesn't exist." Before Max could reply, she switched her gaze to Antony. "Isn't this where you tell us smugly how you already know all about this?"

Antony shook his head. "Not this time, Miss MacAllister. Worrying about a hidden archaeological site isn't high on my list of priorities." He glanced at Iris. "And no, don't bother asking what they are either, my dear."

Iris glowered, but Emma ignored it to bring the conversation back to their next cache location. "Look, we can all sit here arguing and waste more time or focus on what's most important—winning. It's pure luck that Max could decipher this clue so quickly, and we need to take advantage of it. Not just so I can claim the prize money, but also so that Antony can have his breadcrumbs to who knows what, and Max avoid his rival finding his prize dig site."

Max shrugged and answered, "The site isn't too far from here, actually, in Somerset. We could probably make it before it gets dark and have a look around. And yes, it's a deep cave system that will always be dark, but finding the entrance is bloody difficult without the sun."

Iris raised her brows. "So we'll just stroll in? It can't be that easy."

"No, of course not. It's a hidden section of the Wookey Hole Caves, which is always crawling with visitors. My site is a set of previously undiscovered rooms. Even if it's a little away from the main cave entrance, it takes timing to slip in unnoticed."

Emma studied Max again. Clearly this male was more than she'd thought before.

Of course, given what she'd learned of Antony, maybe Max had learned quite a bit from his much older brother.

Speaking of the devil, Antony strode toward a small room off to the side. "I'll have what we need to access the caves brought here within twenty minutes. Use the time to eat, sleep, whatever you wish because it's going to be a long night."

He closed the door, and silence fell for a minute. Her dragon spoke up. *Well, there goes my chance to best Logan's dragon tonight.*

Calm down, dragon. Once we finish this hunt, I'm stepping back for a while. We'll have plenty of time with Logan then.

Her beast grunted. *We'd better. I want to keep him.*

Ignoring the small flare of panic, she did her best

to reply calmly, *Don't get ahead of yourself. One step at a time, aye?*

Fine. Now, let me nap and dream about how to win over Logan's dragon.

Logan hugged her tighter to his side and she looked up at him. He raised his brows. "All right?"

Leaning into him, she sighed. "Mostly. We're so close to finishing this, and yet, we could still fail."

He kissed her brow. "Aye, I know, angel. But now's not the time to give up."

She raised an eyebrow. "Of course I'm not giving up."

He smiled, moved his hand to her arse, and lightly slapped. "There's my fighting lass."

She stuck her tongue at him and he chuckled. She raised her chin. "And here I thought I might kiss you a bit before we left. But now I'm not so sure."

He guided her to the far side of the room and murmured into her ear. "Oh, aye?"

Logan nuzzled her cheek and she sucked in a breath. His touch had become addicting so quickly. "Aye."

As his jaw brushed against hers, the slight bristling of his late-day whiskers made her shiver. His husky voice made her body heat up as he said, "As much as I love your lips, I think I've neglected kissing your pussy, angel. Maybe if we find somewhere more private, I can rectify that."

"Logan," she scolded half-heartedly. Only half-heartedly because she remembered the last time he'd gone down on her, and before he'd fallen unconscious, it'd been bloody amazing.

Iris spoke from the other side of the room. "Max is the only one who can't hear you two. Either find a room or change the subject."

The door on the side opened and Antony strode out. "There's no time for that. Come, we're going to recharge in the kitchen and get ready to leave."

Iris drawled, "Is that an order?"

Antony smiled. "Why yes, it is, my dear. I was going to have Miss Watson stay behind to act as a go-between for communications, but I thought maybe you could do it."

Iris glared. "I'm the senior Protector, and I'm going. Someone has to look after Logan and Emma."

As they argued a bit, Emma moved her lips to Logan's ear and whispered so no one else could hear, "How much do you want to bet that at some point, they're going to rip off each other's clothes and have a good ol' hate fuck?"

Logan snorted. "As long as they don't set us up as some sort of bloody referees, to judge who is better at fucking, I say let them have at it."

Emma bit her lip to keep from laughing. "Let's merely calm them down for now, though. I want to find the last cache before doing anything else."

Logan kissed her lips gently. "Come, love. Let's play peacekeeper."

And as they managed to get Antony and Iris separated and into the kitchen, it wasn't long until they'd eaten, refreshed, and headed out for another drive.

But this time Emma didn't complain about being trapped in the car. Because in roughly two hours, they could be on the cusp of finding the last cache and claiming the prize.

Chapter Twenty

As Emma followed Logan down a small passageway, lit only by the torch in his hand, she wished her keen dragon-shifter eyesight could see in complete darkness. But, alas, dim light was fine but not pitch black.

While she was doing her best to remain calm, she didn't relish being stranded where she couldn't see anything beyond a faint outline, should the torch fail.

Logan reached back his hand, touched her arm, and whispered, "Don't worry, angel. I have spare batteries in my pocket, along with another wee torch as a backup. We'll be fine."

Of course Logan would know about her uneasiness concerning total darkness, given the past. "I'm not twelve years old this time. I won't scream and cry that I'm going to die. Well, at least not straight away."

He snorted. "That was quite impressive back then. Of course, if you'd listened to me about not going into that cave by yourself, you wouldn't have had us all searching frantically for you."

Even when Logan had been fifteen, he'd been protective of her. "Aye, well, one of the lads at school said there might be a treasure there, but only the bravest would look. I couldn't pass up the challenge. Although…"

"Although what?"

"Well, I didn't exactly learn my lesson then. I went back later, but with my brother Ian in tow. To say I was disappointed when we found nothing was an understatement."

He chuckled. "No doubt. And I suspect your sense of adventure has always been there, angel. We probably wouldn't be here if it wasn't." She was about to open her mouth to defend herself, but Logan added, "And that wasn't a dig at you, love. *We* probably wouldn't be where we're at now without your sense of adventure."

Her anger faded. "Aye, you're probably right. And whilst I love that you're chasing this adventure by my side this time, I'm looking forward to the end of this bloody competition. I've had enough secrets and danger for a wee while."

His hand found hers and squeezed. "Aye, me too. So let's keep our eyes peeled and see if the clue makes more sense as we go along."

On the drive to Somerset, Max had shared the clue in full, and Emma had it memorized.

QUEENLY SECRETS, cloaked in darkness
  Dragon eyes forever watching
  The answer lies in the steady gazes
  If one can bear to look, and face the consequences
  Seize the heart and victory will follow

IT HADN'T MADE much sense until Max had shown them inside the cave and she'd seen the first mural.

Dragons in every color flew overhead as a queen sat on a throne, conferring with others around her. Max said it was only one of the murals, and that they spread all through the hidden set of rooms. Most of them told some sort of history concerning Queen Alviva, or so he could tell.

However, he hadn't yet explored in great detail the other rooms and passages off the main one. And so they'd split into three groups: she and Logan, Iris and Antony, and Max alone since he knew the place already.

And currently she and Logan were going down the left passage Max had only briefly checked out without studying the walls, let alone had looked for specific clues in any of the murals. The largest one they wanted to examine was at the end, through a tight passage.

As Logan stopped right in front of a narrow slit in the wall, he shined his torch inside. She asked, "Will you fit through there, do you think?"

"Aye, no matter what. Because I won't let you go through first."

"Logan…"

He turned his head to meet her gaze. "Not because I think you're incapable, angel. No, I don't want you to get stuck in there if I can't follow you. The thought of you being trapped and me not being able to help will drive me fucking mad."

She nodded. "Max did say to ensure we could enter any space in pairs, just in case." She held up her walkie-talkie. "Especially since this is the only way we can communicate inside the caves. Mobile phones are useless here." She eyed his broad shoulders. "Although I'm a bit worried about you making it through in one piece."

The corner of his mouth ticked up. "Would you prefer that I had smaller shoulders? I rather thought you fancied mine."

As she thought of gripping them while he fucked her, her cheeks heated. "Aye, maybe I fancy them a wee bit."

He laughed. "We're going to explore that more in depth later. But for now, here, hold the torch."

She took it and frowned. "Are you sure you want to go in without any light?"

"I have the wee one in my pocket, just in case." He patted it and then turned to face her, barely able to do so in the tight space, and kissed her gently on the lips. "Wait for me to get through before you follow, aye?"

She bobbed her head. "Be careful."

He grinned. "Now who's warning whom?"

Fighting a laugh, she rolled her eyes and gave him a playful shove. "Just go on with you."

After one more kiss, Logan went to the narrow opening in the rock.

It took him a minute of slowly moving his arms and body to get through, but he did. Emma shone the light into the space. "What do you see?"

"Aye, there's a grand mural in here, on the far side. Let me quickly switch on my torch and ensure it's safe before you come through as well."

She saw the wee light go on and roam around the room, catching a grand mural in the distance. The room was massive, nearly as big as the main one they'd entered through.

Logan took a few steps deeper inside when something clicked.

Dread pooled in her stomach. But before she could warn Logan, there was a small explosion and dust filled the passageway.

Emma choked and coughed as she crouched down, protecting her head, dropping her walkie-talkie in the process.

As she tried to breathe, she noticed nothing had collapsed on her side of the opening. Yet.

The initial sound dampened and it turned eerily silent. Too silent.

"Logan!" she shouted as she coughed, trying to move and shine her torch inside the area.

But the bloody dust kept the inside hidden from her. She shouted his name again, but no answer.

Oh no, no, no, no. Not again. Logan couldn't be hurt again.

When the dust settled enough that she could mostly see, Emma tried to look inside the opening again. But all her light revealed was a pile of rocks, as if there'd been a cave-in.

If so, she probably wouldn't be able to dig him out on her own.

Her heart pounded and her throat closed up. But somehow she managed to push back her fear, knowing she couldn't help Logan if she fell apart. "Logan! Answer me, aye? Shout to let me know you're okay."

Nothing. Just nothing.

She was about to start shouting some more, determined to get a response, when her dragon spoke up. *We should contact the others and get help.*

But that means leaving him. What if he's dying? I don't want to leave him alone.

Neither do I. But staying here and not getting help might kill him.

The thought of leaving Logan alone, in pain, and maybe dying choked her throat with emotion and made her eyes heat with tears.

Her grand fear of losing someone she loved might have just come true.

But rather than worrying about future pain, all Emma could think about was how she'd wasted what time they'd had together.

And because of her caution, Logan might never know how she felt about him.

Her dragon growled. *Worry about that later. Get help.* Now.

She shouted, "Logan, if you can hear me, I'm going to find the others. I dropped my walkie-talkie in the collapse and can't find it. I'll be back as soon as I can. Don't you dare think of dying on me, aye? I won't have it."

Silence.

A single tear rolled down her cheek, but Emma brushed it away. "I love you, Logan. And I'll be back as soon as I can."

And as she ran—or attempted to run when able, given how narrow some parts were—Emma did her best not to focus on how everything could go wrong.

Until she'd seen Logan's body, and saw he was dead, she was going to believe he was alive. They had too much left to do, too many wasted years she needed to make up for.

And Emma was nothing if not stubborn.

So she pushed her legs until she found Iris and Antony down one of the other passageways.

Iris frowned. "What's wrong?"

Emma explained what happened and asked Antony, "Tell me you have people who can get him out of there?"

"I do, but it sounds like it was boobytrapped. It's going to take time to clear the rubble."

She growled. "We don't have time. He might be dying, and every second wasted lowers his chance of survival."

She swore a look of sympathy flashed in Antony's eyes, but it was gone before she could be sure. He answered, "Here's what I can do—you keep looking for the clue with Iris and I'll see what I can do to rescue Lamont."

"But—"

"No buts. There is more at stake here than merely prize money. We need to win this."

She was about to argue some more when Iris put a hand on her shoulder and squeezed. "If there's one thing I've learned about Antony Holbrook, he knows how to do the impossible. Let him work his magic whilst we keep searching, aye?"

"But Logan's all alone…"

Antony said softly, "I know what it's like to be helpless to save someone you love singlehandedly, and how it can feel like the worst failure. However, let me assure you that having me reach out to my contacts will give him a much better chance of survival, Miss MacAllister. I promise you that."

She barely noticed Iris's frown. No, Emma couldn't believe the sincerity—and was it pain?—Antony seemed to radiate.

Her beast spoke up. *Don't be stubborn. Let him help.*

Antony *had* seemed to do the impossible so far.

And if her having to stay away from Logan for a short while meant she could ultimately save him, she'd do it. "Aye, then I'll do as you say. But I want constant updates, or the deal is off."

He nodded. "I will give you that. Now, let Iris fill you in on what we were doing. I have some calls to make. Oh, and be careful. There are bound to be more traps, I'm sure of it."

As Antony walked away, Emma fought the urge to race after him. Relying on help had never been easy for her. But it seemed she needed to get past that to give Logan his best chance.

She looked at Iris and took a deep breath. "I'm going to be a wreck, but I'll do what I can."

"Aye, I know, Emma. I know. Come on."

And as she tried to focus on studying the next mural, her thoughts kept going back to Logan and how he could be suffering, or dying, or already dead.

No. He had to be alive. He just had to. She refused to believe that just when she'd admitted to herself how she loved Logan that he would be gone.

Chapter Twenty-One

L ogan woke up coughing, the dust so thick in the air he almost felt like he was suffocating.

His dragon spoke up. *Hurry, get up and get us out of here. Emma will be worried.*

Emma. No doubt she'd be frantic. *If* the cave-in was only on his side of the opening.

Not wanting to think about the worst-case scenario, Logan slowly tried to sit up, but his leg wouldn't move. It didn't hurt, though, so he reached into his pocket and pulled out the wee torch. Relief crashed over him when it turned on.

A few rock shards pinned his trousers to the ground, nothing more. Although as he coughed and slowly pulled at the material until it ripped free, he noticed that if he hadn't jumped away at the brief flash of light before the explosion, he'd be buried under the mound of rubble blocking the entrance.

Score a point for dragon-shifter reflexes.

Once his leg was finally free, he slowly scooted backward. The last thing he needed was for the rocks to settle further and fall over him.

It was then he noticed a faint breeze low on the ground, coming from behind him. Searching with his light, Logan spotted water on the far side.

Then he remembered how a river ran through the Wookey Hole cave system. Apparently, it even went through the hidden dragon chambers.

He needed to get to the water and see if he could swim out.

As he stood, he wobbled a second before regaining his balance. On top of the difficulty breathing, his head pounded and ears rang, but he refused to let it hold him back.

Not just because Emma had to be worried about him. No, the brief light before the explosion meant it had been caused by *someone*, planted to go off by a certain trigger. Either the competition organizers had lied about the rules or someone had wanted to stop them from winning. Permanently.

Logan started toward the sound of water and his dragon said, *And if that's true, Emma's in danger.*

I know that, dragon. But I can't help or protect her unless we get out of here.

I wish I could shift and dig us out, but the room isn't big enough.

He'd noticed that too. If he tried to shift, it could cause a further collapse, not to mention injure his beast. *No worries. We grew up swimming in Loch Naver. If I can handle an icy loch in the Scottish Highlands, this shouldn't be too bad.*

Or so he hoped. Logan was no cave diver, but even he knew that sometimes the distance between two open-air areas of water in a cave system was more than a person could handle.

Even dragon-shifters had their limits when it came to holding their breaths.

Not that he was going to let it stop him. He needed to reach Emma before it was too late.

Reaching the edge of the water, he shined his light around and noted it was only a seven-foot-by-five-foot opening, with maybe an inch between the water's surface and the enclosed sections to either side—the source of the breeze. However, he had no bloody idea which way to go, or if he could even reach a different section without drowning. For all he knew, the inch of precious air could disappear a few feet down the line.

And even if he could make it, he needed to be careful not to materialize in front of any lingering humans and draw the Department of Dragon Affairs' notice.

His beast sniffed. *We'll deal with that when we get to it.*

Aye. Although no matter what, we need to make sure

Emma is safe and knows what's afoot. His beast grunted and Logan stared at the water. *Time for a swim.*

His torch wouldn't work in the water—they hadn't thought they'd need to go diving, given how the clue should be in a mural—and so he kept it on but laid it down on the floor. His shoes, socks, shirt, and trousers followed. While dragons didn't care about nudity, he didn't want to offend any humans, so he kept his boxers on.

He slowly slid into the cool water and treaded in place. Given how awful the air quality was after the cave-in, Logan didn't know how deep a breath he could take. Still, he did the best he could, and ducked under the water.

Swimming to the left, he struggled to move forward, stroke after stroke, into complete darkness. He wasn't afraid of the dark, but as his lungs burned, the pitch blackness triggered a slight panic.

Not wanting to fail on his first attempt, he tamped down the panic and turned back. His lung burned more and more until he was sure he'd have to swallow water.

At the last second, he saw light and broke free of the surface. Taking huge gulps of air, he made it to the side where the torch was and propped his arms on the raised surface. He'd failed his first attempt.

But he was far from done; Logan refused to give up. He couldn't give a fuck about winning the competition, but Emma had only recently become his female. And he was going to be reunited with her, even if it killed him.

And so once he caught his breath, he tried again, to the other side. Came back, rested, and tried again and then again.

He refused to die alone in this cave. Somehow, someway, he was going to find a way out.

EMMA'S MIND wandered for the millionth time to Logan. She still didn't know what had happened to him. All she knew was that Antony had someone coming, some sort of diver, apparently, and he'd let her know of any progress.

Iris had said it was a good thing a diver was on his way because it must mean the river ran through the room Logan was in.

Not that the tidbit helped calm her at all. If Logan was injured, or dying, it wasn't as if they could take him underwater and gently transport him somewhere. Antony might have contacts, but it wasn't like they had a personal submarine pod or some such thing he could summon on a whim.

And in that case, Logan would die and there was nothing she could do about it.

Tears threatened to fall as her dragon sighed. *Stop it. You're usually not so pessimistic.*

Aye, but my way of thinking is more realistic, you can't

deny it. Besides, it's more than that. He's hurt, or worse, yet again because of me and my stupid geocaching.

Don't start that up again. Antony had been watching for this one, and I'm sure he would've recruited us to continue, no matter what. And you know it.

She mentally grumbled. Given how it seemed that Antony got whatever he wanted, her beast was probably right.

Thankfully she didn't have to argue more because Emma stopped in front of the next mural in the long, tall room she and Iris were examining.

Even though her every instinct called to race back to where she'd left Logan, she made her feet stay in place. If she found the bloody clue, then Antony could use even more resources to save Logan. Or at least she hoped so.

Doing her best to focus, Emma studied the images, paying extra attention to any dragon eyes.

The scene depicted Queen Alviva on a raised dais, a near-identical female standing behind her throne—Edwina—and a number of dragon-shifter males kneeling at her feet.

They seemed to be doing that in all the murals. No doubt one of Alviva's requirements. Not necessarily because of vanity—although probably a wee bit so—but more because dragon females always had a hard time getting the males to take them seriously in positions of power. Alviva wanted to remind everyone of who was in charge, for both her meetings and posterity.

But since none of the eyes of the human forms held any sort of secret, Emma focused on the dragon ones, both on the ground and in the sky.

However, she instantly noticed something different about this mural. None of the ones before had included a white dragon, but one flew in the sky of this scene. White dragons were rare, and Emma only knew of one from Clan Stonefire. But whereas in real life their eyes were like any other dragon-shifter's, this one seemed to glint a wee bit.

If only she could see it better. She scanned, saw a rock nearby that could be moved with two people to give her a stool of sorts, and she said to Iris, "I think I found something, but I need your help."

Without a word, Iris came over and raised her brows. Emma gestured toward the white dragon. "Does his eye seem sparkly to you?"

Iris squinted as she shined her torch at the dragon in question. "Aye, a bit."

"We need to get a better look. Help me move this rock so I can inspect it."

The two of them managed to scoot a step-level-like rock over and Emma stood on it. She studied the white dragon's eye, and aye, the slit was shiny black, as if it were made of obsidian.

She hated to think she had to damage the mural to get to the clue, but it was the only way to end this.

Antony had repeatedly said how important it was for all dragon-shifters for her to win. Not because of her senior center plan, but rather for some mysterious threat Antony was trying to vanquish.

And after all they'd gone through—all Logan had endured—she wasn't going to quit now. "Keep the light on the eye so I can try and see if the slitted section comes out."

Iris didn't bat an eyelash as Emma removed a versatile pocketknife from her trousers. It wasn't the first time she'd needed one wee tool or another.

Unfurling what she desired—a flathead screwdriver—she started poking around the edges to see if the stone wiggled loose.

It was slow going, but at the very top, there was a small area for the screwdriver head to slip into. Carefully, she moved back and forth, until the black stone started to come out. It took a few minutes—the stone was fairly thick—before it finally popped out. Iris caught it, but Emma didn't even notice. Instead, she took her torch from her pocket, pushed the On button, and looked inside the opening where the stone had been. The only thing she saw was some scratching at the end: Stone = Key

For fuck's sake. This wasn't the end?

Her dragon growled. *Check the rock. It had better be. I'm tired of this.*

Emma never would've thought she'd agree, but she did in this case. It was hard enough for her to focus and lose her shit over Logan. But she absolutely refused to leave him here if it turned out there was another clue they needed to solve.

Irritated, tired, worried, and hungry, she jumped down, took the dragon eye slit-shaped rock, and felt it. There were some engravings on the back side. Taking out her mobile, she turned on the light and magnifier app, and inspected the rock. She quickly found the message inscribed with tiny markings:

CONGRATULATIONS, you win. Take this rock and present it to the address below and you'll receive instructions on how to claim the prize. The real stone will be returned after the fact.

"THANK FUCK," she muttered. Emma quickly explained the message to Iris as she pocketed the stone and said, "Now, let's get this to Antony and hopefully he'll let me help rescue Logan now."

Antony was waiting outside the cave, needing to use his mobile phone to coordinate Logan's rescue. He was also keeping watch since Zoe was further afield, waiting for any nod to come help.

It didn't take her and Iris long to reach the fresh air. However, they'd barely stepped outside when a gunshot rang out.

Iris grabbed her, pressed her down, and scanned the area.

Another shot rang out, hitting a few feet away, and Emma's heart nearly exploded out of her chest. Even if the competition wasn't always completely legal to begin with, it was against the rules for another competitor to shoot another, let alone steal the grand prize away once it'd been claimed.

So who the bloody hell was shooting at them? And where the fuck was Antony?

Iris murmured, "Stay low. When I say run, you hide over there, behind those boulders, aye?"

Emma wanted to ask what Iris planned to do—dragon-shifters weren't allowed to own guns, unless they were in the army—but she noticed the dragonwoman's fingers had already morphed into talons.

Then it hit her—Emma was one of the fastest shifters inside Lochugard, but Iris was *the* fastest. And it would take several machine guns firing at once before bullets would do any real harm to someone in their dragon form unless they had armor-piercing bullets.

Which she didn't know for sure. But Iris had better judgment of those things having served with the human British Army and Emma trusted the dragonwoman.

She murmured back, "Aye, I'll do as you say for now. But if things turn to shite, I won't sit by and do nothing."

Iris said quickly, "Before anything, let Zoe and

Finn know we're in trouble." She glanced at her. "If it gets truly bad, then call Honoria too."

The Skyhunter female leader had given her contact information, in case of emergencies. And Skyhunter was still the nearest clan to Somerset. Even if Emma didn't know Honoria well, if Iris said to contact her, Emma would.

"Aye, I understand."

"Good. Now, get ready."

She moved to a crouched position and as soon as Iris shifted into her purple dragon form, Emma ran.

A few shots rang out, but she ignored them, sprinting as fast as she could.

Somehow she made it to behind the group of boulders and quickly peeked around them to see if Iris was okay.

As she watched a human male fly through the air and hit a tree, Emma reckoned so.

Taking out her mobile, she sent messages to Zoe and Finn. As she debated contacting Skyhunter as well, a wee drone came into view. It shot something at Iris, and within a few seconds, Iris slumped to the ground in an unconscious heap.

She nearly cried out but instead, gripped her phone so hard it should've cracked. She murmured to herself, "Keep it together, Em. Keep it together. Iris needs help, so get it."

And so she typed off a message to Honoria, and another to Zoe and Finn.

Everything on the other side of the rocks was eerily silent. Emma peeked around the boulder, scanning the area to see if anyone waited for her. And even though she didn't see anything and burned to run to Iris, if Emma was wrong, she'd become a target.

Her phone buzzed and replies were in from everyone. They all essentially said the same thing: help was on the way.

With another look around the boulders, the scene now showed a few humans surrounding Iris. They must've been hiding in the trees to see if any other threats would emerge; good thing she'd stayed hidden.

As her heart pounded, she ducked back into her hiding spot and did her best to not freak out. She couldn't let them kill her friend. But what could she do? She wasn't a Protector, or a soldier, or some secret spy with combat training. She was just Emma, the computer nerd who liked to look for silly geocaching treasures.

Treasure. Maybe that's what they wanted. If she could distract them with the stone, they might leave Iris alone until help could arrive.

Quickly she remembered her phone could do a text-to-speech function. So Emma quickly typed up a message, and started moving slowly through the nearby brush and trees. She needed to put her phone somewhere, have it start reading aloud, and get as far away from it as possible. The distraction wouldn't be very long, but every second counted.

And so she kept moving slowly, her heart thundering in her ears, hoping she wasn't in way over her head.

Chapter Twenty-Two

Logan had lost track of how many times he'd pushed his body a bit farther through the water. However, as his lungs burned and he swam with everything he had, he knew this would be his last attempt for a while.

If ever.

So despite his lungs screaming for oxygen, or the lights dancing behind his eyelids, he pushed on, taking the silent strength from his dragon the whole way.

Just as he thought he couldn't keep going, light brightened the inside of his eyelids. With a renewed strength, he opened his eyes and went a bit farther, toward white and purples lights.

Knowing he had a few seconds, at most, before he'd lose consciousness, he tried swimming toward the top. As black dots started to fill his eyes, his head broke the surface.

A few gasps sounded from somewhere, but he barely heard them above his greedy gulps of air, his lungs starved to the point Logan was still lightheaded after a few beats.

When someone's voice filled his ears, it took him a second to make sense of it. "Where the bloody hell did you come from?"

After a few more breaths, he turned and noticed a human male standing nearby, with lights shining in various spots behind him.

It took Logan a second to process, but between the multicolored lights and the wee rowboat in the water, he recognized the space from the Wookey Hole website. This was the public visitor area, and the exit wasn't too far away from this chamber.

A new rush of energy filled his body as he swam to the edge of the water and somehow pulled himself up. The human drew closer, and Logan put out a hand. "My friends are in trouble and I need to warn them."

The human scowled. "You're a dragon-shifter."

There was no point hiding the tattoo marking on his arm. "Aye. And you can interrogate me later. For now, I need to save my friends."

"None of the other night guards reported trespassers."

Logan slowly stood up. He didn't have the

patience to be polite. "Let me use your phone and help my friends. Then you can ask your questions." The human opened his mouth, but Logan beat him to it. "My name's Logan Lamont, from Clan Lochguard in Scotland. There. Report me to the DDA later. I bloody well don't care. But my friends' lives are in danger, so loan me your damn phone."

After the longest second of his life, the human nodded. "Fine. But if you run off before telling me where you swam from, or why you're here after hours, I will call the DDA straight away." Logan nodded. "Then follow me. I'll show you where you can get a signal."

Climbing the stairs after his exhaustive few hours —maybe? He had no idea how long he'd been trying to escape—was excruciating. But he made it to the top and through another chamber until the human stopped and offered his mobile. "Call them, but I'm staying right here."

Not caring what the human heard, he punched in Zoe's number, and she answered on the first ring. "Who's this?"

"Zoe, it's Logan."

"Logan! Are you okay? Reinforcements will be there any minute now."

"Reinforcements?" he echoed.

"Aye." Without asking why he didn't know what she was talking about, Zoe explained about Emma and Iris, and the attack. When she finished, he growled, "Fuck. There has to be something I can do to help until the others get here."

"If you can think of some sort of distraction to put the attackers off guard, it should help. For now, I need to go. Skyhunter's calling me. Hold tight. Help is on the way."

The line went dead and he lowered the phone.

The human spoke up. "I don't know exactly what's going on, but I don't want anyone killed on my watch. Maybe I can help."

He eyed the human, a male in his thirties or so, who had the look of someone who'd once been a soldier and now was a night guard. "Why would you offer?"

He said one word, "Holbrook."

Logan blinked. He had no idea if the human was friends with Max or Antony, but Logan didn't care. Right now, the mention was good enough. He replied, "Aye, well, then I need your help to distract those trying to kill my friends."

The human gestured. "Follow me."

And as they walked toward one of the staff rooms, the human explained what they could do. It only reinforced his guess that the human was tied to one of the Holbrooks in some way.

Once he had some trousers on and the gear the human male had given him, Logan followed him and hoped he had enough adrenaline remaining to keep him from collapsing and allow him to help Emma and the others.

EMMA HAD CLIMBED up a sturdy enough tree and watched the humans as they studied her phone. Before pressing Play on it, she'd started the erase features she'd long ago encrypted on the device. Once it finished, no one would be able to retrieve anything, no matter how good they were.

But now the humans kept scanning the area, trying to find her location. Emma kept her ears open, hoping to hear dragons approaching in the sky. However, there was nothing beyond the humans murmuring to each other, some rustling branches, and even a few wild animals scurrying through the brush and trees.

She was still on her own. All she could do was hope the humans below wouldn't start looking up into the trees too closely.

Her dragon spoke. *For now, all that matters is that Iris still breathes.*

Even from her perch, Emma watched her friend's dragon form to be sure. *Aye, I know.*

She may still not know what had happened to Logan, let alone Max or Antony, but at least Iris was still alive.

Emma gripped the branch in her hands harder.

When she'd first accepted their help for the competition, she never would've imagined how she'd end up happy to have at least one of her team mates still alive.

Before guilt could come crashing down, music blared nearby, followed shortly by some flares.

She said to her beast, *What are they doing? I didn't hear any dragons flying, did you?*

No, but that doesn't mean they're not here.

Another flare shot into the sky, all but shouting, "Come find me."

The humans below split into two groups. Four of them went toward the flares and music while the remaining three stood near Iris's body.

She heard a twig snap not far from her tree, and she looked down. She pressed her fingers to her lips to muffle her cry.

It was Logan.

He was alive. Wet hair, wearing new clothes, and doing his best to sneak through the trees, but still breathing.

All she wanted to do was climb down, pull him close, and kiss him. To tell him how she loved him, and that she'd been a fool to resist both him and her feelings for so long.

However, as the music blared louder in the distance, it reminded her of the current dangers.

Iris. Saving her friend was more important right now. And while Emma burned to ask Logan how she could aid his plan, she didn't want to draw the three remaining humans' attention. So she stayed put and watched as Logan crept slowly, something in his hand she couldn't make out, waiting to see if a moment would pop up where she could help.

When it became clear he meant to take down the three humans, Emma made a split-second decision, and she quietly made her way down the tree. She'd been climbing them since she was a wee girl and knew how to keep it from moving too much. And given the slight wind, a mere human shouldn't notice the difference.

But all she knew is that she had to be at the ready in case anyone needed her. She may not have extensive training or anything, but she was still a fucking dragon-shifter. And against humans, it was one massive advantage.

Remembering what Iris had done to allow Emma to hide, she instantly knew she needed to do the same to give Logan the greatest chance of success.

The humans might shoot her with the same thing as Iris since Emma had no idea where the drone was, but she was going to risk it. Logan was alive now, and she was going to ensure he stayed that way. No matter what.

She tugged off her clothes, took a deep breath, and said to her beast, *Like we've practiced hundreds of times before, aye? A fast shift will give us the best advantage.*

Aye. Let's help and protect our love.

It was still strange to think of Logan that way, but it was true. *On my count. One, two, THREE!*

L<small>OGAN</small> <small>GRIPPED</small> the tranquilizer gun in his hand he'd received from the strangely prepared security guard and waited for the right moment to strike. Even if the human male—named John Lane—had gone through the instructions twice, Logan was still nervous.

If he froze, or missed too many times, he'd end up captured or dead.

But seeing Iris's unconscious body in the clearing stirred the anger of both man and beast.

His dragon spoke up. *There's only three of them remaining. If it comes to it, we'll shift and overpower them.*

Let's hope it doesn't come to that. We still don't know if they have Emma, and they might harm her if we attack.

His dragon grunted. *Lane said he could take down the other humans if we handled these ones. Capturing them and interrogating them will be the best way to find Emma.*

If she wasn't already dead was left unsaid.

For a beat, fear gripped his heart. He'd loved Emma for so long and had only recently had his feelings reciprocated. If he lost her now, after finally claiming her heart, he might never recover.

Stop it. He couldn't wonder about what-ifs. Even in the medical field, that line of thinking could end up hurting someone, even if unintentionally. It was doubly true now as well.

Gripping the tranquilizer gun tighter, he crept the last few feet to the edge of the scrub, until he found an opening where he could shoot while still having some cover.

Just as he lined up his first shot, a dragon form grew nearby. After a few mere seconds, a red dragon stood there.

But not just any dragon. No, it was Emma.

His relief at seeing she was alive was quickly replaced with anger. What the fuck was she doing, putting herself in danger?

His dragon growled, *Fire and help her before they do the same as what they did with Iris.*

Since he still had his tranquilizer gun aimed, Logan made the final adjustments and fired. The dart hit the nearest human's back and he fell to the ground.

Emma's dragon form didn't even bat an eye at it either.

Before his mind could go down the road of how she knew he was there to help and not some stranger, Logan focused on another human. One had pulled out a strange-looking gun, with a larger-than normal barrel.

Or so he thought, given his limited knowledge of firearms.

And the bastard had it pointed at Emma.

Oh, not today, motherfucker. He loaded and fired off another shot.

The dart hit the human's arm, but the male instantly pulled it out. And while he staggered, he still had the strength to fire his weapon at Emma before collapsing.

Her beast roared, but still managed to bat away the remaining human. Once the male hit the tree and stayed still, Logan raced out toward Emma. He was nearly there when she tilted sideways and then fell over.

"Emma!" He rushed over and stroked her snout. While she was still breathing, she didn't respond. Even when he reached behind her ear to scratch the patch of unscaled skin—the most sensitive on a dragon—she didn't react.

He continued to caress her face. "Don't you bloody die on me, angel, do you hear? I'm not ready for you to be my guardian angel in truth."

Silence.

Fuck, fuck, fuck. To avoid his emotions taking over, he fell into his nurse role. A cursory examination said her heartbeat was strong, and her breathing even. While Logan had no idea what the aftereffects might be, Emma seemed stable for the moment.

All he wanted to do was stay there, murmuring words of encouragement, until either Lane came to help him, or Max and Antony finally showed up.

However, he couldn't ignore Iris's form about ten

feet away. Even if he didn't have any tools or drugs to help her, just knowing someone cared could mean life or death in some situations. And Iris had been nothing but loyal to them all.

So as much as it pained him, he left his female to run over to Iris and examine her. He quickly determined she was in the same state as Emma.

Drugged, but not dying, the best he could tell.

Still, some dragon-shifters had been drugged in the past and had soon gone into a steady decline; Layla often studied those cases and discussed it with him. They didn't always end happily.

After telling Iris she'd better pull through and he'd be back to check on her, he raced back to Emma's red dragon form. As he stroked her scales some more, he murmured, "If you need to fight, fight it. I know you're stubborn, so bloody well use it, angel."

Emma didn't reply, of course.

Staring at her unconscious form, Logan debated leaving her and Iris to find Lane and a phone when several dragons glided into sight, swooping in and back up, until a white one descended and carefully landed. He could barely blink at the sight—he'd only heard of but never actually seen a white dragon— before the beast shrank into the pale, blonde-haired human form of Honoria Wakeham.

She ran toward them, neither of them caring

about nudity. All Logan wanted was to help Emma. "Honoria, please tell me you have a doctor nearby."

The dragonwoman nodded. "Our clan doctor is hovering not far away, waiting for word from either me or Asher." She looked up, made a series of hand signals to the dragons above, and a green one flew away from the rest. Honoria looked back at Logan. "Robin will fetch him. But in the meantime, you mentioned you were a nurse training to be a doctor. So what did you find out about them?"

As he tried to calmly recite what he'd learned, Iris convulsed.

He rushed over and managed to find her pulse. *Fuck.* It was too fast. He needed access to medical supplies, and quickly. All he could do was stroke her snout and murmur reassurances.

It seemed far too long before a blue dragon slowly landed, laid down the bag in his talons, and shifted into a male. Just as the dragonman with dark skin and curly black hair approached with a medical bag, Emma started convulsing.

His heart stopped beating a second before he dashed over. The unknown doctor shouted something, but Logan couldn't focus on anything but Emma.

Seeing her familiar red dragon form twitching sporadically made his gut churn. *No, no, no.* She'd better not fucking die.

He stood next to her head and kept an eye on her mouth. Dragons didn't vomit often, but drugs sometimes caused it and he needed to ensure she could breathe. "Ssh, Emma. I'm here. You can get through this, I know it. Just hold on a bit longer, angel."

He finally looked up at the doctor and glared, but the male finished whatever he was doing with Iris before heading over.

On the fringes of his consciousness, he noticed that Iris was still again, except for the rise and fall of her chest.

However, Emma's convulsions were stronger than Iris's, and it was taking everything he had to keep murmuring in a strong voice and not show his fear. "Come on, Emma. Just a wee bit longer, aye? You're a strong lass. And if you don't want your brothers to kill me for allowing this to happen, you need to hold on and have my back eventually, aye?"

The doctor nodded at him, and without a word, took out a vial and syringe. Logan wanted to ask what it was, but he merely kept talking to Emma. Sometimes, the voice of someone a person cared about was the strongest tether to staying alive.

Only once the doctor administered the drug and Emma calmed again, did he finally let out a sigh and stroke Emma's snout.

The doctor spoke in the same south of England accent as most everyone from Skyhunter. "The shots I administered will help counteract any of the known drugs the dragon hunters or former Dragon Knights have used in the past. However, they could've been hit with something new. In that case, I need to get them back to Skyhunter ASAP and run a series of tests."

Logan nodded. "I'll help if you need it. I'm a nurse on Lochguard."

The other male raised an eyebrow. "I think not." Before Logan could protest, the doctor continued, "I'm guessing this female means something to you. And you know it's best not to treat those you have a strong emotional connection with, if possible."

His dragon spoke up. *He's right. Just let him do his job.*

Even if he still didn't know if Emma was out the woods yet, there was no reason to be an arse to the male just trying to help. "Aye, you're right, Doctor…?"

The male put out his and. "Dr. Elijah Harper." Logan shook his hand and then Dr. Harper said, "You can help for her transport, though. If you can ride with her, talk to her, it couldn't hurt."

Honoria strode up to them, now wearing a simple stretchy dress. "Apparently the Holbrook brothers are busy with something, and no one will talk. However, Emma said she'd found the final clue. I don't want to bother about it, but if I don't try to find it, the DDA Director won't be happy. Especially given the cleanup the DDA has to do here."

His first instinct was to growl. Who cared about the bloody clue?

But as he stared at Emma's still form, he knew she'd want them to finish this thing properly. Especially if the stupid thing would help as many dragon-shifters as Antony had hinted at.

Not that Logan wasn't going to try and throttle the human the next time he saw him for leaving Emma and Iris on their own against so many enemies.

His dragon spoke up. *Forget about that for now. Help Honoria and Emma both.*

He ran a hand through his hair and then pointed to the nearby trees and brush. "She came out of there. Find her clothes and you might find the final piece of this bloody treasure hunt."

Honoria ignored his tone and went searching. "Found it!" She returned and glanced up at the sky. "Ah, Asher's here with the transport crew." She looked back at Logan. "Try not to growl at everyone. We just want to help Emma and Iris. The quicker we can get them back to Skyhunter, the better."

He nodded. "Aye, I know."

Honoria's face softened. "She's in excellent hands with Dr. Harper. And the other dragon doctors allied with us and Lochguard are all on standby for video conferences. Try your best not to worry, okay?" Dragons started to descend lower, with four hovering. They dropped a net to the ground at the same time

Asher King came out of the trees in his human form. He nodded at his mate, and then barked, "All of us are going to have to shift and move one of the two dragons on the net, and then the other female. Ready?"

Even though Logan was still bone-weary from all the swimming, a second wind came over him. He'd do anything for Emma. Anything.

Once they'd all shifted, it took some maneuvering to get first Iris onto a net and lifted, and then Emma onto another. Right before the dragons above were to carry her off, Logan shifted back to his human form and crawled on top of Emma.

Laying his head on her side and holding onto her wing bone to keep from falling, the four dragons above slowly lifted them into the sky.

And as they made their way back toward Clan Skyhunter, Logan stroked his female's scales the entire time, murmuring all the things he wanted to do with her when she woke up.

The rhythmic sound of dragon wings lulled him and exhaustion finally set in. But he fought sleep until Emma was safely on Skyhunter's land, inside a makeshift medical tent erected around her. As soon as Dr. Harper and the other medical staff converged on her, Asher placed a hand on his shoulder, squeezed, and pushed him toward the exit. "Come on." Logan opened his mouth to protest, but Asher beat him to it. "No, you need sleep. And whilst you're on Skyhunter, I'm temporarily in charge of you and your welfare. Sleep, recharge, and then you can help us understand everything that happened and be there for your female when she wakes up."

It was the "when she wakes up" that caused Logan's protests to die in his throat.

His dragon spoke up. *It's true. Emma will need us and we nearly died ourself today. Sleep, heal, and we'll be better to help our love.*

He replied to Asher, "But don't you need details from me now?"

Asher shook his head. "We've received some from Zoe Watson, and a call from Antony Holbrook."

At the mention of the human's name, he growled. "Where the fuck did he run off to?"

Asher merely raised an eyebrow. "I have no idea. But the DDA said it was for them and was told not to ask more. Trust me, I wanted to." He shrugged. "But you know the history of my clan. I have to be careful."

Even if Logan knew that Skyhunter had been a fucking mess a few years ago, complete with a leader who'd killed some of his own clan members to try and frame someone else, he still didn't like Asher's answer. "Then I need to call Finn."

"No. Finn said you need to rest before you contact him." Asher's voice held the ultimate form of dominance, one almost every dragon-shifter would obey. Begrudgingly, even his dragon recognized Asher's position.

They stopped in front of a cottage. "You'll stay here. And don't try to sneak out to see Emma. My Protectors will keep you away from her until the doctor clears it."

He narrowed his eyes, wanting to say he wasn't a child. But his dragon spoke up first. *Stop antagonizing him. Both he and Finn gave us the same orders. Rest, regain our strength, and that way we can help Emma, no matter what the future holds.*

Fine, but I don't have to like it.

Once Asher left him alone, Logan showered and lay on the bed. He expected to be awake for hours. However, the ordeals of the day finally washed over him and his exhausted body passed out.

Chapter Twenty-Three

Emma heard some kind of beeping and slowly opened her eyes. She was lying in a bed in someplace unfamiliar. But beeping was coming from some sort of medical machine, and she put together the white, pristine walls with the equipment—she was in a hospital of some sort, although she didn't know which one.

Her dragon's sleepy voice filled her head. *Can't they turn those blasted machines off? It's bloody loud and irritating.*

The normal soft beeps were like daggers in her head, although she tried to remember why.

Then it came back to her—shifting, trying to help Logan, and her being shot with something.

Logan. Emma tried to sit up, but as soon as she lifted a few inches from the bed, she cried out in pain and collapsed back.

In the next beat, Logan hovered over her, searching her gaze. He must've been sitting to the side of the room.

He murmured, "Emma? Are you okay?"

Of course she wasn't, and it was on the tip of her tongue to be snippy. However, the circles under Logan's eyes and his disheveled clothes made her wonder how long she'd been out.

And if he'd been by her side the whole time.

That, combined with how her male looked worried, and exhausted, and far too serious, erased some of her foul mood. Instead, the devil rose up in her, wanting to tease him and break the tension. "Who are you?"

For a second, he blinked and the color drained out of his face. Then she managed to reach a hand out and grab one of his. "No, no, it was just a joke, aye? I couldn't resist. Of course I know you, Logan. I'd better not forget the male I love."

The flicker of irritation faded and his gaze turned soft and warm. "Oh, aye? Say it again."

She smiled. "I love you. But…"

He raised an eyebrow. "But what?"

She narrowed her eyes. "If you ever nearly get yourself killed again, I will murder you myself first, aye?"

He smiled and stroked her forehead, the bridge of her nose, and finally her cheek. Each light touch helped relax her. "And I should say the same for you.

What were you thinking shifting and making yourself a target?"

Emma sighed. "Oh, don't play that game. You would've done the same for me, if I needed help, aye?"

He muttered, "Maybe."

His reluctance made her grin. "At least you're honest."

"I'll only ever be honest with you going forward, love." He continued to caress her face, almost as if he were afraid she would fall unconscious again if he didn't.

What she wouldn't give to be strong enough to kiss him, and more. Much more.

As if he could read her thoughts, he gently kissed her lips and whispered, "You'll have to wait a few more days for that, angel." He kissed her again. "But for now, how about I fill you in with everything that's happened?"

"Only if you sit next to me and hold me." He hesitated a beat and Emma added, "Please? You won't hurt me, I promise."

With a sigh, he gently moved her over, propped himself up on some pillows next to her, and gently pulled her against his side. As she laid her head on his chest, she let out a breath and melted against him. "Now, tell me what happened, all of it."

As he stroked her hair, her back, and even her hip, Logan told her about how they were on Clan

Skyhunter still. Both she and Iris had reverted to their human forms after a day or so, and had been carefully monitored; they both would be okay. The doctors hadn't shared everything with him, but apparently all the clan doctors had worked together to find the antidote to the drug cocktail the humans had used on them.

He still hadn't heard from Max or Antony, and no one would say where they were or why the males had abandoned them.

However, the clue had been turned in by Zoe and a few of Skyhunter's Protectors, under some secret instructions Logan didn't know. Regardless, the money was waiting for Emma in a specially created offshore bank account for her—no doubt to be untraceable—and it was anybody's guess as to whether Antony Holbrook had gotten the information he'd wanted.

At this point, Logan paused. Emma looked up and noticed a mixture of amusement and exasperation in his gaze. "What? There's something else you're not telling me."

He smiled. "Aye. Let's just say your brothers are here and have been, shall we say, bloody ridiculous."

She groaned. "Oh, no. What have they done now?"

Logan shook his head. "Nothing too drastic. They've all tried to pull rank over me, saying they have priority. I told them to fuck off."

She laughed. "I'm sure that went over well."

The corner of his mouth ticked up. "As you can imagine." He put a finger under her chin and tilted her head up. "All of your family is here, actually. I've held them off so far since Dr. Harper wanted to limit your visitors, and I can do so for a wee bit longer, if you need more rest."

Part of her wanted to stay here in her room with Logan, reveling in the beat of his heart and the fact he was still very much alive.

However, the thought of seeing her family after everything filled her with both yearning and shame. "I don't know if I can face them yet. Reckless as always, I nearly got you and Iris killed, after all."

Logan's gaze turned fierce, and his pupils flashed as he said, "Don't you fucking dare blame yourself for everything that happened. At first, aye, it was your competition and project. But that all changed once Antony basically forced us all to keep going. Iris knew what she was getting into, at the very least. Being a Protector is filled with a massive amount of risk."

She looked down and fiddled with Logan's T-shirt. Emotion choked her throat, and her voice came out scratchy as she said, "But you…oh, Logan. I'd thought you'd died back in that cave."

Tears trailed down her cheeks. Logan wiped them away with his thumb. "Shh, angel. I'm alive and here now, aye?" He hugged her closer against him. "And I love you more than ever before."

His words only made her cry harder. After all she'd done to him, both long ago and recently, he still loved her.

Logan merely held her as she let it all out, and when she finally calmed down a bit, he asked, "Tell me what you need, angel. I can't stand more tears."

After a few deep breaths to pull herself together, Emma tilted her head up. At the fierce love and warmth in his eyes, her breath caught.

Her dragon spoke up. *He's not lying. I think it's time to forget all the stupid mistakes of the past and try to forge a new future, aye?*

Could it really be that easy? Not just the danger she'd put him in, but also her years-long fears of losing someone she loved?

Then she remembered when the explosion had happened, and how frantic she'd been afterward, afraid she'd never have the chance to tell Logan what she felt.

How she'd been a fool to wait so long to start a life with him.

And here they were, both alive and mostly well, and Emma needed to seize the moment and her future. Because if she didn't do it now, she might lose him forever. And she couldn't bear losing her best friend, her lover, her perfect match in so many ways.

She cupped his cheek. "What I need is you, Logan Lamont. Will you be my mate?"

After a blink of surprise, he grinned slowly. "Care to repeat that, angel?"

She glared half-heartedly. "You heard me." He laughed and she couldn't help but smile again. "You're a bit of a bastard at times, aye?"

He sobered a bit and his eyes turned heated. "If I remember, you liked that about me when I didn't have my memories."

Even if her body was too tired to do anything about it, his words still heated her skin and made her heart race. "Aye, maybe."

He kissed her nose. "But to answer your question, aye, of course I'll be your mate. You're mine already in my heart, and I can't wait to proclaim it in front of everyone else as well."

His words softened both dragon and female all the more.

With no trace of fear, or apprehension, either. All she wanted was Logan, no matter the risks.

He leaned down to kiss her when the door opened. A dragon male she didn't recognize walked in. His nearly black eyes widened and then narrowed. His accent said he was probably from Skyhunter. "I now see why her heart rate elevated. I thought I told you to alert me as soon as she woke up."

Logan cleared his throat. "I was about to, I

promise." He gestured at the frowning male. "This is Dr. Elijah Harper, Skyhunter's head doctor."

Emma had barely nodded at the doctor in greeting when a familiar male voice boomed down the hallway—her brother Connor. "The doctor was in the middle of telling us what's going on, and then raced off. I'm not going to wait around any longer. I want to see my sister."

Logan barely sighed before her brothers Connor, Ian, and Jamie entered the room. Her sister Cat was on their heels, her bairn in tow and mate Lachlan right behind her. Then her mum, stepdad, and wee baby sister entered.

The room wasn't very big and was now close to bursting with MacAllisters.

Dr. Harper frowned as he checked the monitor screens. "I told you lot to wait. Does no one from Lochguard listen to instructions?"

As her stepdad apologized to Dr. Harper, her mum handed wee Sophie to Jake and came to the side of the bed. She took Emma's face in her hands and then kissed her brow. "There's my lass. I knew you'd come back to us."

As her mum stared at her with love, tears threatened to fall again. Much like with Logan, Emma now recognized how she'd bloody well taken for granted how wonderful her family was. "Aye."

Before her mum could say anything else, Dr. Harper's firm tone filled the room. "I don't know how it's done in Scotland, but I want everyone but her mother, stepfather, and whatever Lamont is out. Now."

Her siblings grumbled, but when Dr. Harper gave them all a "look," they each told Emma they'd be back soon, they loved her, and they left. The doctor followed, saying he'd be back shortly.

Once alone with her parents, Logan bristled at her side and squeezed her tighter against him. "I'm Emma's mate-to-be, that's what I am."

While she might've liked to better ease into it, her mum's eyes lit up. "Is that true?"

She didn't hesitate and merely snuggled closer to Logan. "Aye. I love him, Mum."

Her mother and stepdad shared a smile before Jake put out a hand to Logan. "Then welcome to the family, Logan. We've got to keep the men outnumbering the women as long as we can. Because with two human men mated to female dragon-shifters in this family, our odds favor having daughters."

Jake waggled his brows at her mum, and her mother lightly hit Jake's arm, and Emma couldn't help but laugh.

She was happy to have her mum and stepdad here. Not just because Jake could be silly on occasion, but because she better understood why her mother had taken a second mate and risked her heart again for love.

Logan finally shook Jake's hand and then replied, "Aye, thank you. Although don't expect a slew of grandchildren for a while yet. I plan to keep Emma to myself for a wee while."

Her cheeks heated. "Logan."

He laughed, and then leaned down to whisper in her ear, "It's true. I'm going to be a bit selfish for a bit. I've built up a lot of fantasies over the years."

Emma's cheeks were burning. Jake couldn't hear, being human, and if her mother had heard, she didn't show it. She murmured back, "Behave."

Chuckling, Logan carried on some small talk with Emma's mum and stepdad, until Dr. Harper returned and said that Emma needed to rest.

And when she couldn't stay awake much longer, she laid down with Logan, murmured, "I love you," and fell into the most peaceful sleep she'd had in a long while. Being with Logan completed her in a way she hadn't known she needed. But now that she finally understood it, she was never giving him up.

Epilogue

One Month Later

Logan had somehow survived dinner with Emma's family despite his impatience to whisk her away for her surprise.

Aye, the dinner had been a celebration of their mating ceremony and finding the site for Emma's senior center project. Which were, of course, important to him. However, his inner dragon hummed as they drove up to a secluded manor house situated a few hours from Lochguard.

As he turned off the car, Emma frowned as she looked at the massive three-story sandstone building. "Where are we? I hope you didn't waste money on a night at a fancy place when we have our own cottage back home."

He smiled, took her hand, and kissed the back of it. "I know we agreed no honeymoon, at least for now. But you'll like this place, I promise, Mrs. Lamont."

She glanced at him and raised an eyebrow. "I thought there weren't to be any secrets between us."

"Wee ones can be fun, aye? And you'll find out the truth soon enough." He gestured toward the building. "Now, come on. I'm sure your dragon is all but bursting with curiosity right now."

Emma grumbled, and exited the car. Logan retrieved the wee bag he'd stashed in the boot, and took Emma's hand, threading his fingers through hers. "Don't bother asking what's in the bag. You'll find out after we're inside and shown to our room."

She squeezed his fingers. The action was as natural as breathing now, but his heart rate still ticked up whenever his mate did it. Sometimes it was still hard to believe how Emma was his and even carried his name now.

His dragon spoke up. *She's our mate, our heart, and tonight she'll become ours in a whole different way.*

Aye, I know, dragon. Trust me, my cock's been hard for weeks waiting for this.

As they reached the door, it opened, revealing a man who served as the greeter-slash-butler for the house named Graves. He nodded at Logan, recognizing him from an earlier visit. "Right this way, Mr. Lamont."

As the human male guided them up a set of stairs and down a hallway, Emma whispered, "How many times have you been here before?"

"Only a few. And never to meet with a partner, only to watch."

Her gaze turned puzzled at that. But then a male dressed as a gladiator exited a room, nodded at them, and headed down the stairs.

Emma frowned. "What the…?"

Thankfully Graves stopped in front of a door, preventing Logan from having to explain what sort of place this was just yet. The human unlocked the door and handed Logan the key. "Everything is set up and the room will be open to viewing in ten minutes."

Logan nodded. "Thank you, Graves."

He tugged Emma inside and watched as her eyes widened and mouth dropped.

The room was fancy, aye. A giant bed stood in the center of the room, chairs lined the walls, and a series of golden rectangles lined the walls at roughly chair height. The ceiling was the grandest, though, with a large mural of humans watching a female on her hands and knees as a male fucked her from behind.

Tastefully done, or so everyone pretended.

His dragon snorted, but after Emma had circled

the room and stared at the ceiling for a few beats, she met his gaze again. He tensed, wondering if she hadn't really meant the fantasies she'd told him. But at the curiosity and heat he saw in her blue eyes, he relaxed a fraction. He spoke before she could. "Whilst we've made love outside before, you've mentioned more than once you wished someone would watch." He gestured at the golden rectangles. "In about five minutes, those golden slats will open and anyone who's a member of this place can watch what happens here."

He studied her closely. Emma had shared many a fantasy with him, and he wanted to make all of them come true for her. However, if she needed more time, or balked, he'd take her away immediately. After all, Logan had learned of this place years ago. And while he'd been a voyeur many a time, this was his first visit with a female.

Some part of him had wanted to bring Emma here and hadn't wanted to spoil it with memories of others.

As soon as Emma beamed at him, he let out the breath he'd been holding. "Interesting." Her eyes moved to the still-closed slots and then the chairs. "I don't think I could handle someone sitting in a chair just yet, but the peepholes intrigue me."

At her flashing dragon eyes, he closed the space between them. "Oh, aye?"

She ran her hands across his still-clothed chest.

"Aye." She stood on her tiptoes and whispered, "If my words don't convince you, then confirm it another way."

At the thought of fingering her pussy and finding her already wet, Logan's cock went hard. "I just might have to do that."

He nibbled her earlobe as he ran his free hand down her leg, to the hem of her dress, and then slid it up oh so slowly, inch by inch across her warm, soft skin, loving how her breathing sped up.

When he reached where her thigh met her hip, he growled. "No knickers?"

Her hand lightly stroked his cock through his jeans. "We *were* just mated. I figured they'd just be torn off anyway."

With a growl, he took her lips at the same time as he ran two fingers though her cunt.

At her wetness, he murmured, "You're dripping already."

She lightly squeezed his dick. "It doesn't take much when it's with you."

His dragon growled. *Strip her and fuck her already.*

Soon. I want to tease her and let her enjoy being watched a bit first.

He kissed her lips one last time before stepping back and holding out the bag. He nodded toward the tall screen in the corner. "Go change, angel. We only have a few minutes before those slits open."

She turned around and overemphasized the sway

of her hips as she walked away. He called out, "Emma." When she met his gaze again, he licked the two fingers he'd had between her legs. Her pupils flashed faster and he added, "I plan to devour you slowly, aye?"

Her cheeks flushed and she dashed behind the screen. Not because of being embarrassed—he knew her too well for that—but because she was probably impatient to get started.

Logan quickly shucked his clothes and placed them on an empty chair. Standing near the bed, he lightly stroked his cock as he waited for the female of his dreams to fulfill one of his many fantasies.

EMMA'S HEART raced as she changed out of her dress and put on the black, barely-there negligee. It was see through, cupped her breasts, and then opened into a slit in the front.

There weren't any knickers to go with it.

Aye, it was impractical and would probably come off within minutes, but the lace made her feel pretty and the sheer material brushing against her nipples made her even hotter.

She still couldn't believe Logan had followed through on one of her fantasies. A lot of dragonmen were possessive to the point they'd murder anyone who saw their mate naked in a sexual way.

But then Logan was different. Her sexy mate and best friend had slowly understood what she'd needed with constant sex over the past month, and he'd helped Emma to accept how her desires were valid and important as well.

Not a day went by when she didn't love Logan even more.

Her dragon growled. *Aye, aye, he's bloody amazing. But right now, I want his cock.*

I hope you know the first time is mine, dragon.

Just as long as you share.

"Emma? Are you ready?"

Taking a deep breath, Emma put her shoulders back and waltzed from behind the screen to where Logan waited by the massive bed. It now made sense why it was on a small platform—the better to give people a chance to see what was going on.

She darted her eyes and saw that the peepholes were still closed. A thrum of anticipation went through her, and she got even wetter at the thought of people watching her and Logan.

As soon as she reached her mate, Logan lightly caressed her cheek with the back of his fingers. "So bloody beautiful."

She pressed her body against his, loving the hardness of his cock against her belly, and put a hand on the back of his neck. "Kiss me."

He took her lips in a rough kiss, his tongue dominating her mouth, his teeth nipping her bottom lip, and his hands firmly on her arse, holding her close.

She kissed him back just as fiercely, but all too soon he broke it. Before she could say a word, he lifted her onto the bed, and spread her thighs.

As he rubbed back and forth on her skin, a clicking sound filled the room. She noticed the golden rectangles were gone, and blackness was in those areas.

Logan leaned to her ear. "Tell me now if this isn't what you want, angel. All I want is to make you come so hard you forget your name, and it doesn't matter where we do it."

She cupped his cheek and kissed him gently. "I want you now, Logan. To make my claim on you, letting anyone watching know I'm the only female for you."

His pupils flashed to slits and back before he spread her legs wider. "Then I'm going to be extra thorough, leaving no doubt that you're my female and mine alone."

Her dragon hummed as Logan nuzzled her cheek and then kissed down her neck.

Emma threaded her fingers through his hair, arching into the whisper of his lips, the sting of his teeth, and the soothing flick of his tongue.

So when he pinched her nipple through the sheer fabric, Emma cried out and arched her hips.

Logan lifted his head, his gaze intense as he

lightly toyed with one taut nipple, and then the other. In the brief silence, she heard whispers from some of the peepholes.

At this rate, she was going to soak the bed before Logan ever fucked her.

As if he'd heard the whispers as well, he lightly traced the strap of her negligee, and slid it down her shoulder inch by inch, until one of her breasts popped free.

His gazed zeroed in on her. In the past, she'd always felt rather small-chested. But with Logan, she only felt beautiful.

He cupped her boob. "Mine, all mine."

He leaned down, lightly flicked her nipple with his tongue, and then kissed above her areole. His teeth bit her and she cried out at the sting; not from pain, but at how it only made the throbbing between her legs pound harder.

He drew her nipple into his mouth. As he suckled, his gaze met hers and she gripped his hair with her fingers. Her other hand moved down his chest and lightly brushed the tip of his cock. She rubbed the wetness there a few times before lifting her fingers to her mouth and sucking off his precum.

Logan groaned, released her nipple and took her mouth in a bruising kiss.

His hips pressed against her pussy, and she gripped his firm arse cheeks to keep him close. As he ground against her, Emma cried out. "Do that again. I'm close."

He froze, pulled back, and she reached for him.

But then Logan was on his knees in front of her, pressing her legs as wide as they would go. As he stared at her cunt, he murmured, "So wet and plump, begging for my tongue and cock." He ran a finger through her center and Emma arched her hips again. "Make sure to scream extra loud, angel. I want everyone watching to know your male pleasured you well."

Before she could say anything, his tongue fucked her a few beats before he moved to her clit. Threading her fingers through his hair, she arched into every lick, and swirl, and light nibble.

And as he suckled her tight bud, he thrust two fingers inside her, curling them upward so when he thrust, he hit her G-spot. Between the teasing inside and his mouth on her clit, Emma felt the pressure building and soon she screamed his name as wave after wave of ecstasy coursed through her. Not once did Logan let up as she came, drawing it out with slow, sweet torture.

When he finally stopped, he wiped his mouth, stood, and kissed her. Even though she'd just had a bloody intense orgasm, the musky taste of herself on his lips made her throb all over again, craving much more than his tongue or fingers.

She broke the kiss and whispered into his ear, "Will you fuck me now?"

With a growl, Logan tossed her back on the bed and then covered her body with his. "If I don't, my dragon is going to take control."

Her dragon growled. *Aye, aye, I'm the same way. He'd better get to work, or I'm going to straddle him and ride his cock until it hurts.*

She smiled at him, drew her legs back to lay her feet on the bed, and said, "My dragon is a wee bit threatening too." She caressed his cheek. "Claim me for the first time as your official mate, Mr. Lamont."

He grinned. "With pleasure, Mrs. Lamont."

After a quick kiss, Emma waited to see what her mate would do next.

ALL LOGAN WANTED to do was plunge into Emma's pussy and take her hard and fast. However, he could do that at home, in their cottage. Here, he wanted to draw it out, let her feel eyes on her, and make her that much wetter and aroused.

His beast growled. *Why are you wasting so much time? Claim her. Who cares about being patient? An orgasm is an orgasm.*

Not true, and you know it. Now, shut it, dragon. You'll have your turn soon enough.

Since they'd earlier laid out ground rules for this

night, his beast knew that if he kept pushing, Logan would toss him into a mental maze until he was good and ready to let him out. Just because his inner dragon was a huge part of himself didn't mean that sometimes his beast didn't get fucking annoying.

With his beast silent, Logan leaned back and sat on his heels. He'd already ensured that Emma's head pointed toward where the first voyeur section would fill. As he trailed a hand between her breasts, around her navel, and back up to her throat, he stopped to lightly stroke the pulse there. "Is your heart racing because you're eager for my cock? Or are you a wee bit nervous?"

Her eyes flashed to slits and back several times before she raised a foot to run down his leg. The light caress made his cock even harder. Then she moved a hand between her legs and lightly stroked herself. Logan groaned. "You're going to kill me."

She raised her fingers and he bent forward to suck them into his mouth. As he laved them, licking every last drop of her honey off her skin, Emma arched her hips upward. "Don't make me wait any longer, Logan."

He gently drew her hand away from his mouth and kissed her inner wrist. "As my angel commands."

Before she could reply, he flipped her over onto her belly, and raised her hips into the air. As he caressed her shoulders, her back, and then her arse, he whispered for her ears only, "Let's recreate the mural, aye?"

Emma's answer was to press her bum against his groin. Bloody hell, she'd make him come if he didn't get a move on.

With a growl, he ordered, "On your hands and knees. It'll give them a better show, angel."

His mate didn't hesitate to follow his instructions. Her legs were so wide and her hips raised, that he could see her dripping pussy glistening in the light. He lightly slapped her arse and rubbed it. "Aye, just like that, love."

He ran his fingers through her cunt until he found her swollen bundle of nerves. He pinched her once, and at her cry, his cock let out another drop of precum.

Even if his dragon didn't speak, he roared, signaling the time for teasing was over.

Gripping his dick, he ran it through her swollen pussy, loving the feel of her heat and wetness against them. Dragon-shifters couldn't catch STDs, but ever since Emma had been on birth control long enough, Logan had grown addicted to feeling her without a condom.

He positioned himself at her entrance but didn't thrust. No, he ran a hand underneath to one of her breasts and tugged her nipple. Emma groaned and wiggled her arse in the air. "Please, Logan. I need you inside me."

With a growl, he thrust to the hilt but stilled. Brushing her hair off her back, he kissed the top of her spine, and asked, "Tell all these people who your pussy belongs to, angel."

She wiggled her hips, as if trying to encourage him to move. Logan pinched one of her nipples and she cried out. Her voice was husky as she answered, "You, Logan. Only you."

"Good lass." He leaned back and lightly smacked her bum again. "Now let's see how loud I can make you scream."

Gripping her lovely hips, he pulled back and thrust forward again. Slowly at first, but soon he let go, pounding into her as hard as he could, wanting his mate to wake up feeling what she'd done with him here tonight.

As the sound of flesh smacking flesh filled the room, he heard some groans and moans from the peepholes. None of it fazed him, especially as Emma only grew wetter the more noise the other people made.

His lass really did like people watching.

Soon Logan was lost to the hot, tight feel of her cunt gripping his cock, her moans driving him ever closer to orgasm.

But he wasn't about to come before her. So he reached a hand around and strummed her clit in the rough, hard movements she liked. It didn't take long before Emma cried out his name and came around his cock, her spasms lasting so long that he could barely hold back his own orgasm until she finished. As soon as she did, he pressed against her clit one last time and let go, filling her with his cum, claiming her in a way different from any others. Not just because she was legally his mate now, but also to mark the first of many fantasies he would fulfill with her.

Once his mate had wrung every last drop out of him, he collapsed to the side and took Emma with him. She slowly turned in his arms. And even if he regretted his cock sliding free, the feel of her breath against his neck, her soft breasts against his chest, and her leg thrown over his more than made up for it.

They lay there a few minutes before a loud click sounded, signaling the slits had closed and they were alone again.

Brushing her wild sex hair from her face, he smiled, kissed her lips, and asked, "So? Was it what you imagined?"

She smiled slowly and rubbed her nose against his jaw. "Better. You're going to have to work extra hard to make me come that hard at home."

He lightly smacked her arse. "Cheeky angel." She laughed and he added, "There's plenty we can do at home. After all, next time it's my turn to have my fantasy fulfilled."

She lightly ran her hand against his chest. "And what would that be, Mr. Lamont?"

He grabbed her hand, brought it to his mouth, and lightly nipped her finger. "You tied up and at my mercy, Mrs. Lamont."

She sucked in a breath and he felt her nipples harden again. Oh, aye, his mate was going to be just as adventurous with sex as she'd been with traipsing around on treasure hunts.

His dragon growled. *It's my turn.*

Just a few more moments and then aye.

His beast grunted. *I never understand human things like pillow talk.*

Emma lifted her head, kissed him tenderly, and sighed, garnering his full attention once more. "I can't wait to try that. Although for right now, just hold me a wee bit longer, aye? I want to cement this memory into my brain for all time."

As he hugged her closer, he laid his cheek against the top of her head. "Aye, this is one memory I never want to forget. I love you, Emma Lamont. I have for years and will continue to do so for the rest of my life."

She snuggled into him. "I love you, too, Logan Lamont. And no matter if you forget me again or not, I always will."

Hugging the light of his heart even closer, Logan kissed her head. Sometimes it took losing everything to finally gain what someone wanted. And now that he had it, he was never letting go.

Author's Note

Thanks for reading Emma and Logan's story! I had no idea that when Logan first showed up in *Surrendering to the Dragon* (on a first date with Nikki) that he'd eventually end up here, with one of the MacAllister's. I love me some amnesia romance, and I think it worked really well for this pair (they both needed a jolt to realize what they had right in front of them). And, well, I liked that I could be a bit naughtier with this couple toward the end as well. ;) I've finally, *finally* stopped caring about comments shaming me for the heat and sex in my books. I'm 41 (as of writing this) and too old to care any more, lol. If only I could've told myself five years ago to not stress, my life would've been so much easier. Ah, well. Going forward, I'll do what I want…

You may have noticed how I set up the next book with Iris and Antony. An age-gap, spy mission romance? Yes, please. I'm not sure of the exact release date for their story, but it'll be called *The Dragon Recruit* and will be written after Stonefire #15, *Taught by the Dragon.*

As always, I thank not only my readers but also the people who helped to make this book a reality:

- Becky Johnson and her team at Hot Tree Editing are fantastic. After all these years, they still don't let me down.
- My beta readers Iliana G., Sabrina D., Sandy H., Ash B., and Mel M. are all amazing and help the final book shine. Not only do they catch any lingering typos, they also point out the minor inconsistencies I probably would've never noticed myself.

Thanks again for reading! And while waiting for my next dragon book, I hope you'll give my new series, Dark Lords of London, a try. It's a paranormal time travel series with vampires, shifters, and fae witches. (The first book, *Vampire's Modern Bride*, will release in July 2022.)

Until next time, I'll see you at the end of the next book!

Also by Jessie Donovan

Dark Lords of London

Vampire's Modern Bride (DLL #1 / July 2022)

Dragon Clan Gatherings

Summer at Lochguard (DCG #1)

Winter at Stonefire (DCG #2 / TBD)

Kelderan Runic Warriors

The Conquest (KRW #1)

The Barren (KRW #2)

The Heir (KRW #3)

The Forbidden (KRW #4)

The Hidden (KRW #5)

The Survivor (KRW #6)

Lochguard Highland Dragons

The Dragon's Dilemma (LHD #1)

The Dragon Guardian (LHD #2)

The Dragon's Heart (LHD #3)

The Dragon Warrior (LHD #4)

The Dragon Family (LHD #5)

The Dragon's Discovery (LHD #6)

The Dragon's Pursuit (LHD #7)

The Dragon Collective (LHD #8)

The Dragon's Chance (LHD # 9)

The Dragon's Memory (LHD #10)

The Dragon Recruit / Iris & Antony (LHD #11, TBD)

Love in Scotland

Crazy Scottish Love (LiS #1)

Chaotic Scottish Wedding (LiS #2)

Stonefire Dragons

Sacrificed to the Dragon (SD #1)

Seducing the Dragon (SD #2)

Revealing the Dragons (SD #3)

Healed by the Dragon (SD #4)

Reawakening the Dragon (SD #5)

Loved by the Dragon (SD #6)

Surrendering to the Dragon (SD #7)

Cured by the Dragon (SD #8)

Aiding the Dragon (SD #9)

Finding the Dragon (SD #10)

Craved by the Dragon (SD #11)

Persuading the Dragon (SD #12)

Treasured by the Dragon (SD #13)

About the Author

Jessie Donovan has sold over half a million books, has given away hundreds of thousands more to readers for free, and has even hit the *NY Times* and *USA Today* bestseller lists. She is best known for her dragon-shifter series, but also writes about magic users, aliens, and even has a crazy romantic comedy series set in Scotland. When not reading a book, attempting to tame her yard, or traipsing around some foreign country on a shoestring, she can often be found interacting with her readers on Facebook or TikTok.

And don't forget to sign-up for her newsletter to receive the latest updates and sneak peeks at:

www.JessieDonovan.com